# THE
# BLOODY
# MUDDY

**Tommy Templeton Murder Mystery Series**
*The Coven*
*The Bloody Muddy*

**Other Novels by T. W'ski**
*Stone Blind*
*BlackHeart's Treasure*

**Poetry Books by T. W'ski**
*MACHO*

**Book of Short Stories by T. W'ski**
*T. W'ski's Shorts*

**Novels to come in 2021 by T. W'ski**
*The Laver and the Purple Sand Pirates*
*West of Kansas*

# THE BLOODY MUDDY

*A Tommy Templeton Murder Mystery*

## T. W'ski

iUniverse

## THE BLOODY MUDDY
## A TOMMY TEMPLETON MURDER MYSTERY

*iUniverse books may be ordered through booksellers or by contacting:*

*iUniverse*
*1663 Liberty Drive*
*Bloomington, IN 47403*
*www.iuniverse.com*
*844-349-9409*

*ISBN: 978-1-6632-1856-8 (sc)*
*ISBN: 978-1-6632-1857-5 (e)*

*Library of Congress Control Number: 2021902959*

*Print information available on the last page.*

*iUniverse rev. date: 02/11/2021*

**Marilyn**

The best of what turned out to be just the rest

# CONTENTS

# PROLOGUE

## The Village of High Cliff,
## One and a-half years earlier.

**At the top** of the ancient stairway he stopped and looked back. There on the surface of the lake with a crown of stars surrounding her head was an image of Willow. Out of the surrounding darkness he could hear her speaking to him. "This is the price we witches must pay if our coven is to survive. Remember that I love you, Tommy and will for all eternity."

"Willow why wasn't I taken? Why have I been excluded from the spell brought on by the coven and granted by the Dark One? Why can't I go with you?" he asked pleading in a voice that was just short of a scream of desperation. He was speaking directly to Willow and indirectly to the dark forces governing her existence and he wanted to make sure that they heard him, heard the desperation in his voice that gave clear evidence as to his weary, troubled, and confused state of mind.

"You are your own spirit, Tommy. You were born

outside our coven and therefore not included in the process that ensures its survival. You were however born with some very strong and special powers of your own. They were a gift to you for having been birthed through the union of a witch and a warlock. Remember, Tommy I once told you that it takes a special knowledge to use those powers to their full potential. With the passing of my coven and in appreciation for all that you've done for us the original Wicca have instilled in you that knowledge. It will ensure that when they are needed your special powers will be available to you. They will serve you well in the future. Trust in the knowledge and the power when it opens up for you." Willow's image started to fade from the water's surface.

"Remember most importantly that I love you and will be by your side for all eternity." The smooth surface of Glen Lake now sparkled with the reflection of a million stars. Willow's image was gone. Tommy stood there for a moment longer staring out at the lake looking and remembering seeing in each star someone that had once occupied the now-deserted village of High Cliff many of whom he had become acquainted with.

A smile formed upon his face. Realizing that his head had cleared and the darkness that had attempted to acquire his spirit had been dispelled he turned and walked back through the village. His mind replayed scenes in which the townsfolk of High Cliff moved freely about attending to their daily business as they had once done in this world. *I wonder what will become of High Cliff now that its citizens had left?*

Gathering his luggage from the Witten's house Tommy got into his car and drove away headed for home and the world of the others.

# CHAPTER ONE

**Willow and the events** that had taken place in High Cliff constantly occupied the mind of Tommy Templeton during his final year at Dartmouth. He hit the books as if in a trance trying to shut out the rest of the world and find within himself the reason for his existence. Whenever he started falling too far into the darkness his roommate would do something unheard of to bring him back. It was his roommate that always reminded Tommy of Willow and what she meant to him. Those memories finally led him into applying for admittance to the Federal Bureau of Investigation, the F.B.I. Whenever he contemplated his future and a career path to follow after graduation Willow's words would enter his head followed by the remembrance of what had transpired in High Cliff.

In his mind his acceptance to the bureau had gone unquestioned. There had been one sticking point that was of minor concern the requiring of three years of experience in his chosen field after graduation. His attachments of letters of recommendation from noted professors and acquaintances would he was sure allow for the dispensation of that requirement and allow him to skip over it.

Tommy's weekends and holidays were spent at his mother's house in Lebanon while he attended his final year of college at Dartmouth. He commuted back and forth from his room on campus to her house and always found the drive released the stress of the previous week even when the traffic was bizarre. For a long time after her death he still thought of the house as hers even though he had inherited it upon her dying. At the completion of college and the usual graduation ceremonies he had vacated his room, said goodbye to his roommate, and move in to his house to stay.

It wasn't long after he had moved in when the letter from the F.B.I. arrived. He opened it nonchalantly expecting to read of his acceptance, but was surprised when he was informed that his application lacked the three years of experience and instructed him to re-apply in three years time after he had spent those three years working in his field of expertise in the world outside the F.B.I. Tommy read and reread the letter several times until the implications to his life's course and future sunk in.

Sitting at his desk in the room he had converted into his study he put his head in his hands and let his mind wander. *Now what? I guess I'll have to look for a job?* Then the thought hit him. *Well at least I won't have to rush into anything right away and I don't have to cancel my after graduation, congratulatory vacation. I can now take it and think about what I'm going to want to do for the next three years. Once I've made that decision I can start compiling a list of perspective employers and work on my résumé and while I'm on this after graduation celebratory trip it would be the perfect time to get all three of those things accomplished.*

Two weeks after receiving his letter of non-acceptance from the F.B.I. Tommy collected his mail and saw that his tickets for his trip had arrived. *These past two weeks have flown by. It was a good thing these tickets arrived in the mail today or I might have missed my flight and the boat,* he thought standing in the entryway with the mail still in his hands. He took a deep breath while looking through the glass panels of the front door. *So I guess I had better get ready and thanks to that brilliant spurt of pre-planning during fall term all I have left to do is pack with a full two days to do it in.*

# CHAPTER TWO

**Tommy managed to get** his packing done and make it to the airport on time, their time, several hours early. The first leg of his flight took him to Chicago and after landing he had just enough time to find the terminal and board the plane that flew him to Dallas. In Dallas he had a short layover and was able to walk around some getting something to eat and drink at the airport restaurant. As he was reboarding the plane he had to wait in the area just outside the loading gate and he noticed a young couple waiting along with many others. Taking out his cell phone he dialed 9-1-1 and requested an ambulance at the loading gate. Walking up to the attendant at the gate he said, "There is an ambulance on the way for the young woman in the long, grey, hooded sweat shirt. I suggest and it is imperative that you call security indiscreetly to get here A.S.A.P." The attendant manning the gate looked at Tommy and was about to ask why she should do that when a loud scream came from the young woman.

Her companion was standing over her holding a knife in his hand that was dripping blood on the carpet. The young woman had passed out and was slouching over in her seat. Tommy quickly walked over to the nearest fire extinguisher, broke its protective glass with his elbow and approached the man carrying it in his hands. "Get back," the young man screamed. "She's a bitch and deservers what she got so let her die." Before the young man could say another word Tommy pulled the trigger on the extinguisher and sprayed the young man in the face and continued to spray him until he dropped the knife at which point three other male passengers waiting to board tackled him to the floor.

"Hold him there," Tommy said pulling his handkerchief from his pocket and applying it with pressure to the young woman's wounds. It seemed that in moments the medics arrived along with security who took over the situation.

The young man was taken into custody and the young woman rushed to the nearby hospital. Everything in the waiting area returned to almost normal and got better when the gate attendant announced that the loading gate was open. When Tommy stepped up to present his boarding pass the attendant asked, "How did you know?"

"I had a friend who had the same look on his face just before he killed his wife," Tommy said lying. "I'll never forget that look and when I saw it on that young man's face I took a chance on history repeating itself and made the needed calls," he added smiling.

The flight from Houston to New Orleans despite all the commotion at the terminal arrived on schedule. Tommy hailed a cab that took him to the Quarter and dropped him. Getting out of the cab he grabbed his bags and stood there waiting for a break in traffic.

"Don't get to comfortable," Arch Tommy's old college roommate said as Tommy walked through the open door of his upstairs apartment. "Now that you're here with little time to spend we're going to start making a night of it this very evening."

"How did you ever manage to score a place like this?" Tommy asked setting down his suitcases and walking through the open French Doors of Arch's flat out onto his balcony that was fronted by ornate, iron-laced grillwork and looked down upon the busy street below.

"An uncle left it to me," Arch replied.

"Lucky you. I wish I had an uncle like that."

"He never married and I guess that I was his favorite nephew. Why I'll never know."

"If he was living here he probably thought that your lifestyle mirrored his own or else you're his only nephew and that's why he left it to you," Tommy answered chuckling to himself.

"Is the street down there always this busy?" Tommy asked leaning on the railing and looking down on the street below. "I had a hard time getting out of the cab and for a moment I wondered if I'd make it across the walk to your doorway with my suitcases."

"You are standing in the heart of Cajun Heaven, Tommy. The food is phenomenal here. There is music in the air 24/7 and if you shut up and listen you can hear it. Also if you look down into the throng the 'mounds' are at times breathtaking to behold," Arch added knowing that

Tommy's fastidious dedication to a woman he had been seeing for a short time during his final years of college, a woman who had died, was unprecedented.

"And the throng of people?"

"There 24/7 also. It thins a bit after some of the bars and restaurants close, but there are always people down there coming and going.

"Remind me again when does our ship leave?" Arch asked.

"The day after tomorrow. Did you just say 'our' ship?" Tommy asked looking at his friend.

"You caught that little slip up, huh?" Arch replied smiling. Shrugging his shoulders he explained. "When my father heard that you were stopping in to see me before you sailed upriver there was this look that appeared on his face. It's hard to explain, but it was between a fatherly smile and one you'd see on the face of the devil after having just taken the souls from a church full of people. Believe me it was strange and as you know I know strange."

"Ah, yes I do remember you and your relationship to strange," Tommy said adding "and what do I have to do to get something to drink in this glorious slice of heaven? I haven't had anything to hydrate me since leaving the airport and until I acclimatize I'm going to need plenty of liquid to make my body feel comfortable in this hot, humid atmosphere."

"Beer? Water? Never mind I know what you need," Arch replied heading for his kitchen.

"So what are you doing these days to keep out of

trouble?" Tommy asked listening to the clanking of glassware, ice cubes dropping into what he envisioned was a glass pitcher, and the opening and closing of cupboard and refrigerator doors.

"I'm working for the old man," Arch's voice came clearly from behind the wall after drifting through the arched doorway that led to the kitchen.

"Refresh my memory. What does your father do again?"

"He's a big shot lawyer here in New Orleans."

"We are talking about the same man that saved your educational experience by buying the dean on more than one occasion as I recall."

"The very same man. You've met him more than once, I think."

"I have?"

"Whatever you said or did at those meetings you impressed the hell out of him and he hasn't forgotten you."

"It's always refreshing to see a son following in the footsteps of his father and vice versa."

"If I remember correctly from what you told me after that episode with the love of your life you are doing the same. How's that coming along by the way?"

"I honestly don't know," Tommy answered seeing Arch come from the kitchen with glasses and a pitcher dripping with the sweat produced by its cold contents in the heated atmosphere of a southern city on the shores of the ocean.

"Here let me take those," Tommy said grabbing the ice filled glasses from his friend. "Let's sit out in the shade on the veranda. This time of afternoon we sometimes get a cooling breeze blowing in from off the gulf," Arch said.

After filling two glasses Arch handed Tommy one filled with the liquid refreshment and sat down. Tommy followed his example and sat down in a chair opposite him that was shaded by the balcony's roof.

"What do you mean you don't know?" Arch asked continuing their previous conversation.

"I told you that my mother was a witch and my father a warlock didn't I?"

"You did and it's strange because if I had come from anywhere other than Louisiana," Arch paused, "Well maybe from a few countries to our south and I guess from what I'm told there are a few other places too, but anyway what I was trying to say was that if I hadn't come from Louisiana I'd have thought you were nuts, but having come from here I understood your meaning completely."

"There were those couple of incidents during our last year at uni' that made me think I knew just what I was going to do with the rest of my life, but since then there has been nothing.

"I believe that I told you that the F.B.I. has turned me down?"

"You did mention it during our last phone call," Arch replied.

"I thought that if things were following as I was sure they would that I'd be a shoe-in, but now I just don't know and along with that I don't have an inkling as to what I'm going to do for those three years that will impress them to the point of admitting me." Arch looked at his friend thinking.

"When my father made his gift of my ticket for this trip he also told me that he had upgraded the single room that you had originally purchased to the owner's suite so that we could bunk together just like we had at uni'. When he did that I got the feeling that he was hoping for some kind of a miracle of the kind that he had hoped would happen when he bailed me out on those occasions you spoke of. Now I'm wondering if he didn't have something else in mind."

"I'm not sure that I'm understanding you," Tommy said with a questioning look on his face.

"I'm talking in reference to the miracle. My way of doing things as a lawyer isn't always his old school way. Oh I get results or the old man would have canned my ass months ago, but I'm not so sure that my way of handling the cases he has assigned to me in the past I've handled in quite the manner that he wants cases handled by his firm. And to put a point on that statement I haven't made partner yet," Arch acquiesced, "and I'm his son. Anyway I got the impression that he might be thinking that by spending a month in close association with you, you might change that."

"And you've just alluded to the fact that something has happened to change that assumption. What changed it?"

"While I was in the kitchen mixing the drinks I got to thinking about it since you had just asked."

"And?"

"And at the time that I told him that you were coming I also mentioned the F.B.I. refusal."

"I'm still not understanding? You're not making any sense, Arch."

"It was the very next day the day after I had told him you were coming and while we were at our law offices. He was between clients at the time and called me into his office. When I went in I didn't close the door. While he was in the process of telling me about my ticket and the change to your booking his next client arrived and stood there in the open doorway."

"So what the hell has that got to do with anything?"

"It was his eyes. In the kitchen just now for some strange reason I remembered my father's eyes. He wasn't looking at me, but he wasn't looking at me, he was looking past me at his next client."

"Someone important?"

"You might say that," Arch replied.

"Who was it?"

"Minerva."

"Who's Minerva?"

"She's the local witch, a soothsayer," Arch answered, "and when she predicts something she's never wrong."

"Never?"

"Never."

"So why should her standing there and your father looking at her be such a big deal?"

"Remember what I said about the look on his face?"

"I do," Tommy answered, "and you think that this Minerva had something to do with that look?"

"I didn't at the time, but now I'm not so sure." Tommy looked at his friend, took a drink from his glass, leaned back and closed his eyes letting his mind interpret what Arch had just said.

"Changing the subject, now," he finally said without coming to a conclusion that he'd willingly share with his best friend. "I have a need to know just what you have planned for me on my first visit to New Orleans?"

"Wine, women, and song my friend. I told you to come a good week before you were to ship out, but since you didn't listen to me we'll just have to condense that week into an evening and a-half and continue it once we're onboard."

"You are aware that I haven't changed, Arch. I'm still that quiet roommate that you usually with a friend draped over you for support would wake up at all ungodly hours of the night. No I take that back. It was always at some ungodly hour early in the morning to relive the exploits of your past twenty-four hours. So when I got your text inviting me to stay for that week and I thought about it I didn't think that I could trust you with this body for a whole week. Chances are that if I gave you a whole week's time by the end of that week I'd be so messed up that I'd miss my boat."

"Now you won't have that to worry about will you? Besides I still have hope for you, Tommy Templeton," Arch said raising his glass in a salute to his friend.

"Oh by the way I almost forgot my parents are expecting us for dinner at their place around seven tonight. Would you like a refill?"

# CHAPTER THREE

**The ornamental gates** started to swing open as Arch's Mercedes approached the entrance to his parent's home. Without slowing down he made the turn from the street and slid through them with a fraction of clearance. "Same old Arch," Tommy said being used to such behavior, but taking no chances he braced himself for the crash that one day was sure to occur. Arch's Mercedes flew down the drive, past the moss covered trees that lined both sides of the long driveway. The trees intertwining limbs overhung it and presented patterns of shade and sun as they passed beneath them.

Parking the car across from the front of a huge southern styled mansion Tommy and Arch got out of the car. As they walked through the multi-pillared entranceway that led to the entrance its double doors opened before them. Standing beside them two servants appeared wearing colonial period clothes. "Welcome, Mr. Ponnard," the older of the two gentleman said as they passed through the doors and entered the foyer.

"Good evening, Harvey," Arch replied and nodding to the other servant greeted, "Malcolm."

Standing ahead of them in the lavish, winding, stair-cased foyer were two women. "Hello, mother," Arch said to the older of the two women giving her a kiss on the cheek. "Mother this is my ex-school roommate Tommy Templeton. Tommy this is my mother, Anne."

"How do you do, Mrs. Ponnard," Tommy said.

"It's a pleasure to finally meet you Tommy and call me Anne, please. Arch and my husband have both talked about you so often that I feel that you're a member of our family."

Anne Ponnard turned toward the woman standing beside her. Tommy had noticed the woman's gypsy like appearance when they had entered the house. He now took particular notice of her dark eyes, her blood colored lipstick, her matted, beaded, and braided hair that stuck out from beneath a scarf that she had wrapped around head. She was wearing large, gold, hooped earrings, and a colorful, billowy blouse worn over an ankle length dress that allowed her bare, soil darkened feet to contrast with the shinny, polished floor of the foyer she stood upon.

When she turned her attention in his direction it gave him a chance to see beneath the exterior façade to notice just how young she was. He guessed that she was about the same age as he and Arch. "Tommy I'd like you to meet Menerva another friend of the family."

"A pleasure I'm sure," Tommy replied extending his hand. Menerva took the opportunity and in one swift motion grabbed Tommy's extended wrist with both her own many bangled and ringed wrists and hands. With her eyes closed and her head bowed she held Tommy's wrist for only a moment. Suddenly her head jerked backwards and her eyes opened wide and white. She stood like that looking up at the ceiling finally lowering her head back to one's normal position looking straight into Tommy's eyes. The look of pleasantness that had been on her face had disappeared and had been replaced by a look of shear terror. She pulled back her hands as if they were on fire and took two steps backward away from Tommy.

"Menerva?" Mrs. Ponnard asked seeing the change that had come over her. "Is something wrong, darlin'? What have you seen?"

"I have to go," Menerva replied. "I have to go," she repeated. "Tell Mr. Ponnard that I was wrong," she shouted and turning she ran out and through the barely cracked door as Malcolm and Harvey had seen her rushing their way and only had time to get it open that far.

"Now that was odd," said Mrs. Ponnard.

"Odder still is the fact that she said that she was wrong. Menerva's never wrong," added Arch.

"Your father is waiting for the two of you in his study, son. I have to go check on the progress of dinner," Mrs. Ponnard said leaving Arch and Tommy standing in the entry.

"Did you say something to Menerva to upset her that I missed hearing?" Arch asked.

"No nothing," Tommy answered. "She just grabbed my wrist and then starred straight into my eyes with a look of terror on her face and ran out."

"Did she say anything to you?" Arch persisted.

"The lawyer in you is showing," Tommy said smiling at his friend. "She did mumble something just before she threw her head back, but it was so low and guttural sounding that I didn't catch it. I don't think that what she said was in English though. It sounded foreign, dark and foreign."

"It was probably the language of the gypsies. I've heard her mumble the language of the gypsies before and at those times I always thought that she was putting a curse on me or the person we were talking to."

"Thanks for that," Tommy said looking at Arch whose facial expression showed that he was just short of bursting into laughter.

"What was that with the wrist holding? Does she always do that when she meets someone for the first time?"

"As a matter of fact she does, but it's usually on the sly and not so blatantly out in the open. Come on let's go meet the old man," he finally said slapping Tommy on the back while trying to gather himself.

# CHAPTER FOUR

**Arch's father was sitting** behind his desk reading a sheet of paper, which he returned to its legal sized, manila folder when the two young men walked in. "Hello, son," he greeted.

"Dad you've met Tommy Templeton before," Arch replied introducing Tommy.

"I have on several occasions. How do you do, Tommy?" he greeted extending his hand which Tommy shook.

"I guess you don't scare the socks off of everyone whose hand you shake," Arch said in jest.

"Son?" Mr. Ponnard questioned.

"We've just had something strange happen, dad," Arch started, "when mother introduced Menerva to Tommy."

"Ah so you've met our local soothsayer," interrupted Mr. Ponnard.

"Met her and when she did her wrist reading on him he scared her so bad that she literally ran through the front doors," Arch said.

"Son?" Mr. Ponnard asked again looking at Arch for an explanation.

"Literally, dad. When she did her wrist grabbing

thing whatever vibes she got scared her to the point that she ran through the small crack in the front doors that Malcom and Harvey were able to get open when they saw her coming. If they hadn't got it cracked like they did I do believe she would have gone right through them."

"Extraordinary!"

"She also left a message for you, father." This peaked Mr. Ponnard's already heightened attention. "She said to tell you that she was wrong."

"Menerva said that?"

"That's a direct quote, dad," stated Arch as he walked over to the sideboard and poured three glasses of cognac handing one to his father and one to Tommy. "To the strange," he toasted raising his glass and drinking.

When everyone had taken a drink, Arch asked, "Do you know what Menerva meant, dad?"

"Meant?" Mr. Ponnard returned taking his time before giving an answer.

"By her, 'I was wrong', statement," Arch clarified.

"I will have to talk with her to be sure, but it probably has to do with the lawsuit she is helping us with. You know the one and if that is the case then it could have several meanings none of which need be discussed here." Arch nodded his understanding and raised his glass in Tommy's direction.

"You never cease to amaze, my friend. Life is never dull when you are around," he said before taking another drink.

# CHAPTER FIVE

**A little before eleven** Tommy and Arch left the Ponnard Residence and headed for Bourbon Street. "It's a bit early for the real parties to be in full swing, but I know this place where even at this early hour there is always something going on," Arch said parking his car in its usual spot. "The beautiful thing about this place is that it's just around the corner from my front door."

"And that is important, why?" Tommy asked.

"At four in the morning when you are blind drunk you can feel your way home by leaning on the walls of the building and turning into the first doorway you come to. It's a feat that I am proud to say that I've managed to accomplish more than once" he said looking at Tommy who was shaking his head.

"And once you got inside how many of those times did you end up sleeping at the foot of the stairs?"

"I have to admit that there were times that the key had a mind of its own and refused to find the lock so I had to spend the night outside the door sleeping on the street, but once I got the key in the lock I always managed to pull my way upstairs and onto the bed. Another of those amazing feats that I've accomplished that I hadn't thought of until now. Thanks, buddy."

"Do you know what you need?" Tommy asked as the two men walked through an ancient doorway that looked as if it had been there since the days of Jean Lafayette half a block down from the doorway to Arch's apartment.

"What do I need, buddy?"

"A wife. Someone to keep you on the straight and narrow," Tommy said.

"There's no fun in living life like that with someone always telling you what to do," Arch chuckled as his heart ached at the thought running through his head. "And speaking of that someone whose bosses me around yet remains loads of fun I want you to meet Jennifer," Arch replied walking toward the bar.

"Arch! You made it," Jennifer greeted kissing and hugging him.

"Jenny I want you to meet my friend and old roommate from college. Tommy this is Jennifer."

"How do you do," Jennifer said shaking Tommy's hand. When she tried to let go Tommy held onto it for a bit longer. Jennifer looked at Arch giving him that 'what the hell is he doing look'.

"Not to worry, Jen my boy Tommy here is testing and making fun of me at your expense," Arch replied. "That's it isn't it, Tommy and by the way you're losing your touch, old bud. That handshake makes two people that haven't gone off screaming after you've shaken their hands." Jennifer looked at Arch.

"The two of you must have had quite a few at your parent's house if you're making comments like that," she said.

"Earlier this evening Tommy here offered his hand in greeting to Menerva and right there and then in front of my mother, in the foyer, she did her usual thing, and grabbed Tommy's wrist. She stood there for a bit, threw her head back, got this horrible look on her face, and went screaming out the doors."

"Menerva? Thee Menerva?" Jennifer asked with Tommy noticing a strange look on her face when she pronounced Menerva's name.

Arch nodded and asked, "What are you drinking? I see that your glass is empty."

"Where is Tommy's chaperone?" Arch asked leaning close to Jennifer so that Tommy wouldn't hear.

"You mean Rachael," Jennifer whispered back. "She should be here momentarily. Why did you say chaperone?"

"Someone on the quiet side not expecting anything other than an evening out I did explain Tommy's limitations when I asked you to set him up?"

"You did and Rachael is just as you ordered."

"I thought I knew all your friends and I don't recall a Rachael," Arch said.

"Like Tommy is an old school chum of yours Rachael is an old school chum of mine. She only got into town recently and just called me this past week so since she fits the parameters you requested I thought this would give us a chance to catch up too. You know kill two birds with one night chaperoning your mate." Jennifer smiled as Arch just shook his head.

"And speak of the devil here she is," Jennifer said seeing Rachael walk through the door. Waving her over Jennifer said in introduction, "Tommy I want you to meet an old school friend of mine Rachael and, Tommy I'm counting on you to make sure she has a good time this evening."

"Hello, Rachael I'm Arch," Arch said stepping in and shaking Rachael's hand. "I'm Jenny's and she always does that to me."

"Does what, honey?"

"Haven't you noticed that you always leave me out of the picture and lurking in the background whenever there is another beautiful woman around hoping that I don't notice."

"Don't mind him he's been like this for as long as I've known him," Tommy said. "I'm Tommy," he added moving in on Arch and shaking Rachel's hand. Without letting her hand go he said. "I've met you somewhere before, very recently."

"I don't think that we've ever met before, Tommy," Rachael said. "I'm fairly new to New Orleans."

"See now he's gone and pushed me aside two. Time for me to get some new friends," Arch said smiling. "If you stick with us and you won't be new in town for long," said Arch breaking the bond.

"He's right," interjected Jennifer. "Look what he's done to me."

The darkness of night was filled with the sounds of fabulous Bayou Blues and the bar soon filled to overflowing. Drinks flowed into gullets like the waters of the Mississippi flowed into the Gulf and with the light of first dawn showing through the open front door Arch called it a night. "There is this bakery well it's either a bakery with a bar and a restaurant or a bar with a restaurant and a bakery or a restaurant with a bakery and a bar either way it's two doors down and it serves the most amazing hangover remedies in the World."

"Bell's Place," Jennifer shouted. "Yes!" and led the way toward the door dragging a staggering Arch after her.

True to his words Bell's Place did serve the most amazing hangover remedy. Breakfast was delicious and wolfed down by one and all. While they were waiting for their Mud Pies, "A necessity if you eat at Bell's," Arch assured them just before having an epiphany. "Rachael you may not know it, but tomorrow my good buddy Tommy and I are going to take a riverboat up the Mississippi all the way to Saint Paul, Minnesota. Since we all had such a great time tonight I suggest that you girls accompany us."

"Some of us have regular jobs you know and can't just disappear from it for a whole month," stated Jennifer.

"I happen to know for a fact that you can," Arch said. "I happen to know your boss and I'm sure that he'll let you go and if he doesn't I'll just have to kick his ass."

"He is my boss," Jennifer explained bringing a look from Tommy who noticed that Rachael didn't react to the insight.

"She's my sexatary," Arch said.

"I am certainly not that, but I do find that it's the best way to keep him in line and out of too much trouble."

"As busy as that must keep you I'd be willing to bet that it doesn't work, does it?" asked Tommy smiling.

"Surprisingly it does most of the time. Tonight since you're in town and I've heard him raving about you and your exploits so often I decided to release him to the dogs," Jennifer answered adding looking straight at Tommy. "You must know Arch really well?"

"As for you," Jennifer said turning toward Arch. "Your suggestion is being quite presumptive, boss, honey. There are a few important things that you've forgotten to take into account."

"Such as?" Arch asked.

"You only have tickets for the two of you for starters. I know that money isn't an issue, but they aren't going to let us just tag along for free."

"And from what I've been told those trips are usually solidly booked," Rachael offered.

"So you know about the riverboat trips?" Tommy asked.

"I'm kind of a history buff and when I researched this area before deciding to move here I stumbled upon the riverboat trips, but until I get settled, find a job, and am able to start putting some money aside I could never afford one."

"Jenny was right, Rachael I can and will pay for everything the tickets, the food, and the fun, me," Arch said his comment going without the applause he expected.

"And as far as tickets go I have an old man that

has influence. He was the one that when he found out that Tommy was going upriver fixed it so that I could accompany him. He even got Tommy's room changed from a single to the Owner's Suite. I'll have to check to make sure, but I don't think that accommodations for the four of us or your tagging along will be a problem. So what else concerns you, my precious?" Arch asked looking at Jennifer.

"One word, 'limitations' and then there's Rachael's availability. She might not want to or be able to go," Jennifer said giving Rachael a peculiar questioning look that Tommy noticed.

"I am a cad," Arch said in a way of apologizing. "Rachael I'm sorry for the way I am forgive me, please?" Rachael looked at Arch and just smiled.

"So what are your thoughts on Jenny's misgivings?" Tommy asked Rachael.

"I'm not tied down at the moment, but I have been looking for a job. There's nothing on the horizon as of yet."

"So you're free to go with us?" Arch persisted.

"There are other things to consider so I'll have to think about it and let you know."

"What about you, Tommy?" Jennifer asked.

"I need to talk to Arch, and he needs to get back to you, and you need to get with Rachael."

"I understand," Jennifer said giving Arch her stern look to which he shrugged questionably. The mud pies were eaten in semi-silence as everyone considered the 'Cads' proposition.

# CHAPTER SIX

**"There she is, Tommy** a floating hotel with all the amenities that one out of water and built on dry land has," Arch stated as he and Tommy arrived dockside.

"You can always walk out of one that's on land, but on this one you'll have to know how to swim if you leave at the wrong time. Do you still remember how to swim, Arch?" Tommy asked in jest knowing full well that Arch knew all to well how to swim as he was the captain of the college swim team.

"Let's just say that on this trip knowing how to swim isn't going to be enough. You'll have to be either a damn fast swimmer or the reincarnation of Tarzan 'cause if the drop doesn't get you the gators will," Arch replied.

"It's only a six story jump from our room up there on the top floor. No, that's not right what are floors called on a ship?"

"They are called decks," Arch said.

"Isn't the sixth story deck about the same height as the high dive you mastered in college? Of course the pools you were used to diving into didn't have gators in them," Tommy replied.

"That's true, but they were there sitting in the bleachers watching and waiting," Arch returned causing both men to break out in laughter.

"Damned if you aren't right, Arch damned if you aren't right."

"Shall we check in, and board the boat?" Arch asked.

"Is it a boat or a ship?" Tommy asked as they approached the gangway.

"Anything over sixty-five feet in length is considered to be a ship," the purser taking tickets at the foot of the gangway answered.

"That solves that thank you, sir," Arch said handing the man his ticket.

"The rest of your party has already boarded, Mr. Ponnard, sir all that is except for Mr. Templeton, sir."

"And I am he," Tommy said handing the man his ticket right behind Arch.

"All present and accounted for then welcome aboard, gentleman," the purser said signaling a couple of porters to help them with their luggage and show them to their suite.

"What's with all that, 'sir', stuff and 'your party'?" Tommy asked as they walked up the gangway knowing the answer, but not wanting the fact to go to Arch's head. Tommy had seen him when he thought he was lord and master of all he surveyed and it wasn't that side of his friend that he liked.

"The old man's influence I imagine, but don't fret I know my place in this party of four," he acknowledged.

"Just checking you know how you can get?"

"Remind me if I get out of hand would you please and don't let it slide. You'll be doing me a favor especially if you call me on it before Jennifer does."

"I will, Arch," Tommy said noticing an old colored gentleman sitting in a chair on the bow side of the ship's entryway. "You go on ahead, Arch. I'll catch up with you in a bit."

Walking over to where the old man was sitting Tommy said, "Hello there!" The old man nodded his response. "Mind if I join you?" Tommy asked.

"Another chair's just there," the old man said indicating a folding deck chair leaning against the wall of the main deck beside his. Tommy retrieved the chair, opened it, and sat down next to the old man.

"My name is Tommy Templeton," Tommy said extending his hand. The old man took and shook Tommy's hand.

"Name's Ben. Been expecting you," the old man said.

"Why's that?" Tommy inquired.

"You're the fella that requested fishing licenses for the length of Ol' Miss ain't you?"

"I am that man, yes. And I suppose you're the fella that they told me to be on the lookout for who'd give me tips on and show me how to fish our Ol' Miss?"

"I be he, young fella," the old man said.

"Things have changed a bit since I made the reservation," Tommy said.

"I noticed. Moved up top and you've got company tagging along with you," Ben said.

"Hit the nail right on the head. It'll probably mean

that I'll have less time to just laze about and fish like I had intended."

"Figured as much, but the fish won't mind," Ben assured Tommy.

"How do I get in touch with you when I can find time?" Tommy asked.

"Ask a porter or call the desk. I spend a lot of time fishing or working the spaces in-between if you know what I mean?"

"I think I do," Tommy replied.

"Would you like something to drink?" Tommy asked looking around for a porter.

"Got all I need right here," Ben said offering Tommy an open jar concealed by a paper bag. Tommy took a sip testing first and then a full drink.

"Swamp shine. Always makes sure that I has a case when I comes on these trips."

"It isn't bad tasting, but it's strong I can feel the buzz after just that one drink," Tommy replied.

You gotta sip it, son. Here in the bayou we takes things slow, sips time you might say."

"Thanks for the tip," Tommy said. "I'll remember to do that next time."

"I figure that you've been here since the gangway was lowered so I have to ask what you've observed so far when it comes to the rest of our fellow passengers?"

"Most a them is as expected on holiday and out for a good time some romantic, some not. Then there is a few that is along for the historic interest of the trip always amusing that. Then there are a few that seem to have their problems always is a few of them. Some of them problems be personal some be with their relationships. Can never be understanding why it is that they come on a trip like this when they can't settle their differences on dry land. Comin' on a trip that floats don't ever seem to help fix their problems and for most it just exacerbates it sometimes to a dangerous level."

"Human nature," Tommy replied. "Don't want a good thing to end and trying their damnest to prevent the inevitable." Thoughts of Willow suddenly drifted across Tommy's mind. Ben just nodded his acquiescence took a sip from his bottle and offered it to Tommy. Tommy took the jar in a bag from him and sipped it this time.

"There is always a few that is interesting all in and of themselves," Ben continued. "Them are always fun to watch too. Take the bunch you've boarded this here ship with."

"Oh what about them?" Tommy asked interested in the old man's assessment of his friends.

"Take Ponnard for instance. I've seen him about afore so I knows a bit 'bout him and his old man. I hear it told that his old man sent him along with you on this trip on the advice of a soothsayer."

"That wouldn't be a woman named Menerva?" Tommy asked.

"You've met her then?" Ben asked.

"She grabbed my wrist, held it for a second, and then ran off scared to death. You wouldn't be able to explain the why of that would you?"

"Have a suspicion, but it's better left unsaid for the time bein', but it's very interestin'," Ben said taking his time while taking a good look at Tommy.

"You know that the old man didn't send his son along with you for nothing. There's something in that and it surely needs more watching to figure out the what and why fores of it."

"Then there's the woman."

"The blonde is Mr. Ponnard's secretary and although I don't think that he's totally aware of it I think that she is the love of his life. They ought to be married and if they last, if Mr. Ponnard the junior doesn't go and screw it up somehow, they just might be. I'm sure to get an invitation. Would you like one if it happens? I can fix it," Tommy offered.

"Not talking 'bout her, son talking 'bout the dark one the red-head. Sensed something strange 'bout her. She be on a mission, a secret mission that's known only to her."

"Your senses may not be wrong, Ben. I've got a feeling that there is more to her then she is letting on too, also."

"Be careful 'round her, son she may be dangerous," Ben stated.

"To herself, to others, who to, and why is she dangerous?" Tommy asked. "I haven't sensed the dangerous part, but I do know she has an ulterior motive for coming with us on this trip and then again I could be wrong."

"Just an old man's observation, son. Pay no attention to my ravings. Probably just the shine talking," Ben said. "Sometimes I wrong, times not, but I do know about fishing Ol' Miss. Bring your friends along do them good to sit, sip, and contemplate their lives," Ben said. "Tomorrow morning just as the sun come up before the ship sail be a good time. I be on the river side of the bow with enough poles and chairs for all."

# CHAPTER SEVEN

**"Where have you been,** Buddy. You said in a bit and it's been ages. We're all unpacked and ready for an investigational tour of this here ship."

"I've been sippin' swamp shine and talking fishing with the guide I asked the travel agency to provide me. You do remember me telling you that, that is why I came on this trip in the first place."

"Refresh my memory."

"I came on this trip to reward myself for having completed college. I told you that as part of that reward I intended to spend it working on my resume and sitting on the deck of this ship with a cane pole in my hands fishing," Tommy replied.

"Surely that's changed now that we're all here with you?" Arch asked. "It's party time, time to celebrate in style like we did in college."

"You celebrated that way and dragged me along with you besides you are here because your father took it upon himself to invite you along without consulting me first."

"Are you telling me that you don't want me and the girls here?" Arch asked acting as if he were offended.

"Not at all I'm actually glad that your father did what he did and if he would have asked I would have jumped for joy and given my consent gladly. As for the four of us having decided to stick together and enjoy this once in a lifetime experience I couldn't be happier, but and that's a big but I don't want this trip to be one big party. I want time to sit, relax, reflect, and fish. And when the occasion presents itself I want time to work on my resume once I decide what it is exactly I want to be doing out here in the real world. Most of all and this is really important to me I don't want you-all to be offended when I decide to do any of just that, okay?"

"Well I'm glad we got that out of the way," replied Arch.

"So am I," Tommy said.

"Look, Tommy. I know that at times I can be insensitive toward others and don't always listen to what they tell me, but that's one of those things that makes us such good friends. It's what I've always admired about you while we were in uni' together. You always shot straight from the hip whether I liked it or not and nine times out of ten you were right and set me on the straight and narrow."

"Thanks, Arch and I'm sorry for coming a bit unglued just now."

"Did you say you were sippin' swamp shine? Lucky you. I've had that stuff only once in my life and it really did a number on me so much so that I swore never to indulge again."

"I'd have probably been in those same shoes, but

my experienced guide instructed me as to the right path to take."

"Male or female? The latter I hope," Arch said with a sly look on his face.

"Hate to disappoint, but it was male. He was the old, colored gentleman that I walked over to talk to when we boarded the ship. He's my fishing guide," Tommy said.

"I'll bet it was old Ben," Rachael said stepping out of one of the bedrooms. "Couldn't help but overhear your conversation as the two of you were kinda loud."

"Sorry for that," Tommy said wondering how she knew old Ben if she were as new to the area as she made out to be, but he wasn't about to ask not yet anyway.

"We realize that this was your planned reward, Tommy," Jennifer said having come into the room right behind Rachael. "We also know that we've injected ourselves into it and we are more than grateful for the two of you to have allowed us to experience it with you. Whenever you feel that it's time for you to do the things you came on this trip to do, do them and we'll understand. Won't we, Arch?"

"Of course we will, babe," Arch said. "Isn't that what I just said?" Jennifer walked over to him, put her arm around him, and squeezed more than hugged him bodily.

"Okay so now that we are all understanding of one another what have I missed while I was out playing hooky?"

"You and I are in the room on the left," Rachael said. "It's the one with the nicest view. We thought you deserved it since this trip was your idea and it has two 'fulls' in it. We can talk about that later when we're alone."

"We can always change the arrangement if you're not comfortable with it," Jennifer said.

"No not at all the arrangement sounds great," Tommy said as an old saying popped into his head. *Keep your friends close and your enemies even closer.*

# CHAPTER EIGHT

**"So where are we** off to?" Tommy asked.

"You haven't unpacked yet," Rachael said.

"Plenty of time to do that later," Tommy replied.

"Okay then we are out of here," Arch said picking up the cabin's phone and dialing up the desk.

"The captain has offered to give us a personal tour of the entire ship, bow to stern. Isn't that correct?" Jennifer asked seemingly of no one. Arch on the phone nodded the correctness of her statement.

"I feel that the presence of Arch's father may be with us this entire trip, which in and of itself may make it a bit more interesting," Tommy said showing his approval by giving Arch the thumb's up sign.

The tour was quite informative as Rachael, Jennifer, and Tommy had never been on a ship of any kind before. Arch on the other hand had been on a large yacht or two, but he had never been on a cruise ship of this size. The tour lasted almost four hours and by the time it was over the entire group found that they were thirsty and famished.

Retiring to the dining room they discovered that

their gastronomical distress was being shared by a goodly number of their fellow passengers as all the tables along the starboard and port window sides of the dinning room were taken. The foursome decided to take up residence at a table center stage, with an aisle on both sides from which they could observe the rest of the passengers at the other tables.

"That must be a worrisome handful," Jennifer the first to comment said. "I would be worried sick about bringing a child that age on a cruise like this. I'd have to have her? It is a her isn't she?"

"Looks like a her to me," Rachael offered.

"Anyway I'd have one of those halter things with a line attached and I'd have to have that line attached to me at all times even in my sleep."

"I'm sure they're all right. They all look like they are in their thirty's so they should be experienced enough," Arch added.

"Which one is the wife or does he have two?" Jennifer asked.

"Could be that the fourth member of their party hasn't arrived yet or maybe he needed a lie down," Arch added.

"He's probably in the bar at wits end over the kid trying to forget why he ever brought her along," Jennifer said.

"If I had to guess I'd say that the blonde is the wife and the woman with the dark hair is either a friend or a nanny that's been invited along to watch the child," offered Tommy.

"A real live nanny you mean? I think you're right. Look at the way she's acting," said Rachael.

"I wonder if she's an au pair?" Jennifer submitted.

"Moving on. What do we make of those two at the table next to and toward the stern of the nanny's table?" Rachael asked. Before anyone could reply a waiter appeared with menus and asked about drinks.

"We should all have something that fits the occasion something with an appropriate name like a 'Bon Voyage', or a 'Black Voodoo'," suggested Arch. "Do you have anything like that?"

"I would have to ask, sir," the waiter said passing out the menus.

"Just bring us a large pitcher of Long Island Ice Tea and four chilled glasses with the appropriate garnish," said Jennifer. The waiter nodded and left.

"That's what I pay this woman for. She always has the right answer no matter the situation." Jennifer didn't reply to his comment, but just smiled back at him.

*I wonder what she's thinking?* Tommy thought to himself seeing the look on Jennifer's face.

"Back to our people watching. Tommy you go first this time and save us all the trouble," Rachael said.

"Thank you for that, but I'm not a fortune teller or a soothsayer." At the word 'Soothsayer' Jennifer gave Rachael a strange look that Tommy caught as he was looking straight at her at the time. His mind drifted and suddenly he was once again walking through the open front doors of the Ponnard Residence.

"Tommy! Tommy, are you going to give us your expert opinion or not?" Rachael asked breaking Tommy's train of thought.

"I'm sorry that high praise got me all flustered and I couldn't think for a moment," Tommy said trying to cover his tracks.

"Okay look at the couple man and wife sitting directly to my left by the windows. By the way he is acting I'd say that he is very domineering to the point of being what we'd call an over-bearing ass."

"How can you tell that by just looking at him?" Arch asked.

"While the three of you were observing the older couple with child and nanny I was watching them," Tommy explained. "It was the way he acted when the waiter, waited on them that drew my attention."

"And?" persisted Arch.

"He did all the ordering and I could see that it wasn't what his wife wanted by the look on her face."

Further delving into Tommy's assumption was interrupted by their waiter who appeared at their table with a full pitcher of Long Island Iced Tea and four chilled glasses that were already filled. He set them down in front of each of them and stepped back. "Have you had time to look the menu over?" he asked.

"Yes and we'd all like the." Seeing the look on his friend's faces Arch smiled and said, "a joke, a joke." Jennifer gave him a jab in the ribs.

"I have," said Rachael returning to the issue at hand. "I'll have the Bayou Gumbo."

"So will I," said Tommy.

"And I," added Jennifer.

"Like I started to say before the three of you so rudely attacked me with your looks and your elbow, waiter we'd all like a very large pot of your Bayou Gumbo with bread bowls and plenty of butter and pepper to go around. You do have bread bowls?"

"If we don't we will send out for them, just for you, Mr. Ponnard."

"You lucky, unimportant, bastard," Jennifer said causing the waiter to smile.

"Make that smug, special, and just plain damned, fall into it, lucky," said Tommy.

"You're all jealous because you're not the only ones that can read minds," Arch said folding his arms across his chest and trying to look smug. Everyone laughed so hard that they drew the attention of the passengers at the other tables. Noticing this the foursome quieted down.

Leading off Tommy picked up his glass of Long Island Iced Tea and held it over the center of the table as the other three followed suit in salute.

"To Arch's new found abilities," Tommy said.

"To Arch's new abilities,' repeated Jennifer and Rachael.

"To me," added Arch smiling, taking a drink, and starting to choke. Everyone else in the process of taking a drink started to laugh and had a hard time from not blowing the drink out of their noses, while Jennifer set her glass down and slapped Arch on the back.

"Are you alright, babe?" Arch nodded and she ceased her back-slapping.

"That's your last bit of frivolity for the rest of the day or you're going to kill us in some undignified matter," Jennifer said bringing nods from all around the table.

"Okay then back to the game," Jennifer said.

"How about the woman sitting by herself at the first table in the same row along the windows on Tommy's left?" asked Rachael.

"I got this one," offered Arch. "I've seen this type at least a hundred times in my short life."

"Your explanation better be good or that short life just got shorter," said Jennifer.

"It's a good thing that no one was taking a drink just then," said Rachael bringing her hand to her mouth as everyone else was trying their hardest to muffle their laughter.

"Whatever they put in this drink it doesn't help," Tommy said while trying to stifle his laughter.

When things had settled down again Arch continued. "You should be able to recognize the type, Jenny. We get them every now and then in the office. She is what's known as a man-killer, but she's the kind of woman who isn't looking for just any man she's seeking a married man. It's my bet that before long she will have picked out a target and start working on him. She'll be fun to watch as we travel upriver."

"How about the single woman sitting at the last table on the opposite side of the room?" offered, Jenny.

"See you do know the type," said Arch. "The two women are much the same except for one major difference. Take a good look at the woman I just dissected." Everyone looked the woman over. "Now look at the second woman that Jen has pointed out." Everyone turned to look her over. When they were finished Arch asked, "What is different about the two of them? Keep in mind that they are both man-killers and out for a score." After a short period of silence Tommy spoke up.

"It has to be something physical about the two of them for that's all we can see."

"You aren't as dumb as you look, buddy," Arch said. "Tommy is correct."

"Then I know," said Jennifer.

"Okay then don't keep us in the dark tell us, Jenn," Rachael prompted.

"The first woman is pretty in a made up way. She uses a lot of makeup to create her beauty."

"That's my girl. Go on," Arch said.

"The second woman uses very little makeup. She is what we girls call a natural beauty."

"Another woman or better yet a man this time?" insisted Jennifer.

"Men are easy they're all so much the same. Let's do one more woman," Rachael said.

"I've got one," Arch said whispering his words as he leaned over the table. "It's the woman sitting alone by the windows on the right side of the ship at about a forty-five degree angle toward the stern. Quietly so she doesn't hear us," he warned.

"She is worried or anxious about something or someone more likely a someone," offered Tommy.

"She's older, late forties, no wedding ring so I'd say she's divorced and could it be?"

"Could it be what?" whispered Jennifer leaning across the table.

"That someone here is her ex-husband and the man that just sat down at her table across from her is her ex's replacement."

"Juicy," Jennifer said.

"Really?" Rachael asked unbelieving.

"She has brought him along on this trip because her ex and his new conquest is also taking the cruise. I'd like to revise my interpretation now that I've watched her and him. I dare to say that they aren't in a relationship, but that she has hired him to accompany her on this trip just to make her ex jealous," Tommy added.

"You really have an imagination, buddy," Arch said holding up his glass in salutation.

At that point their waiter followed by another waiter returned carrying a large tray which they set atop a small folding table that they had also been carrying. Finished they one at a time set a plate with a bread bowl on it, which they took from the trays in front of each one of the foursome. Their waiter then placed a large tureen of Bayou Gumbo in the center of the table. "Tureen refills are free. Is there anything else I can get for you, Mr. Ponnard, sir?"

"You might bring another pitcher of Long Island Ice Tea," Arch said. "Iy looks like we'll be needing one. The waiter nodded and followed his associate back to the galley.

"These bread bowls are hot and smell as if they have

just been freshly baked. You don't imagine?" Rachael asked after smelling hers up close.

"Mr. Majestic? Your opinion please?" Tommy quipped.

"I've already cut out the center of my bread bowl and as you can see am presently filling it with gumbo. It is such a large bowl that I don't believe their will be any gumbo left for the three of you," Arch said.

"Free refills. Free refills weren't you listening again," Tommy said smiling at Arch.

"Watch out, babe," Jennifer said when Arch's grip on his plate started to tip gumbo over the edge of his bread bowl onto it.

"I don't need a nurse," Arch stated.

"I'm not too sure about that and I happen to know how you can get one full time," commented Tommy getting looks from both Jennifer and his good buddy, while Rachael oblivious to what he was referring to completely ignored the comment as a private joke between Tommy and Arch.

There was a lot of dipping, chin dabbing, drinking, and slurping with very little talking during the meal except for the repeated comment: "God this is good."

"And how was everything?" The waiter asked upon returning to the table.

"Do you have a hand truck that we can use? I think that my companion is unable to walk back to his cabin," asked Jennifer.

"Is there any thing else I can get for you?"

"Could you please have four Bloody Mary's sent to our suite can you, please?" Arch asked. "And which after consuming I think it'll be time for a nap."

# CHAPTER NINE

**The Bloody Mary's were** waiting for them when the foursome arrived at their suite. On their way to the bedroom with Arch on her arm Jennifer asked Tommy to bring one of them and follow her. In the bedroom she sat Arch on the edge of their bed took the Bloody Mary from Tommy and handed it to Arch. In four gulps he drank it down after which Jennifer took the glass from him handed it back to Tommy and laid Arch back on the bed. Crossing over to the patio door that led out onto the balcony she closed its blinds. "He'll sleep for a couple of hours and be as good as new," she said to Tommy. Leaving Arch to sleep it off they left the room.

Out in the main compartment they found Rachael half-way through her drink.

"I'll be getting up an hour before dawn tomorrow," Tommy said.

"What on Earth for?" Jennifer asked.

"I'm going cane pole fishing with my guide. He claims to be an expert and I'm going to find out if he's told me the truth. He's invited you all to join me and you're more than welcome to come along. I've arranged with the Purser to have breakfast ready for us in the dinning room at five o'clock so you might think about it."

Jennifer's prediction was right on, for after a few hours of sleep Arch was up and raring to go. "I thought since this is your last night in New Orleans I'd treat everyone to a special night out."

"Not too special I hope," said Tommy. "I'm going fishing in the morning, early, and besides how much more special can any night be after the one we spent last night?"

It was dark when the foursome left the ship and took a taxi into the heart of New Orleans dropping them off in front of what appeared to be an old church. "If it weren't for the neon sign above the door that reads: *Lucifer's* and the banners on each side of the entrance I'd think you were taking us to a prayer service of some kind," said Tommy.

"This isn't any prayer service, old buddy," said Arch opening the door allowing the sounds of Southern Rock to infiltrate the home of Jazz and Southern Blues.

Inside the joint was jumping and packed with people that seemed to fill every available bit of space. Arch spoke to a waitress who grabbed four menus. "Stay close to me," she said as she started making her way through the crowd to an area of tables on the balcony. Ushering them to a table at the railing that had a perfect view of the stage and dance floor she waited while Tommy and Arch seated their companions and sat down themselves before handing each of them a menu and asking if they'd like something to drink to start off their evening. Taking their order she disappeared.

"Would you like to dance?" Tommy asked Rachael.

"Love to," she replied and taking Tommy's hand followed him down to the dance floor.

"I'm a little rusty at this," Tommy said. "It's been more than a few months since I attended a dance at uni'."

"You seem to be doing just fine," Rachael replied.

"I hope you aren't offended by my decision to sleep in separate beds. Maybe once we get to know each other better we can change that arrangement, but until then I just can't."

"Jennifer has filled me in. Someone you knew at uni' died?"

"Something like that. I had just lost my mother and then there was a series of deaths and they were all friends of mine followed by a woman named Willow who left soon after," Tommy explained.

The song ended. "We should probably get back," Rachael said turning to head back to their table. Following after her Tommy suddenly stopped. Rachael had taken a few steps further before she realized that Tommy wasn't behind her. Turning around and taking a step back she noticed Tommy looking up at the ceiling of the old church turned nightclub and turning his body around in a slow circle. She noticed that an area of the ceiling over where the tables on the balcony were located particularly interested him. Seeing one of the security staff nearby Tommy walked over to him with Rachael following on his heels.

"I need to talk to whoever is in charge here tonight," Tommy said. The individual talked briefly into his lapel transmitter.

"What's going on?" Rachael asked stepping up beside Tommy.

"Go get Jennifer and Arch and meet me outside across the street. Don't take no for an answer from either of them." The security individual overheard Tommy.

"What's going on here," he asked.

"The manager?" Tommy said not answering his question.

"He's over by the bar. This way," the security guard said heading for the bar and talking into his transmitter.

"What's going on, Carl?" the manager asked.

"I'm Tommy Templeton and you need to close down for the night and clear the building including the band, every member of your staff, and yourself."

"Are you some sort of lunatic. Why in the world would I want to do that?"

"Because if you don't you'll be responsible for the deaths and serious injuries to an awful lot of people."

"Are you threatening me? What do you want?"

"Look at me," Tommy said. And when the manager did Tommy leaned toward him and whispered. "On the inside of your left wrist under your watchband there is a white rabbit with very large pink eyes."

"Who are you kidding? I ain't got no tattoos or any

rabbit on my wrist pink eyes or not. How much have you had to drink? Carl see this gentleman to the exit."

"I must have been mistaken. Excuse me," Tommy said walking toward the entrance with Carl right behind him unawares that Rachael had stayed and overheard his talk with the manager.

"What the hell is going on, Tommy?" Arch asked once he and Rachael had been rounded up by Rachael and joined them on the corner across the street. "Do you know how hard it is to get a dinner reservation at this place?"

"I was impressed, Arch thank you, but I have an early morning appointment to go fishing."

"Well you go fishing then. I'm going back in there. They serve the best BBQ'd ribs in the whole of the United States."

"If tomorrow I serve you the best BBQ'd Ribs you've ever had ones that are even better than those served by *Lucifer's* will you come with me now?"

"Forget it. I'm in the mood for ribs right now. Tomorrow I'll be wanting some of those fish you're going to be catching early in the morning," Arch said crossing the street with Jennifer on their way back to *Lucifer's*.

Rachael had returned to retrieve Arch and Jennifer when she saw Tommy exit *Lucifer's*. Now after having hurriedly made up her mind to stay with Tommy she watched Arch and Jennifer walk up to the entrance of *Lucifer's*. Before they got there Rachael noticed that Tommy had closed his eyes and could hear him chanting something that she couldn't quite make out.

Arch reached the entrance, opened the door, and was stopped by security. "You ain't coming back inside," one of two burly individuals said. "Anybody associated with that weirdo ain't welcome at this club tonight or ever."

"I'm a personal friend of the manager." Arch tried to say. "He knows who you are, Mr. Ponnard and he extends his apologizes, but you ain't getting back inside not tonight anyway." Shaking his head Arch with Jennifer on his arm re-crossed the street to where Tommy and Rachael were standing.

"Thanks a lot, buddy. You've got just got me black-balled from one of my favorite hangouts. No one has ever gotten me black-balled before not in all my years of raucous behavior," Arch started to say in a loud voice even before he reached the corner on which Tommy and Rachael stood.

"That's what friends are for, old buddy," Tommy said smiling.

"Who's for *Bell's* and some Mud Pie?" Jennifer asked looking at Rachael for some sort of explanation as to what had happened. Rachael mouthed the word 'later' and shrugged her shoulders.

# CHAPTER TEN

**Morning came early** and when Tommy left his bedroom he found Arch waiting for him in the common area of their cabin. "All ready to catch a few," Arch said.

"Is Jennifer coming?" Tommy asked.

"The girls figured that after last night we might need some buddy bonding time together without them.

"Listen, Tommy I want to apologize for the way I acted last night. I really didn't mean whatever it was I said. You know me, Mr. Spur of the moment with his mouth running full tilt."

"Forgiven long before it ever happened," Tommy replied. "I'm famished. Let's go eat some breakfast."

With breakfast behind them Tommy and Arch headed for the deck of the riverboat. There on the river side of the bow they found old Ben. "Morning, gentlemens," he greeted.

"Morning, Ben," Tommy returned.

"Ready to catch some fishies for lunch?"

"You bet."

Ben showed Tommy and Arch how to bait their hooks. "Now just drop the line over the railing and every once in a while raise the cane up about a foot, hold it there for about a minute, and let it back down slowly in one smooth motion. After you do that five, six times, and you ain't caught anything pull your line up so you can check to see if the bait is still on the hook."

"That's what you hired a guide for?" Arch asked Tommy under his breath not wanting to insult old Ben.

"Yup! The secret to cane pole fishing is how to fix the bait on the hook and the movement of the pole. I heard it told once, but didn't know the just how's. Now I do and it's thanks to my guide, ol Ben here," Tommy replied sitting back in his deck chair and putting his feet up onto the railing. "Time to just sit back and." At that point the line on his pole jerked so hard that it almost pulled the cane pole right out of his hands. Regaining his grip he raised the line out of the water and at its end was a large Catfish.

"Swing him over the railing and let's get that hook out of his mouth before he swallows it all the way down," Ben said. "He's of a good size too." Ben pulled out a pair of long-nosed pliers from the sheath he had on his belt and removed the hook. "If when you get him this side of the railing and you find that the hook is too far down to reach with your pliers just cut the leader and leave the hook in. You can get it back later when you cleaning him." Putting the big Catfish on a stringer he threw the stringer into the Mississippi. "Catfish that size is mighty good eaten. Some say it be better than most chicken."

Tommy re-baited his hook with Ben watching him to make sure he did it right after which he dropped his line back in the water. Just as he did so Arch got a hit, but when he raised his pole the hook was bare. There was no fish on the line and no bait on the hook. "When you feels the fishies a nibbling on the line wait just a wee bit. Let them do a bit of swallowing first so that when you raise the cane you've got him hooked good," Ben said. "Sometimes you can feel 'em a chewing on the bait, but they don't want no part of that hook. That's why we raise the line every so often it entices them fishies to go for it and take it all in one bite and prevents them from nibbling the bait off the hook."

The morning progressed and within two hours Tommy caught one more, Arch caught two, and Ben caught a total of four Catfish. I'm thinking that we should call it a day, gentlemens," Ben said. "We have enough for a fine meal and besides soon the captain he'll be a pullin' away from the shore and he'll be wanting me to show him the way out into open water. I'll clean up them fishies and see that they get to the chef to fix up nice for lunch."

"Thank you for taking care of that for us, Ben," Tommy said. "When we have them for lunch won't you join us after all you caught as many as Arch and I did together."

"Mighty kind of you, gentlemens. Give the desk a call and if I'm free I'll shows up.

"Before we go though how about a sip of the shine?"

"Swamp shine I swore that I'd never let another drop of that stuff cross these lips," Arch said. "Got so very, very wasted once when I was drinking it. For three days I didn't know where or who I was. Now though

Tommy here has told me that you've told him the secret to drinking swap shine without getting wasted so I'll have just a sip. Thanks, Ben," Arch said as Ben handed him the jar in a paper bag.

"Now I didn't tell your friend here that he won't ever get wasted if'n he sips the shine, but he'll at least know he's getting wasted and just how wasted so he can stop getting so very, very wasted. It won't jump on 'em like a swamp cat jumpin a big buck." Ben passed the jar around and then passed it 'round once more.

"Got a present for the two of you afore youse go," he said opening a door to a storeroom behind them. "Here be a box of swamp shine for the two of you. Since we ain't left port I had time to fortify my own reserve and I got a case for the two of you."

"Thank you, Ben," Tommy said taking the cardboard box full of paper bag, wrapped jars of swamp shine from him. "I'll lock it in my trunk so the lush here doesn't sip it all away by himself." His comment getting him a look from his good buddy.

# CHAPTER ELEVEN

**"Whew!** It's a good thing we had breakfast before we went fishing. Those two sips of Ben's swamp shine really had a kick to them," Arch said as he and Tommy headed back to their cabin. "You gonna lock up that shine like you said?"

"Okay you can have one jar to nurse between taking your naps," replied Tommy. "But the rest, yes I am locking them up in my locker."

"Let's see we're on this riverboat for twenty-one days counting today. How many jars are there in that box?"

"Eighteen," answered Tommy after stopping in the hallway outside their cabin to count the jars.

"If we divide them equally that makes?"

"One jar every three days so make that one last you your first three days," said Tommy.

"Daddy's back and he's got goodies that he'll share for some sugar," Arch said opening the cabin door. No one answered. "They must still be in bed," he said heading for the bedroom. "There's no one in my room," he said walking into Tommy's room. "I see that Rachael isn't here either. They must be down having breakfast."

"You really are locking that case of shine in your trunk," Arch said watching Tommy clear room in his trunk for the bottles of shine.

"And the lock on it says 'See you in three days'," Tommy answered.

"Be that way then," Arch replied turning his back so that Tommy wouldn't see him smiling.

"I think I'll give my old pal Freddie a call and see how he's feeling this morning."

"Who's, Freddie?" Tommy asked.

"He's the manager of *Lucifer's* the fellow that wouldn't let me back into his place.

"Freddie you son-of-a-bitch how are you this morning? What? What? Whoa slow down or you're going to have a heart attack."

"He's still mad, huh?" Tommy asked from his chair across the room. "Maybe I was wrong."

"How did he know? How did he know? Tell me," shouted Freddie so loud that Tommy could hear him. "And the white rabbit? Ask him how he knew about the talking white rabbit with the large pink eyes? Ask him? Ask him?" Freddie shouted even louder into his cell phone.

"I don't have a clue as to what the hell you're talking about, Freddie old pal," Arch assured him.

"You don't know?" Freddie asked. "Have you not seen the television morning news or read a god damn newspaper? Where do you live in the dark ages? How could you not know?"

"Know what for god sakes?" Arch shouted back.

Settling back down an octave or two Freddie continued, "*Lucifer's* this morning is nothing but a pile of ruble. And your friend knew that it was going to happen and warned me. I haven't told them yet, but when I do the police will want to know how he knew too." "They're a little late for that, Freddie our ship has just sailed," Arch replied feeling the cavitations of the riverboat's paddle wheel as it moved forward from her mooring. "We'll have to talk to them when we get back from our trip up the Mississippi."

"How about that," Arch started to say, but was cut off by Rachael entering the room.

"How did you know?" she asked Tommy looking straight at him.

"A lucky guess," Tommy answered throwing his arms sideways his palms in the air.

"Lucky guess my ass," Rachael returned.

"I wouldn't know about lucky, but I'd say it's a beautiful one. Wouldn't you, Tommy?" Arch interjected. "I've seen him naked." He tried to explain and lighten the mood.

"Not funny, Arch," Rachael replied.

"Would either of you ladies like to fill us in?" Arch asked. "And put in all the particulars because between what I've just gotten from Freddie and now from your screaming lungs I still don't have a clue as to what the hell is going on."

"Tommy knows," Rachael said in a toned down voice taking a seat in the main room.

"It seems that last night shortly after we left *Lucifer's*

your pal Freddie shut down the club ordering everyone including the staff, the band, his security, and the night watchman to go home with full pay. He told them all that he'd see them tomorrow," Jennifer said. "His girl friend."

"That would be Taffy. Remember her, hon? We had dinner with them at Freddie's place about six months ago." Arch interjected.

"I do remember her and that whole night and thanks for reminding me of one of the most horrible of evenings we've ever had," Jennifer replied.

"Yes it really was, wasn't it," Arch answered screwing up his face at the thought.

"Anyway," Rachael continued, "Freddie's girlfriend Taffy told reporters that he had, had one of his security staff show a lunatic out the door and when she asked him what the commotion was all about he nonchalantly slipped his watch from off his wrist. Taking his eyes off her he starred down at his wrist for the longest time. All the while he was doing so he had the strangest look on his face as if he was seeing a ghost or was witnessing a murder or something really terrible. Whatever he saw or thought that he saw it scared him so badly that he dropped his forty thousand dollar *Rolex* onto the floor and immediately started to scream at everyone, closed down the club, and sent everyone home."

"Sometime during the night *Lucifer's* imploded and when Freddie returned to open it up there was nothing there but a pile of rubble," Jennifer said. "The television news said that the police are looking into arson and insurance fraud," she added. "It seems that Freddie is in over his head and owing everybody huge sums of money."

"The good thing is that no one got hurt," offered Tommy.

"What does a white rabbit with large pink eyes have to do with any of this?" Arch asked.

"Nobody has said anything about a white rabbit with pink eyes," said Jennifer. "What the hell are you talking about now and where in the world did you come up with a white rabbit with large pink eyes from?"

"It wasn't me it was Freddie on the phone just now. I just got off the phone with him. I was hanging up as the two of you walked into the cabin.

"Where were you by the way?"

"Having breakfast," Jennifer answered.

"And learning that we had just escaped death last night," added Rachael.

"What do you mean, 'just escaped death'?" Arch asked. Freddie said it was a pile of rubble this morning."

"The news said that the building collapsed between one and two o'clock closer to two they think. If we hadn't left and if Freddie hadn't sent everyone home when he did hundreds of people would have died including us. We never leave there until four or so," said Jennifer who started shaking so bad that she had to sit down. Arch went into the bedroom got a blanket from the bed and bringing it out wrapped it around her.

"Are you all right?" Tommy asked Rachael.

"Can I talk to you alone in the bedroom?" she replied.

"Sure," Tommy said following her into their room. When he got past the door Rachael shut it behind him.

"What's up?" Tommy asked.

"I want you to tell me how you knew that building was going to collapse and how you got Freddie to close down the club and send everyone home?"

"What makes you think that I had anything to do with any of that?" Tommy asked.

"I was standing behind you when you were talking to Freddie. I heard everything."

"You heard what you think you heard. That place was so noisy I'm surprised that you heard anything at all. How the waiters ever manage to get their orders straight I hate to guess."

"Stop the bullshit and tell me what it was that you actually did say?"

"I was just making a suggestion to the manager whom I had just been introduced to that the club should be renamed, *The White Rabbit* because of all the sexual interplay that I had noticed going on between its patrons."

"Oh really?" said Rachael.

"That was it and Freddie didn't take my suggestion any too kindly as the next thing I knew he was having me ejected from the club."

"But you had all ready told me to get Jennifer and Arch out of the club and across the street. Why?"

"I have all ready explained that at the last minute I changed my mind and wanted to leave instead of having dinner out because of my early fishing appointment.

"The riverboat is moving. Can you feel the churning

of the paddle-wheel? I'd like to go out onto the lower deck and get up close to it. Would you care to join me?" Tommy asked.

"Only if you don't throw me overboard," Rachael answered.

"A lovely witch like you, no way."

*A witch not a witch a soothsayer there's a world of difference,* Rachael thought to herself.

"Not a big enough difference that you wouldn't have been burned at the stake back in the day," Tommy whispered low enough for Rachael to catch only part of what he said. She was about to ask him to repeat it, but something told her that she best not so she let it go.

# CHAPTER TWELVE

## "Mr. Ponnard?"

"Yes, Mr. Templeton," replied Arch as he, Tommy, and the girls were sitting on their private rooftop patio watching the shoreline of the Mississippi River glide by.

"Would you be so kind as to call the kitchen and have them start preparing our catfish for lunch? While you are doing so ask them if they could estimate a time it will be ready to serve, and have them call our guest, and inform him of the time."

"Certainly, Mr. Templeton, anything for you" Arch answered grabbing his cell phone from the table beside his chair to make the call.

"We are having a guest joining us for lunch?" Jennifer asked.

"It's a surprise," Tommy answered.

"Lunch will be at or a little after one o'clock," Arch announced.

"That's in half-an-hour," exclaimed Jennifer. "That hardly gives me time to change."

"You look fine just as you are," Arch said smiling at Jennifer.

"For you yes, but if we're being joined by a guest I should at least run a comb through my hair," Jennifer replied getting up with Rachael following right after her.

"Mr. Ponnard right this way," one of the ship's waiters said leading the Ponnard group to one of the larger, round tables by the windows. As they were seating themselves Ben arrived.

"You're looking dapper, father," Rachael said as Ben took a seat.

"You can quit that 'I'm-a-know-it-all' smile, son," Ben said to Tommy as he sat down. Tommy whose ear to ear smile was clearly evident composed himself.

"So do you like the jacket, daughter? I'm afraid the pants don't match, but I'll just keep 'em under the table," Ben commented creating chuckles among those gathered.

"Arch? Had you met Rachael's father before we joined him on the bow earlier today?' Tommy questioned.

"Can I lie?"

"No."

"Then I haven't met him before," Arch answered.

"Jennifer?"

"Yes once when he came to pick up Rachael," Jennifer paused looked at Ben who nodded his understanding and took a drink of water. Continuing she said, "When he picked Rachael up at the office. She was there doing some consulting work for Mr. Ponnard, Senior."

"I thought that I recognized you," said, Arch. "But why?" he suddenly stopped as Jennifer kicked him in the shin under the table and he let the rest of his question drop unasked.

The events of the night out on Bourbon Street followed by the Cad's epiphany at Bell's ran quickly through Tommy's mind bringing up several questions on statements that had been made. He reviewed each of them and was about to raise the first question when his inner voice instructed him to leave it alone.

"And you really did catch these fish?" Jennifer asked questioning Arch as the stewards brought and served lunch to everyone.

"We did just for you to enjoy," answered Arch.

"Actually Arch caught two, and I caught two, and the expert, our guest showed us both up and caught four," stated Tommy.

"Still the greatest angler of all time?" eh, father. "Did you all know that my father has actually won fishing contests and has a room full of trophies to prove it. He also has two specially equipped fishing boats a small one and a big one."

"Now, daughter I'm sure they aren't interested in my past exploits or what I have or don't have and by the way you forgot the row boat and the swamp skiff," Ben said chuckling which brought smiles 'round the table.

"He's right," stated Arch. "All we care about is that he keeps finding fish for us to catch and devour. These Catfish are delicious."

"I can't take all the credit for that. The chefs we have onboard this here riverboat really know a thing or two about cooking," Ben said.

"Speaking of cooking didn't I hear someone presently

sitting at this very table promise me the best BBQ'd ribs I've ever had in my entire life?"

"That was only if you bent to my will and took me away from *Lucifer's* immediately," Tommy reminded his friend.

"So it was, so it was," Arch deferred.

"But in joyous celebration of the fact that the two of you are still alive," Tommy said raising his glass to Jennifer and Arch, "I will if you can arrange it with the chefs and they have the necessary items provide for this evenings meal the best BBQ'd ribs this side of heaven."

"A tall order, son," Ben said. "I've had some awfully delicious and some just plain awful ribs in my time. In that light what may I ask is your secret?"

"You'll have to ask the colonel, Ben," Tommy replied.

"I'll bet that if you shared a jar of your shine with him he'd tell you," Arch suggested.

"Are we talking this colonel fella or the young fella sittin' at this table?" Ben asked.

"Either, Ben either," replied Arch. "And by the way if you're free why don't you join us."

"I will make a point of it just give the desk a call and for the honor I will judge the level of excellence these BBQ'd ribs present," Ben answered looking at Tommy.

"You know, Ben I requested a fishing guide not a food judge."

"Well ain't you lucky, son you'll be getting your money's worth then 'cause you got both," Ben answered bringing smiles and laughter from all.

# CHAPTER THIRTEEN

**Lunch was over** and as everyone pushed themselves away from the table Tommy announced that he was going to have a talk with the chefs and then make a couple of laps around the different decks. "I'll come with you to the galley," Ben said.

"Anyone interested in doing the deck laps with me?"

"I've had my tour and it almost did me in besides the beans inside my watch are telling me it's time for a siesta," answered Arch.

"Ladies?"

"We thought that we'd check out the library and then lay out in the sun for awhile. You know that us girls need our quality tanning time," Jennifer replied.

"Okay then see you all later."

Ben led the way to the galley and introduced Tommy to the Chefs. "I've promised Mr. Ponnard a meal of the best BBQ'd ribs this side of heaven and I was wondering if I could talk you into serving them up that is if you have all the necessary ingredients." The chefs said they would make it the 'Special' for the evening going over the ingredients and BBQ'ing instructions with Tommy.

"We're all set for tonight, Ben thanks for the introduction."

"My pleasure, son. Where are you headed first?"

"I thought that as long as I'm here I'd do the main deck first and work my way up."

"Mind if I walk with you for a bit?"

"No not at all," Tommy replied.

"Tomorrow we'll be stopping at *Oak Alley* and that evening might be a good time for us to do some more cane poling if you catch my drift," Ben said starting the conversation.

"Sounds like a plan, Ben. About what time were you thinking?"

"After dinner when it's good and dark. I'll bring the lantern it draws the big fish to its light."

"There's something else I'd like to talk to you about."

"Anything what's on your mind?"

"It's about my daughter. When we talked for the first time I told you that she is on a mission known only to her and I stick by that. I know that she is my daughter and that somehow you and her have some kinda connection, but like I said before be careful around her for I know how dangerous she can be."

"Dangerous in what way?" Tommy asked.

"In occult ways, dark ways, she always has had a connection with the devil like her mother does." Tommy considered what Ben had just said. *Maybe that is why I keep getting these vibes when I'm around her. Willow! How about some help figuring her out*, Tommy thought in his head.

"And you, Ben. What motivated you to come on this voyage?"

"Your request for a fishing guide. I've worked for this company before and when you requested a guide they called me. If I had known that my daughter would be on this voyage too I would have told them to find someone else. Don't get me wrong she and I get along just fine it's just that we don't exactly appreciate the way each other live our lives." A beeper on Ben's belt sounded. "This is as far as I go my captain calls. See you tonight at dinner if not then tomorrow after dinner," Ben said walking away.

Tommy did his deck walk meeting some of the other passengers onboard and thinking about what old Ben had just said to him. When he got back to the owner's suite he found that it was deserted. Going to his trunk he removed a jar of swamp shine and went out on his balcony to take in the view.

# CHAPTER FOURTEEN

**"Sir!"** A steward gently shaking him said.

"What?" Tommy asked waking up.

"I was sent to see if you are coming to dinner, sir. The rest of your party are already seated and the galley is about to serve."

"Thank you, steward. I must have fallen asleep. Tell them I'll be down in a second or two." The steward left and Tommy went into his room, changed his shirt, put on a jacket, and headed down to the dinning room.

"We thought that you might have abandoned ship, mate," Arch said as Tommy sat down. Everyone else at the table hardly noticed his appearance as they were indulging in the BBQ'd ribs that they had already been served with zest accompanied by the constant use of their napkins.

"Your ribs, sir," a steward said serving him his plate of ribs with their accoutrements.

"Ladies and gentlemen may I have your attention please," the ship's captain said after standing up at his table while clinking his water glass with a spoon. "It isn't often that a passenger requests a special meal to be served aboard my ship since we employee only the best chefs available who bring with them a menu unsurpassed anywhere, but today Mr. Templeton, stand up, Mr. Templeton." Tommy took the cue and stood up at his table. "Not only did, Mr. Templeton here request tonight's 'Special', but gave our chefs the recipe for it. So to you, Mr. Templeton a toast for providing us with the best BBQ'd ribs I or my chefs have ever tasted and believe me that is saying something." The captain raised his glass as did everyone in the dining room.

"My pleasure and thank you, captain," Tommy said sitting back down.

"Now that is a testimonial of the highest order. One I have never witnessed before," said Arch.

"I'm much more interested in your testimonials," Tommy said. "Ben?"

"I'm afraid that what the captain said wasn't exactly to the point. He forgot to say that these are the best damn ribs this side of heaven."

"And to that we all agree and to you we thank and again toast. Cheers, ol buddy and a personal thank you," Arch said. "If I had known last night that you weren't pulling my leg and that I could have missed these I'd have succumbed to your demand outside *Lucifer's* immediately. Now excuse me I have ribs to finish."

Dinner was over and everyone in the dining room that had, had the BBQ'd ribs were sitting back with loosened belts enjoying a complimentary round of drinks served especially for the occasion. "You've become quite the celebrity," Rachael said. "Master Chef tonight and savior of the masses a few nights ago so what's the next miracle on your agenda?"

"Fireworks," Tommy answered without thinking.

"What kind of fireworks are you talking, son?" Ben asked.

"The kind that enlightens a questioning soul and fills them with the wonders of creation," Tommy answered. "Now if you'll excuse me I have something to take care of."

Everyone thought that Tommy had meant that a trip to the little boy's room was in order but when he didn't come back. "Where do you think he went?" Jennifer asked.

"No idea, Jenn. Probably went to arrange for that fireworks show," Arch said. "With Tommy you never know," he added.

When Rachael, Jennifer, and Arch returned to their cabin after having spent several after dinner hours in the Paddlewheel Lounge they found Tommy out on the balcony sitting in a deck chair wrapped in a blanket. "Have the fireworks started yet, ol buddy?" Arch asked.

"Later, Arch."

"I think I'll miss them then. You can tell me all about it in the morning."

"Night, Arch," Tommy said as Arch headed for bed.

"Do you mind if I sit up with you?" Rachael asked.

"Not at all," Tommy said. Rachael retrieved a blanket, pulled a chair next to Tommy's, and sat down.

"Is there really going to be a fireworks show tonight?" Rachael asked.

"There will be, but it won't be your usual fireworks show. It's not going to be the kind they have on the Fourth of July."

"I don't understand. What other kind of fireworks show is there?"

"Wait, watch, and be amazed," Tommy said. Rachael looked at him, shook her head, and sat waiting and wondering what this strange man had in store.

Around three in the morning with the sound of the paddles churning the water lulling everyone into a deep sleep the heavens suddenly came alive. A ring of stars seemingly larger than all the others appeared and as it rotated in the night sky the individual stars of the ring began dancing off from and back to that circle. From their center shot what appeared to be three multi-colored, corkscrewing comets which crossed the sky, while spewing stardust that lingered in the sky longer than normal finally falling into old Miss. The largest of these comets came right down the middle of the Mississippi, disintegrating and spewing the riverboat with stardust as it passed over it.

"What do you think caused that? It was amazing," asked Rachael.

"I saw a poster before we boarded the riverboat which said there was to be a nighttime Civil War re-enactment of the battle of somewhere or other. I can't put my finger on the place right now, but when I was in the chart room today I noticed that during the night we'd be passing close by so I hoped we might see some of the fireworks, cannon fire, old time rockets used back then, etc.," answered Tommy. Rachael looked at Tommy and didn't quite agree with him, but it was late and she was tired.

"Well thank you for the show. I'm going to bed now. Are you coming?"

"No the night air is warm so I'm going to sleep out here tonight. Besides it's almost morning. I'll see you at breakfast."

"Goodnight then," Rachael said going inside the cabin.

"Did you get to see the fireworks?" Jennifer asked.

"Oh, you scared me," said Rachael jumping at the sound of her voice.

"I'm sorry. I woke up and saw that the two of you were still sitting outside so instead of butting in I just sat here in the dark."

"You didn't see how light the sky became? It was as bright as daylight and the sky was filled with comets."

"Really?"

"Tommy said it was some nighttime Civil War re-enactment, but I don't believe that for a minute. It was just like his explanation of why he suddenly wanted to leave *Lucifer's* and his explanation of the white rabbit."

"Why does everyone mention that stupid white rabbit?"

"Because the white rabbit talked to Freddie who is deathly afraid of rabbits. It's something from his childhood that he never got over. Anyway this rabbit appeared on his wrist and told him to close the club."

"Who told you that bunch of malarkey?"

"Taffy did," said Rachael, "When I called her and asked her what made Freddie close the club earlier than usual. Goodnight, Jennifer."

"Goodnight, Rachael."

# CHAPTER FIFTEEN

**"This is _Oak Alley_,** folks," the tour guide from the riverboat announced as most of its one hundred and eighty plus passengers disembarked for the day's tour. It was the ship's first tour stop of the many it would be making on its long journey northward. "The alley is a quarter of a mile long and the Oak trees that border it are over three hundred years old. At the end of the tunnel created by these magnificent trees you can see what was called the Big House. It is a wonderful example of Greek-revival Antebellum Architecture. You are invited to stroll the grounds and enjoy its wonderful gardens or join one of the tours of the Big House. There will be complimentary Mint Juleps and pâté filled sandwiches served in the gardens at tours end."

"I don't know about those sandwiches, but I could go for one of those Mint Juleps," Arch said.

"Not until after we tour the Big House," said Jennifer. "I want to see how a real slave owner lived."

"You've been to my father's house, Jenn. You see one you've seen 'em all."

"You're terrible," Jennifer replied.

"So you keep telling me and yet you continue to be my slave," Arch said taking Jennifer's hand and kissing it.

"Flattery helps, but a ring on the finger of that hand you're holding would be even nicer."

"Stab me where it really hurts why don't you. I thought that we've decided to keep our relationship on a slave and master level?"

"In the past, but lately I've realized especially after our near death experience that I'm not going to live forever and neither are you. Maybe it's time to start thinking along family lines."

"Are you talking kids, a dog, and all that kind of family stuff lines?"

"Yes."

"Really?"

"Really," said Jennifer with meaning after which Arch continued to hold Jennifer's hand, but did so as they walked on in silence the wheels in his head turning.

The tour was a walk through a time long past. "Have you every experienced anything that even comes close to this?" asked Rachael.

"Tommy has. Haven't you, old buddy?" Arch said turning his head around to look at Tommy when he said it.

"Tell us about it," prompted Jennifer.

"Later when the tour is over," suggested Tommy.

Leaving the Big House the foursome walked out with the rest of the tour group onto a beautiful lawn covered area upon which tables had been set. The lawn was surrounded by a garden on one side and an area of Oak trees on the other. Through the trees you could see the out buildings in which the plantation's main crop of cotton was ginned and baled. "Let's walk through the gardens before we sit down," said Jennifer leading the group down the path.

"Think of all the work that a garden like this must take," said Jennifer as the foursome finished with their tour of the gardens headed for the table serving English white bread sandwiches from which the crust had been cut and spread with pâté and served along with a complimentary Mint Julep. "I wonder who takes care of the gardens now that slavery has been abolished?"

"A slave of a different kind," suggested Arch smiling at the witticism of his own joke.

"Wouldn't you know it there's a line," stated Arch, "and me dying of thirst."

"There are a lot of people here, honey. I'm sure they won't run out."

"And if they do I'll race you back to the ship, Paddlewheel Lounge, last one there buys," Tommy quipped getting in line behind the women. The line moved and when it was time for his group to plate a few sandwiches Tommy suddenly stepped in front of the girls deliberately tripping himself over Rachael's foot. As he fell forward he upset the nearest plate of sandwiches most of which he watched land on the ground. Those that didn't he unobtrusively brushed off the table with the hand that had been placed upon it to prevent him from falling to the ground.

"I'm terribly sorry," Tommy said in apology. "I didn't know I was so clumsy. Is there any way I can make reparation for the loss of those sandwiches?"

"It's alright, sir," one of the waitresses dressed in old time southern attire said. "We usually have an accident or two and allow for them. It never fails to happen, but it's usually one of our older customers who lose their balance."

"You're awfully kind. Thank you," Tommy said.

"Come down to this end of the table," the wonderfully forgiving woman said in her best southern drawl. "There are fresh sandwiches down here by the glasses of Mint Juleps."

"Now you're talking," Arch said from the rear of the group.

"What the hell was that all about?" Rachael asked looking at Tommy while taking a drink of her Mint Julep. They had found an empty table and were sitting in the shade beneath the tall Oaks. "You just about knocked me over in your haste to get at those sandwiches. Were you that hungry that you had to be the first in line?"

"I don't know what got into me. I wasn't paying attention and for some reason I thought that the line had moved and I was all alone holding up those behind us. When I rushed to catch up I found much to my chagrin that the line hadn't moved. I didn't hurt you did I?"

"No, I'm quite alright," Rachael answered looking questionably at Tommy. *One of these times I'm going to get you to tell me the truth Mr. Templeton*, she thought.

"Okay Tommy time to tell all. You said later and it's later," prompted Jennifer changing the subject.

"Not much to tell really. I lived for a few months in a town that was more middle ages than those of a modern time."

"You mean candles, lanterns, wood stoves, things like that?" Rachael asked.

"Yes and they made almost everything they consumed, including the candles, lanterns, clothing, and baked goods. They even grew and harvested their own crops, milled their own flour, raised and slaughtered their own livestock and poultry. It was quite the place.

"How did it make you feel?" queried Jennifer

"The only feeling Tommy had when he was living there didn't come from his heart it came from his penis," Arch said laughing at his own comment while getting a disastrous look from Jennifer, Rachael, and Tommy all three.

"I wouldn't go quite that far, Arch. You're forgetting what was going on among the folks that lived there at the time," replied Tommy.

"And what precisely would that have been?" questioned Rachael.

"The principal characters who were in charge of running the town were all being simultaneous murdered one by one," Tommy answered which took away the jovial atmosphere they had all been sharing.

# CHAPTER SIXTEEN

**The passengers** of the riverboat, slowly, individually, and in groups returned to the ship. When the last of the stragglers came aboard the gangway was raised and the ship proceeded on its way. Half-an-hour later one of the passengers a man sitting with his wife in the Magnolia Lounge suddenly grabbed at his chest, started gasping for air, and fell off the barstool he was sitting upon. Tommy and the rest of the foursome were sitting in the Magnolia Lounge when it happened trying to quench Arch's thirst and observed the goings on. The ship's doctor was called for immediately, but by the time he arrived the man was dead.

"I'll bet it was a heart attack," Arch suggested.

"I have my suspicions, Arch," said Tommy.

"You would have, old buddy. It comes from that investigative streak you have embedded in the human side of you.

"It would be interesting to know who the man was and anything else anyone knows about him. I'll bet that Mr. Ponnard with all his influence could find that out for me."

"I'll see what I can do, but no promises," answered Arch.

"Wait until tomorrow before making your inquires. That should give everyone involved time to regain control of their senses, get over the loss, and have the correct facts."

# CHAPTER SEVENTEEN

**Day three** and the riverboat pulled into shore for another historic tour. This time it was the *Houmas House* better known as *The Sugar Palace*. "The house has sixteen rooms of Antebellum Period, antique furniture and thirty-eight acres of gardens, ponds, and majestic Oaks," the tour guide announced to those passengers who had disembarked the riverboat for the tour. "Tommy ask the tour guide if the ponds have fish in them and if they do can we try to catch a few," Arch suggested.

"Sorry, Arch not interested," Tommy replied.

"Tommy didn't get to bed until early this morning," Rachael added. "He was up with my father fishing all night in the dark and drinking that awful swamp shine that my father concocts in his secret still."

"Can we anticipate another mouth-watering meal of catfish then?" asked Jennifer.

"We only caught three last night which isn't enough for a meal. However they were of exceptional size and Ben said their meat would be the consistency of chicken so he'd have the chefs add them to tonight's salad.

"Today I was thinking that we should mingle with the

other passengers and see what we can find out about the man that died in the lounge yesterday," Tommy suggested.

"I thought I was going to do that tomorrow?" Arch asked seemingly displaying an air of disappointment.

"You still are, but I want your influential self to question the crew especially the captain and the ship's doctor."

"So that's the plan now I gottcha," Arch said.

"I want you two boys to understand that we girls are very interested in these tours and when they occur we will make the plans for the day," Jennifer said. "Is that understood?"

"Tommy's got his times, you girls now have yours, when do I get mine?" Arch asked trying to look sad and left out.

"When you decide that you want time for your lonesome all you have to do is ask, honey," replied Jennifer.

"Then we'll decide if we can do without your presence during that time," Tommy said. "After all it's your presence that is the spark and coherence of our group. What we'd do without it I haven't the slightest idea. We'd be lost."

"Oh just shut up for Pete's sake, Mr. Templeton," Arch said.

"Who's this Pete and when did he join our group?" Jennifer asked causing laughter to erupt among the group.

The group toured the house and strolled the gardens sitting for some time under the shade of the majestic Oaks enjoying views offered by several of the ponds. During their stroll they engaged several individuals in conversation, but found out nothing about the dead man or his wife.

"I thought that I'd gain a few pounds on this trip with all the rich food, but so far with all the walking we've been doing on these tours and aboard ship, and with the mainly sensible meals we've been having, I've actually lost weight," claimed Jennifer.

"Speaking of food I'm getting thirsty," said Arch. "You don't suppose they're serving something complimentary somewhere around here do you?"

"I haven't noticed any tables anywhere," Rachael offered. "Besides I think that I've had enough sun for one day. What say we head back to the ship? I could use a dip in the pool to cool off."

"I've got a better idea," said Arch. "Follow me," he added leading the group away from the house through the garden. "When I was a teenager we used to visit an aunt that lived near here. Since teenagers aren't especially noted for their ability to converse with adults for longer than a few minutes if at all I used to do some exploring of the area and during my explorations I found this place, well you'll see," he said.

Crossing the fence that bordered the gardens and walking a short distance along the bank of the river Arch led his friends back toward the river away from the riverboat. "There it is. See that old rope hanging from that branch that sticks out over the river."

"You're not suggesting," said Rachael stopping in her tracks. When the others didn't stop she hurried to catch up.

"This rope isn't all that old, Arch," Tommy said after inspecting and carefully putting all his weight on it by hanging from the rope. "I think someone else has discovered your secret swimming hole and has replaced the rope you originally hung here."

"Let's see if it'll hold the two of us," Arch said as he and Tommy both hung from it lifting their feet off the ground. "We're good to go. Last one undressed is an old maid," he added starting to remove his shoes and socks.

"You're not expecting us to get naked are you?" Jennifer asked.

"Underwear only children," Arch said pulling off his shirt and removing his trousers.

"Gangway," Arch shouted taking a run at the rope, and grabbing it he swung himself out over the Mississippi, let go, and cannon-balled into the river. "Come on in it's warm," he said swimming back toward the bank for another go. Tommy went next followed again by Arch and finally after a bit of teasing both of the women gave it a try.

After several more runs with Arch doing some fancy dives from off the rope and daring the others to try and match him Tommy took the challenge, failed, and ended up belly-flopping into the Mississippi. "Enough," he cried out calling it quits. "That was great. Now I can say that I actually swam in the Mississippi," he stated lying on the bank in the sun drying off.

"I was reluctant at first but now I have to agree with

Tommy. See what we mean when we say that you are the spark of our group," said Rachael.

"I agree with Tommy and Rachael, Arch. Without you this would have been just another day, but you have made it a very special one."

"Thanks guys," Arch said. "Either of you wouldn't have something to drink in one of your pockets would you? I think that I'm thirstier now than I was before and hungry too."

"Ladies you might want to put on your shirts as we are about to be rescued from death by thirst and starvation," said Tommy pointing to the two stewards from the riverboat that were each carrying a picnic basket and making their way toward them.

"Afternoon, Mr. Templeton," one of them said.

"Good afternoon, gentlemen. You couldn't have timed it any better. Please set those baskets down right here," Tommy replied indicating a spot and reaching into his pants for a couple of fifties. "Thank you," he added handing a fifty to each of the stewards.

"Picnic anyone?" he asked turning back to his companions as the two stewards returned from whence they had come.

"How? How?" Rachael tried to ask in a state of flabbergast.

"Arch and I had it planned," Tommy said looking at Arch who shook his head slightly while giving Tommy a questioning look.

"Did you plan this, honey," Jennifer asked taking a blanket from one of the baskets while Rachael started taking the fried chicken and other goodies from out of the other.

"I was telling Tommy about visiting here when I was growing up and it was actually his suggestion," said Arch.

"I think that Arch is just embarrassed to admit that he has a human, caring side," said Tommy.

"Well it's a wonderful surprise," said Jennifer giving Arch a hug and a kiss.

Tommy reached into a basket and pulled out four bottles of ice cold, spiked Lemonade handing one to each member of the group. "This is perfect. Thanks, buddy," Arch said.

"There's more lemonade so you can guzzle that one down, buddy," Tommy said.

"They even included watermelon sticks," exclaimed Rachael rather excitedly.

"You do know how to take care of your friends, old buddy."

For the next couple of hours the four friends spent a lazy sun filled afternoon, eating, talking, laughing, and just plain enjoying each others company. Finally it was time to go. "We don't want the ship to have to send out a search party," Tommy said starting to repack the baskets.

On the walk back Arch said to Tommy. "I didn't tell you about the swimming hole. I didn't even remember it myself until Rachael suggested that we head back."

"It was ages ago when you told me back when we were at uni'," Tommy said. "And when you lead us here and everyone was in the river I called the ship on my cell phone and ordered the picnic."

"And they put that all together that fast? They are good, but how did they know where to find us?"

"It's amazing what the GPS on these new phones can do," Tommy said.

"Don't sweat the little things, Arch. Take some of the credit. You're a hero in the eyes of the women especially Jennifer's and you'll always be one in my eyes."

"You're such a bullshitter, Mr. Templeton," Arch replied smiling at his friend.

# CHAPTER EIGHTEEN

**"Later that same evening** the Louisiana State Police River Patrol came and took the body of the dead man off the riverboat so that the morgue could do an autopsy and determine the exact cause of his death. His wife went with them I was told," Arch informed everyone at breakfast. "I talked to the captain on the way here that's why I was late."

"What else did you find out?" questioned Tommy.

"The man and his recently married wife were on their honeymoon."

"Oh my god! Remember when we were playing the passenger guessing game and Tommy said that that one woman looked like she was recently divorced and looked anxious about someone else being onboard this ship," Jennifer said recalling their conversation to the group.

"I remember you said that you believed she was anxious about her ex and his new wife being onboard this trip too," Rachael added.

"You don't suppose that she poisoned him do you?" asked Jennifer.

"It was just a game," answered Tommy. "You girls certainly do have a fertile imagination.

"You know now that I think about it I remembered that the dead man and his new bride were standing in line right behind us when Tommy destroyed that plate of sandwiches."

"Are you sure it was them?" Tommy asked.

"Positively," Arch assured him. "I remember turning around and was talking to them when you took your trip," he added expecting at least a chuckle but got nothing as everyone else was deep into their own thoughts.

"What's on the itinerary for today?" Arch asked.

"Baton Rouge," said Jennifer.

"I suppose that you girls have the events for the day already planned?"

"We do," Rachael said. "We've decided that we want to go on the tour to the Cajun Heritage and Rural Life Museum."

"It's supposed to be an outdoor living history of what it was like to be a slave back in the day. It has slave cabins, kitchens, and even a grist mill where they milled grain into flour," Jennifer added.

The foursome found the museum to be an interesting tour and quite different than the previous two. There last stop was the Grist Mill. "Smell the history," Arch said. "It's as if the old mill is still a functioning entity. I can even smell the freshly harvested grain."

"You were out in the sun too long on that wonderful picnic yesterday," said Jennifer. "The smell of all that wild grass you were lying in must still be stuck in your nose."

"Make fun go ahead I can take it," Arch returned, "just as long as you all had a good time."

"I wonder what's back here?" he suddenly asked seeing a strange reflection in the darkened room opposite the one they were in. Leaving the group he stepped through the room's open doorway.

"Stand up and grab each other's wrist as tight as you can," Tommy suddenly shouted grabbing Jennifer's wrist and pulling her and Rachael toward the doorway that Arch had just passed through.

Stepping into the darkness Tommy held onto Jennifer's one wrist while Rachael held onto her other wrist with both of her hands. Inside the dark room Tommy stretched out his free hand and grabbed Arch's belt. Arch himself was standing on one foot teetering on the edge of an even darker abyss. "Gottcha, old buddy," Tommy said pulling Arch backward toward himself by his belt and changing the leverage of Arch's body from one of certain death in the black abyss to safety in the main room. "Move back into the main room," Tommy shouted to the girls. Following his instructions the wrist-linked, human chain side-stepped their way back into the main room.

"What kind of a game is it that you think the four of you are playing at?" an employee of the Rural Life Museum asked. "Can't you read?"

"What are you talking about?" Tommy asked.

"The sign that says: DANGER – KEEP OUT! What do you think the warning tape and the closed door say: Come play inside me?" he asked.

"The door was open and there was no sign or any warning tape," Arch said.

"There should be," the employee said pushing past the foursome. "The floor in there is weak. Any weight at all even a child's would cause a body to fall right through that floor and if that happened that would be the end of them," the employee added standing in the doorway shinning his flashlight around the room looking for the sign and the warning tape. "I don't see the sign or the tape anywhere," he said closing and locking the door. "That's strange the sign isn't on the door either. I wonder where they went?"

"It could have fallen into the hole when the floor gave way beneath me," Arch said.

"You are a very lucky person," the employee said.

"All my luck comes in the form of that man right there," Arch said indicating Tommy. "His quick thinking saved me."

"Can I ask the four of you to do me a favor? Wait right here and don't let anyone into that room while I go get a hammer, some nails, and a couple three boards to nail across that door along with a new sign and some warning tape."

"We'll wait, but first tell us what's under that floor?" asked Arch. "I have to know."

"It's part of an old cistern that has collapsed. It's the moisture from it that has rotted out the floor above it. We've been trying to decide what to do with it for several months now. There have been times when we've been inspecting the room that we've seen gators down there and some of them have been fairly large," the employee said. "Is there anything else?" the employee asked.

"No go," said Arch, "that's more than I really wanted to know. Thank you."

"It won't take me long, ten, fifteen minutes tops," he said hurrying away.

"What was it that you said to me when we were talking about diving from our deck on the riverboat, Tarzan?" Tommy asked Arch. "Oh yes I remember. 'If the fall doesn't get you the gators will'."

"Very funny, Mr. Templeton. It would have been quite the dive though I must say."

"And your last," said Jennifer. "We just can't let you out of our sight for even a minute before you get yourself into some kind of trouble, can we?"

"Thanks, Tommy. I owe you," said Arch.

"It's just a good thing that you haven't lost that magical sense of balance that you used to thrill us students with on the high dive board. You girls really missed something there Arch was a king in that element."

"I'm just glad that my king is right where he is and alive for me to hold," Jennifer said.

"How did you know that Arch was in trouble?" Rachael asked.

"I heard him inhale. It was the kind of large inhale a person makes when they are in imminent danger. I've heard it before and it's a sound I won't forget."

"How did you know to hold hands then?" Rachael persisted.

"Intuition. You sure ask a lot of questions for a person

who is supposed to have such an intuitive sense herself," Tommy said, but Rachael missed the implication.

"There's something about you that I haven't quite figured out, but I will," Rachael said.

"Is it that important?" Tommy asked.

"It is if we are ever going to have a serious relationship," Rachael said giving Tommy a flirty look before walking away.

"I'm all for a cab back to the ship. I think that I've had enough touring for the day," Arch said when the employee came back with his boards, nails, new sign, and more warning tape.

"Downtown is closer to a bar than the ship," said Rachael. "And I know just the place."

# CHAPTER NINETEEN

**Rachael had the cab** drop them off at *Grumpy's* a bar located in the heart of downtown Baton Rouge. "Go sit at that table in the corner," she said as they entered the bar. "I'll order the drinks and four baskets of food," she added disappearing behind the bar.

"Hello, beautiful," the bartender said in welcome. "It's been a while."

"Hi, Chappie. Is Chantel in?"

"In the back room," Chappie answered.

"Four Voodoos and four Shrimp baskets to the table in the corner. Make it the large sized Shrimp and double 'em up," Rachael said disappearing through a curtain behind the bar.

Walking down the hallway Rachael came to a door with a hexagram painted on it. Opening the door she went in without knocking. At a table in the back of the room sat a woman displaying individual Taro Cards from a deck she held in her hand onto the table's top. She had a bandanna wrapped around her head with large earrings dangling from her ears. By the rest of her attire she looked every part of a gypsy fortune teller. "Hello, mother," Rachael said.

"Look at you child all clean and neat looking. Have you become civilized and given up on the trade?"

"No, mother I haven't given up on the trade. My clothing is a disguise as is the name I am using."

"Which is?" Menerva's mother asked.

"Rachael, mother. I'm using grandmother's name. I'm doing this so that I can learn something that is troubling me deeply."

"Sit down and let's see if the cards can help," Chantel said reshuffling the Taro Cards and spreading them out onto the table's top.

Rachael picked one of the cards and turned it over. "I see that this trouble of yours concerns a young man a special young man in your eyes. Does this mean that I might finally get to hold a granddaughter in my arms before I die?" Rachael gave her mother 'the look' and picked another card. When she turned it over the look on her mother's face told her that her mother now understood her plight. Looking from the overturned card directly at Rachael Chantel asked. "Do you know what you are getting yourself into, child?"

"When I met him for the first time I was immediately inclined to hold his wrist and when I did I was so disturbed by the way I felt that I turned and ran away.

"Today he rescued his friend from a certain death by forming a human chain of inter-locking wrists. He didn't grab mine, but even through the body of another person that was between us I still got the same disturbing vision.

"He's a warlock isn't he? And not your ordinary warlock, but one protected by the Dark One herself." Chantel nodded as Rachael drew another card.

"What are you doing?" her mother asked grabbing Rachael's wrist before she had a chance to turn the card over.

"I need to know more, mother. He does these things most of which are very strange, straight out of the blue, no soothsaying, no visions, but in a direct line to events and circumstances. When I ask him about them he always has a logical answer one that I know and feel is a lie."

"For instance, child."

"We sat up together on the riverboat we are traveling on to watch a fireworks show, but it wasn't an ordinary fireworks show it was a star and meteor show that came straight out of the heavens above. When I asked him about it his explanation was that it was caused by some Civil War re-enactment behind the trees on the shore.

"Now today when he saved his friend. There was no cry for help, no earthly reason for him to suddenly dart into a dark room to save his friend, yet he knew he was needed and when I asked for an explanation once again he gave me a most reasonable explanation for acting the way he did, but I know it was a lie."

"Leave go of the card, child." Rachael did as her mother instructed. Chantel quickly gathered all the cards up, straightened the deck, and put them into a drawer in the table. "This man is here isn't he? I too can feel his presence. I can also feel the presence of your father on you. You have seen him."

"The young man is here and father is working on the same riverboat that we are traveling upriver on," Rachael replied.

"I want to meet this young man bring him back here to me."

Rachael left the room and went out to where the others were sitting. "I have someone that wants to meet you, Tommy," she said.

"Why don't you sit down and have something to eat and drink first," Tommy said.

"My mother doesn't like it when someone keeps her waiting."

"Your mother wants to see Tommy? Why can't she come out here we'd all like to meet her," said Jennifer.

"Maybe later, but she asked to see Tommy first."

"A woman of mystery your mother? Does that trait run throughout the entire family? How many generations back does it go?" Arch asked without Jennifer giving him a kick in the shin that he half expected to get.

"Are you coming?" Rachael asked looking at Tommy.

"Not right now. I'm enjoying my? What's this drink called?"

"It's a Voodoo."

"And these shrimp they're amazing," Tommy stated. "Sit down, Rachael and have some."

"I know what they taste like," Rachael said sitting down. "I spent quite a bit of time in my youth here in this very bar."

"With or without your father present?" Tommy asked.

"When he was here, he was here, but that was very seldom."

"Why?"

"Why what? He was working. His work kept him away a lot," she answered sitting down and biting into one of the shrimp that she took from her basket. Taking a drink of her Voodoo all the while seeming agitated at keeping her mother waiting.

"Why did you bring us here?" Tommy asked Rachael.

"I thought that you'd all like it," she answered, "And I've been wanting to visit with my mother anyway." Chappie appeared, set another chair at the table, and when he stepped aside behind him stood a short woman with long, flowing, gray hair, dressed in a plain, button-up, stone washed, denim dress.

"Mrs. I don't know your last name or Rachael's for that matter," Tommy said getting up and pulling the chair out for her. "Just call me Chantel," she replied as Tommy pushed her in her chair up to the table.

"It's a pleasure to meet you, Chantel," Jennifer said.

"That goes for me too," Arch added.

"These are the friends that I'm traveling upriver with, mom," said Rachael. "This is Jennifer and Arch."

"Your Archibald Ponnard aren't you?"

"Yes, ma'am I am. Do you know my father?"

"So you must be Mr. Templeton?" Chantel asked ignoring Arch's question and addressing Tommy.

"Yes, ma'am I am," Tommy said. "Can we get you something to drink?" Tommy asked just as Chappie set a glass of iced tea down in front of Chantel. "If you're hungry help yourself," he said trying to regain face by pushing the basket of shrimp and curly fries a little closer to her.

"Can I read your fortunes?" Chantel asked producing her deck of Taro Cards from a pocket in her dress.

"Mother's quite good at reading them. People come to her often and pay good money to have their future foretold," Rachael assured her friends.

"What the hell I'm up for it," Arch said. "Do me first." Chantel shuffled the cards as Tommy and Rachael cleared a spot for her to spread them out.

"Pick a card and turn it over," Chantel said. Arch did as she instructed.

"I see that you are," she stopped mid-sentence and looked from Arch to Tommy.

"Mother?" Rachael questioned seeing the look on her mother's face.

"This was a bad idea you'll have to excuse me," Chantel said pushing back her chair and hurriedly leaving the table and returning behind the curtain behind the bar.

"I'd better go and see if she's alright," Rachael said following after her mother.

"Do you scare off all the women you meet?" Arch asked Tommy.

"It was your future that scared her not mine, old buddy," Tommy replied.

"I wonder what she saw that was so upsetting?" Jennifer asked.

"Mother what did you see?" Rachael asked when she caught up to her mother in the hallway behind the bar.

"When you get back onboard that ship of yours gather your things and leave immediately. Every second you stay with these people you are putting your life and your entire future in danger."

"In danger from what or from whom? My powers don't show me anything about being in any sort of danger," Rachael emphasized.

"You are too close. Your powers are being manipulated by the warlock. He knows who and what you are and will destroy you."

"If that were so I'd know. Even in a weakened state I'd know. So what is it, mother?"

"Leave me be, child. Go and do as I've asked."

"I can't, mother. I can't," Rachael answered leaving her mother standing in the hallway and rejoining her friends.

# CHAPTER TWENTY

**"This is the captain** speaking," Captain Lyle said over the riverboat's intercom. "As you are all aware we had a man die several days ago after taking the *Oak Alley* tour. So we are asking that anyone who has any information about him or his movements please contact either myself or the ship's doctor, Dr. Stevens. Thank You."

"Arch?" Tommy asked as they sat in deck chairs out on their balcony taking in the scenery.

"I'll find out later. If I wait we may learn more," Arch answered without moving a muscle or opening his eyes.

"Why all the interest in that man's death anyway outside the fact that it's in your nature?"

"Intuition. I've got a feeling that there is more going on then meets the eye."

"You mean the ex-wife thing?"

"No, much, much more than that," Tommy answered.

"Are you boys ready?" Jennifer asked appearing in the doorway.

"Ready as we'll ever be," answered Arch. "What do you have in store for us today?"

"This is Francisville it is claimed to be one of the 200

most beautiful small towns in the United States. It has seven architecturally unique plantation homes complete with gardens," said Rachael.

"You don't happen to have any relation here?" Arch asked a wry smile on his face.

"Rachael doesn't, but I do," said, Jennifer. "I have a grandmother that lives here."

"Are we visiting her before or after the tour we are taking?"

"We will visit her after if there's time, but first we want to go to see the Rosedown Plantation. It has almost four hundred acres of elaborate, flourishing gardens, and is supposed to be of some historical significance."

The bus dropped off the foursome and the rest of the tourists from the ship it had picked up at the Rosedown Plantation where they proceeded on investigating what made this place so special. "It is a wonder that with all the old plantations along the Mississippi offering tours that any one of them make enough money to keep them looking as good as they do," commented Jennifer.

"Think government subsidies and a lot of volunteer work," offered Arch in explanation.

"You all will have to excuse me. I see someone that I want to talk to. I'll catch you all up later," Rachael said walking away from them to join up with another group that was headed into the gardens.

"What do you think she is up to?" Arch asked.

"It's more like who she is trying to catch up with," queried Jennifer. "Rachael and I have decided to do our part in helping you, Mr. Templeton in finding out what happened to that man in the lounge. If I'm not mistaken Rachael is going to talk to the ex so you boys are stuck with me. You may have status with the captain and the good doctor, Mr. Ponnard, but we girls have the ability to talk to each other at any time."

"So I have noticed, dear," Arch replied.

"I don't see what you women see in touring one garden after another. They all look alike to me," commented Arch as they continued on. "The layout may be different, but the flowers, trees, shrubs, and just about everything else all look the same."

"Now that grove of trees with all its hanging moss is different. I don't think we've seen anything like it before," offered Tommy.

"You're right. All we need to do is wait for it to be late evening, produce a thick fog rolling in off the river, and a vampire or two lurking in the trees for it to really be different. What say we stay 'till after dark and find out?" suggested Arch chuckling at his own joke.

"You two stay. I see another group forming to tour the gardens so I am going to join them and spare the two of you all the anguish."

"How good of you for thinking of us," Arch responded.

"They always leave us, Tommy no matter how hung we are," Arch said still in that good-naturedly mood.

"The only thing hung that I see around here are these trees," Tommy replied referring to the moss hanging from their limbs.

"Let's go see if we can find something to drink up at the house," Arch said.

"I'm right behind you," Tommy replied following after his jovial minded friend.

Tommy and Arch entered the plantation's main house looked around for a watering hole and finding none took the half-circular stairway up to the second floor. Walking through a bedroom they opened the French doors and stepped out onto a balcony with a view of the gardens behind the house. "Hey look. I can see Jenn and Rachael from here. They're over there by that pond," Arch said pointing to two separate groups of people.

"Where away my captain?" Tommy asked stepping up to the railing beside him.

"See that low stone causeway what you might call a bridge that crosses the pond at ten o'clock?"

"I see it," answered Tommy.

"That's weird," Arch declared rubbing his chin.

"What's weird?" Tommy asked.

"The man right behind Jennifer is wearing a shirt and shorts that are almost identical to mine. He even has a hat on just like the one I'm wearing. I wonder who his tailor is. If it's mine I'm going to have to have a talk with him about his claim to only be selling me original combinations."

"That helped. I see Jenn. Now point me to Rachael?"

"She's about a hundred yards ahead of Jenn and at about your high noon," Arch directed.

"I see her," stated Tommy. "She looks like she may be learning something."

"I hope so. I don't want to be the only one sending someone to the gallows." His comment caused Tommy to chuckle as the two men returned to and proceeded back down the staircase to the first floor.

"You know, Arch god must have forgotten or just plain miscalculated when he set your being in motion? In fact he may have played a joke on you," Tommy commented on an observation he had made.

"How do you figure?" Arch asked.

"Well I was just thinking that as thirsty as you always are he could have given you the nose of a bloodhound or better yet the instinct of a camel to find water, alcohol in your case."

"That's what you call a curse, old buddy. It's one of several that I've had to live with all my life," Arch replied.

Time passed and only lemonade was found to quench their thirsts. "I wonder what is keeping the girls?" Arch asked pulling out his cell phone and calling Jennifer. The look on his face told Tommy that something was amiss. The call over Arch put the cell phone back into his pocket which gave Tommy the signal to ask.

"What's going on?"

"It seems that someone in the group Jenn was walking with suddenly keeled over as they crossed one of those bridges and fell into the pond. By the time they were able to get the individual out of the pond they discovered that he was dead. The police are their now and Rachael has joined her to keep her company. She said that we should go back to the ship and as soon as the police release the two of them they'll join us back onboard.

"And here I was half looking forward to visiting with Jenn's grandmother."

"Really? Why? I thought you hated that sort of thing," said Tommy.

"Usually I do, but this is Jenn's grandmother on her mother's side."

"So?"

"So seeing her would allow me to form some sort of an idea of how Jenn will look when she starts to age into her later years."

"You're terrible. Do you know that?"

"Hey it's one of those things you have to consider if you're going to ask a woman to be your wife."

"Arch is there something you're holding back from your old buddy?"

"Recently Jenn has said that she has changed her mind about kids, a dog, a house, and caring for a husband of her very own."

"I see," replied Tommy smiling and holding back all the comments that were circulating through his head.

# CHAPTER TWENTY-ONE

**"It was the strangest** thing," Jennifer started after finding Arch and Tommy sitting on their cabin's balcony, sipping swamp shine, and enjoying a game of guessing at what was making the shipboard sounds they were hearing. Pulling up a deck chair she continued. "The group I was in were all walking and talking when suddenly there was this loud splash behind us. We all turned to see what had caused it and saw this man lying face down in the pond. Funny thing was that at first I thought that it was you, honey," she said leaning over, pulling Arch's head closer to her, and giving him a kiss. "And I don't have a clue as to why I would have thought that," she added. "Anyway by the time someone managed to pull him out he had drowned."

"With all the old people taking those tours and as hot out as its been I'd be surprised that things of this nature aren't a common occurrence. I'm sure that the people who run those plantation tours must know how to handle those sort of incidents and more," Arch said trying to comfort Jennifer. "I'm sure that he'll be well taken care of," he added.

"On a little lighter note how did your talk with the ex turn out?" Tommy asked including Rachael into their conversation as she joined them.

"I found out that the two women the ex and the widow of the now dead man are sisters and after talking with the one still with us on our trip I have come to the conclusion that either one of them may have poisoned the now dead man."

"Why do you think that?" asked Tommy.

"I think that these two sisters were working the man for his money," Rachael suggested.

"No, no I don't see it," said Tommy, "Not after seeing the ex's face when she was sitting in the dining room on the day of our arrival. She looked completely surprised at seeing the two of them onboard our ship. It would not surprise me that in order to lessen the amount of suspicion that must now be hanging over the two of them that they have reconciled and joined forces being sisters and all."

"The sister I talked to said that the coroner has told her sister the widow that her husband's death wasn't a heart attack, but that he was poisoned."

"Arch when you talk to the captain press him as to the 'what and how's' of the poisoning. Would you, please?"

"Anything for you, old buddy," Arch replied still in his jovial mood.

# CHAPTER TWENTY-TWO

**"Sorry I'm late,"** Arch said when he joined the others for dinner in the ship's dining room. "I ran into the good ship's doctor, Dr. Steven's on my way here. "Have you ordered yet?" he asked keeping the others in suspense.

"Yes and I've ordered for you too, honey," Jennifer said with that 'it'll be quite the surprise' look on her face.

"What am I having?" Arch asked having caught and recognized the look.

"A big bowl of grits steeped in Rum and Brown Sugar and topped with several layers of gator meat."

"My father was out fishing today and caught us a gator for dinner," Rachael said adding to the fun Jennifer was having with Arch for making them wait on what Dr. Stevens had told him.

Not knowing whether they were kidding or not Arch decided to let it go and continued his explanation of the conversation he had, had with the good ship's doctor. "Dr. Stevens told me that the dead man had been poisoned with arsenic. It was the coroner suspects in a pâté sandwich that he had eaten a few hours earlier while he was on the *Oak Alley* tour."

"Remember I told you all that he and his wife were right behind us in line waiting for sandwiches and something to drink," said Arch.

*I must not have gotten them all, but I'm sure I did. I should have been more conscientious in my efforts to destroy them all unless they put some of them back on another tray? Could the man have picked one up and ate it?* Tommy asked himself.

"What are you mumbling there, old buddy?"

"Nothing, nothing please go on continue," Tommy said not realizing that he had been talking aloud to himself.

"Another thing the good doctor told me was that the man who fell into the pond was also a passenger on this voyage. The good doctor didn't want to say, but when I pressed him he confessed that the man was known to be a boozer, which probably led to his undoing. The police will let him know as soon as his autopsy is completed."

"You've done well, grasshopper," said Tommy. "Ah and here comes our gator now."

The steward's placed a large silver serving tray with a mid-sized alligator on it that had his back split open, the meat removed, cooked, added too, and stuffed back into his cleaned out and processed carcass. They also placed on the table large bowls of Cajun rice, shrimp, and other complimentary dishes. "Compliments of the chef and old Ben," the steward said. "Is there anything else that I can get for you all?"

"I think we're good. Thank you," replied Jennifer, "it smells wonderful."

"You really weren't kidding were you?" Arch asked. "Did Ben actually catch this rascal?"

"He did," said Rachael.

"It's been a long time since I've had gator, but as I recall it was delicious," Arch added scooping out a big portion from the gator's back and putting it onto his plate along with servings from the other dishes. The rest of the diners at the table sat in silence and watched as Arch took his first mouthful. "Mmmm good. Go ahead try it, it's delicious," he said noticing that everyone's eyes were upon him watching and waiting to see what his reaction would be.

"I've never had gator before," Tommy said putting half a forkful into his mouth. "Arch is right. It really is good," he added after his initial taste. Putting his fork down he added a huge scoopful to his plate.

"How can you doubt anything that the chefs aboard this ship put out," stated Arch shaking his head at his friend's indifference.

# CHAPTER TWENTY-THREE

**"Well what's on** the agenda for today?" Tommy asked.

"Tanning our wonderful bodies at poolside," said Jennifer.

"What no tour?" Arch said.

"The ship will dock below Natchez, Mississippi. It's the oldest city on the Mississippi. It has the largest concentration of antebellum period housing in the United States. It sits high on a bluff that overlooks the river," Jennifer said reading from the ships itinerary for the day. "You can take a tour of downtown Natchez and view the impact that the Civil War had on the city or go on the Frogmore Plantation Tour. The Frogmore Plantation is an eighteen hundred acre working cotton plantation that has eighteen restored antebellum period structures."

"Enough already," shouted Arch. "I get the picture. Enough antebellum is enough antebellum."

"On top of that if you were born and raised down here in the South and reached our age you've had enough of all that Civil War crap that you can take," added Jennifer.

"Now Tommy on the other hand might want to go and if he does so do we all, willingly," Jennifer added.

"Tommy has an invitation to go fishing. You girls go sit by the pool and make yourselves more beautiful than you already are, but I must warn you that a full body inspection will be called for upon our return."

"Tommy Templeton you are a dirty old man," responded Rachael, "And I love you for it."

"Arch want to come along and see if you can catch another gator? That meal last night was delicious."

"I'm game," Arch replied.

# CHAPTER TWENTY-FOUR

**A knock** on their cabin door disrupted their conversation. Tommy went over and answered it. "Come on in doctor," he said when faced with the presence of Dr. Stevens.

"I'm not interrupting anything am I?" the doctor asked.

"We were just thrashing about the insignificance of the Civil War upon our generation," said Arch. "You understand of course that we've had it drilled no not drilled, but pounded into our heads since we were infants."

"What can we do for you, doctor?" Tommy asked.

"I come with some disturbing news."

"Oh," said the occupants of the cabin almost in unison.

"We've been informed of the results of the autopsy of this voyage's latest victim," the good doctor said.

"He didn't drown," said Rachael.

"Oh he drowned all right, but only after he was paralyzed by a substance injected with a syringe into his spine at the base of his neck."

"I want to know if there was any video surveillance

of that bridge," Tommy said stepping in front of the rest of the group.

"I can check, but I doubt it," the doctor replied. "Can I ask your interest in all this? I have gathered from the questions asked of me and the captain by Mr. Ponnard that you all are somehow involved. I'm not only talking about this latest victim, but the previous one as well."

"Our interest goes back a lot farther, doctor," Tommy replied. "And if you don't mind we'd like to leave it at that for the time being."

"Very well, but I will have to inform the captain and the state police of your interest."

"I'd be very glad to talk to them," Tommy said.

"What the hell was that last bit all about?" Arch asked after the doctor had left.

"If you'd stop and think about it you'd know, but I'm not sure if you'd be willing to face the facts right now or that you just can't see them and I'm rather surprised at that with you being a lawyer and all. Although this is close and things that are close and obvious are sometimes hard to see."

"Go to hell," Arch said.

"As you've already pointed out to me you and I are already here," Tommy said walking away into his room and shutting the door behind him.

"What was that all about, Arch?" Jennifer questioned.

"Old university debate stuff. It's really nothing," Arch replied.

# CHAPTER TWENTY-FIVE

**Shortly after Tommy entered** his and Rachael's room the door opened and Rachael walked in closing the door behind her. Tommy was sitting by the room's desk and as she walked across the room and sat down on the bed he turned to face her. "My mother confirmed my suspicions about you," she said.

"And she finally opened my eyes to who you truly are," Tommy said. "I also know that you are only pretending to be this Rachael person. I know that it's a disguise and that your real life persona your New Orleans persona goes by the name of Menerva."

"My mother warned me that you would destroy me if I didn't leave this ship and this cruise, but for some reason I can't."

"Ah, the old moth to a flame bit is that it?"

"It's true there is something about you that draws me to you, but it's not a part of my mind it's here in my heart," she said putting both hands over her heart.

"I haven't said anything up to this point because I've been wondering why especially after what occurred at our first meeting in the foyer of the Ponnard household that you suddenly showed up at the bar. There wasn't much time for you to make that decision only a couple of hours. First you had to decide what you were going to do next. I imagine that the one person that you thought could tell you more about me was Jennifer so you called her. During that conversation she must have said that she was meeting Arch and I and bringing along a date for me. I'm wondering what you told her to get her to change her mind and convince her to let you come with her instead of the other woman whom she had to then call and cancel the arrangement they had at the last minute? Then you had to change your appearance so that I wouldn't recognize your real identity which couldn't have been easy. How long has it been since you had to be scrubbed and dressed like a normal person? Dyeing your hair was a neat trick. I didn't know you could do that in such short time. Even curiouser is why you agreed to come on this voyage with us. Curiosity killed the cat or haven't you heard? By the way your disguise is very good and it flatters you."

"My answer to all those questions is something like that, but it has more to do with that something that has terrified me to an extent to which I have never been terrified before. I had to know what about you that made me so afraid if you. I have always faced my fears in the past. Facing them has always made my soothsaying abilities stronger, but after meeting you and grabbing your wrists I felt completely drained and I suddenly became strongly aware that I was terrified to be in your presence. That terror is what made me run away like I did.

"Once I got away I regained some control, but the terror was still there I could feel it deep inside me. After I thought about it for a bit I came to the realization that I had to know what it was that was causing this intense fear in me. I had to face it and that wanting to find out why is what made me call Jennifer."

"Why come on this voyage?"

"That night we all spent together I was completely taken by surprise with you. You were not what I had envisioned after our first meeting. You were a caring and considerate person and those traits just added to my confusion leaving all my questions unanswered and hanging like moss in the trees. So when Arch suggested that we all come on this trip I was exuberant. It meant that I had more time to understand what was going on within me in regards to the two of us, and also discover why I was wrong if I was wrong, and more time to find out who and what you are, really."

"I see that you have a few questions that you'd like answered. Go ahead and ask them," Tommy said.

"I have more than a few. For example why are you really taking this voyage?"

"I've already told you and it was the truth," Tommy answered.

"I have to ask the next one," interjected Tommy. "Why did you advise Mr. Ponnard to send Arch along with me on this trip?"

"How?" Menerva stopped, closed her eyes, and

answered his question. "Because at the time I had this vision that you could show him that his position in the firm was an important one and that he should be taking it more seriously. Mr. Ponnard was at the point of putting him on the back shelf so to speak because of the nonchalant attitude he had toward the cases he was assigned to handle.

"Mr. Ponnard had told me about you're coming to New Orleans, your importance to Arch, and your trip upriver. That night I had a vision that told me that spending time with you would change his attitude toward his father, the firm, and his life in general. For some strange reason when I held your wrist I realized that I was wrong in my diagnosis and I've never been wrong before not once, not once in all the years of advice that I've given to so many. It too along with the feeling of dread that I got scared me and I didn't know how to handle it so I admitted that I was wrong and ran."

"You know that your vision wasn't really wrong it just mislead you into thinking along lines that were familiar to you. It led you to the wrong conduit so to speak. Arch is a very capable lawyer and has his own way of being one. I asked him about it and he knows that his way doesn't exactly fit into his father's image of what a lawyer should be and how he should act, but he does win his cases and he does it with style and panache. I'm not going to change that. I don't want to change that. It's what makes Arch, Arch.

"Jennifer on the other hand is the one that is going to change Arch's attitude toward life and the way he lives it. It is true that if Mr. Ponnard hadn't dumped him upon me the transition might not have taken place as quickly as it has, but since he has she will change him and I think that in ways she already has. Since we've come on this trip she's had a change of heart when it comes to her relationship with Arch and has told him that she's changed. Right now Arch's mind is considering what she has told him and given time, we'll see.

"I am questioning right now that changing Arch's attitude toward life was Mr. Ponnard, Senior's real motivation for sending him along with me. I suspect that he had a hidden agenda and it just might be that, that hidden agenda was what threw your soothsaying ability slightly off."

"So you think that's why I got such a massive feeling of foreboding the first time that I met you and several times since?"

"In and of itself no. I think that you are trying to explain something that if left alone will explain itself. In other words you've been trying to hard to explain everything from the moment we first met onward," Tommy said, "and those things are accumulating in your psychic causing you to be revisited by what you are imagining to be the cause."

"My senses have just felt the lifting of a great weight caused by the realization that you are right," Menerva said. "Thank you, Tommy," she added a smile appearing on her face as she sat there enjoying the feeling of relief that had suddenly swept through her being upon the revelation.

"Have you figured out what Mr. Ponnard, Senior's

hidden agenda is?" Menerva asked rejoining her place in time.

"Let's just say that I have my suspicion, but for the life of me it doesn't make any sense. Furthermore I haven't been able to gleam a hint as to what would have it make sense. I need more information, but I know that when the time comes it will come to me."

"If you're up to it tonight we should sleep in the same bed. You and I need to hold each other for more than the usual reason. You need to get a firmer grip on your foreboding. You've taken the first step by lessening the tension, but what you need now is a night of close contact with the forces that surround us both. That contact will either increase the foreboding to the point that you'll leave this voyage as your mother has suggested you should or release it completely."

"How did you know what my mother had told me?"

"Once she found out who and what I was she had no other choice if she wanted to protect you.

"Right now though I am going to gather up Arch if he's still talking to me and go meet your father. We will fish and sip some shine and I am going to ask him some serious questions about you and your mother. If you think that the answers he will give me are going to scare you why don't you tag along?"

"I am not afraid of anything my father may or may not have to say and since you know the boundaries of our relationship I will pass on your offer to join the three of you. Jennifer and I will be by the pool if you need either of us," Menerva said rising to her feet and leaving the door to the room open when she left.

# CHAPTER TWENTY-SIX

**"What are we going** to catch today, Ben?" Tommy asked.

"You the only one comin' to fish" Ben asked.

"Arch is having himself a personal crisis, but if he gets over it he may join us later."

"In that case we gonna try and catch us some bass maybe or a mess of crappie. For these we gonna shorten our line keepin' it off the bottom and we ain't gonna raise and dip cause we gonna use a bobber so it can move around on its own," Ben said handing Tommy a cane pole with a hook and bobber already set on the line.

"What are we going to use for bait?" Tommy asked.

"Some of that gator I caught yesterday. I been marinating the meat from inside his legs and tail in a special mixture I come up with in my fishing tournament days."

"You gonna share that secret mixture?"

"We'll see. I usually only share it with family. You gonna become a member of the family, son," Ben asked following Tommy to the side railing and dropping his line overboard.

The two men sat down in their respective deck chairs

that Ben had previously put in place. "You got your shine with you, Ben?"

"I saw that you brought yours so I thought I'd sample it with you."

"You've got good eyes, Ben. I'm going to start early as I've got some thinking to do," Tommy said opening the jar he had brought with him and after taking a sip passed it Ben's way.

"What's in need of all your thinking?" Ben asked.

"I have been gifted from birth with a very special ability."

"That being?"

"I have the knack for solving puzzles created by man and this ability has been enhanced by sources from outside this world we live in," Tommy said.

Ben looked at Tommy and asked, "We talking 'bout them murders that have happened recent like?"

"We are and I am seeing things that connect them to other events that I've experienced since I've come to New Orleans. The only problem is that although I can make certain connections I can't for the life of me figure out what's behind them. If I could do that I'd have the connection and the problem solved."

"Sounds like you've got yourself a conundrum," Ben stated adding, "Pass the shine, son."

"I have another problem that needs figuring out and that problem concerns your daughter."

"Rachael? I warned you to be careful 'round her."

"I'm not talking about Rachael I'm talking about Menerva," Tommy said watching Ben's face as he turned to look at him while taking a sip from the paper bag wrapped jar.

"You figure that out or did she get up the nerve to finally tell you?"

"Both," Tommy said.

"Tell me about her soothsaying ability." Tommy's and Ben's poles both bent at the same time.

"Fish on," Ben said as he and Tommy grabbed their poles. "Wait before you take your hook out of the water."

"Why?" Tommy asked.

"A wager, son," Ben said. "Bigger fish wins."

"What are we wagering?" Tommy slowly asked being afraid of what he was about to commit to.

"A jar of that shine I gave you. I'm starting to run dangerously low."

"Against?"

"Against my daughter's hand in marriage."

"Those days are long past, Ben. Arranged and indentured marriages I don't think are even legal anymore."

"In this case they are," Ben said. "You don't know the ways of us Cajuns." Tommy took his time and considered the offer taking another sip from the jar of shine.

"For the sake of having a little fun you're on," Tommy said raising his catch out of the water as did Ben.

"We should have been watching them bobbers as we'll have to cut the leaders now. These buggers have really swallowed them hooks," Ben said as they both set their catches down onto the deck. Ben stuck his finger through their gills and raised them both up to compare them.

"Two mighty fine bass, but it's going to take a scale

and a tape measure to tell which is the biggest. They both look like siblings to me," Ben said.

"I'll call it a draw if you will," said Tommy.

"Agreed," Ben said putting the two fish into an ice chest that he had brought along.

"Why aren't you putting them on a stringer like you've been doing?" Tommy asked as the two men rebaited their hooks, dropped their lines back into the water, and took their seats along with another sip.

"Know how I caught that gator?" Ben asked. "I'll tell you. He caught himself. Swallowed the fish I had on my stringer and when I lifted it to put on another fish all the metal eyes of that stringer from that first fish I had put on it down to the last eye were stuck inside him." Tommy started to laugh causing Ben to chuckle too. "So today I thought I'd bring along the ice chest."

"That gator was delicious by the way. Arch wanted to come today and catch another."

"If the two of you want to go gator hunting this area we now in be about the last of the gator hunting grounds. Most don't come this far upriver from the bayou so it not be surprising that he ate an easy meal. Want to go gator hunting? That be a good reason to come back to New Orleans and pay us a visit."

"You say that you are running low on swamp shine?"

"That be true."

"Can you call someone?" Tommy's bobber started its dance. "Fish on," he said waiting a bit and when the bobber went down he pulled in another bass. This time the fish was a bit bigger than the last.

"Most be a dumb brother checking up on the last two," Ben suggested taking a sip and passing the jar before clearing Tommy's line and putting the bass in the cooler.

"Can you call someone to bring another case to a designated spot from which someone can pick it up and bring it up here?"

"No one that I can trust," answered, Ben as he rebaited Tommy's hook.

"How important is it that you have a good supply of swamp shine?"

"You up grade my stash and you can have my daughter's hand in marriage," Ben replied offering Menerva to Tommy once again.

"Other than that. Would it be worth say another two cases of shine plus of course your daughter's hand in marriage?" Tommy added half-joking wondering why ol Ben kept trying to give his daughter away.

"It would be indeed, son, it would be indeed," Ben replied.

"Why are you suddenly so insistent on having me marry your daughter?"

"It's something you said," Ben answered.

"What did I say?" Tommy asked trying to think of just what it could be.

"You said 'sources outside this world'. I ain't heard anyone talk like that 'cept my daughter. As soon as you said them words it came to my mind the answer of a puzzle that I been struggling with concerning the two of you and its solution."

"I see," Tommy replied sitting in silence for awhile watching the water and their bobbers floating upon it.

"Can the captain spare you for a day and a-half?"

"Why do you think that my supply has run short, son? It's the captain that's been helping me drink the lot."

"So the answer is yes?"

"Of course, son. Isn't that what I just said?"

"Hi fellas," greeted Arch joining the two fisherman.

"Bad news, Arch. We are too far upriver to catch another gator. The good news however is that if you can get us a fast boat to take you, Ben, and I back to New Orleans leaving no later than noon today Ben has assured me that we can have two more cases of swamp shine to ourselves and that you and I will get to have a double wedding."

"You've been hitting the shine a bit more than usual today, ol buddy," Arch said noticing the way Tommy was acting.

"Can you or can't you get us a fast boat?" Tommy persisted.

"If it's that important I can," Arch replied.

"One that we can lay down in to sleep? We'll be gone a day and a-half down from here and the same back upriver to meet the riverboat at Greensville."

# CHAPTER TWENTY-SEVEN

**"Archie!** It's been too long, man," Bonaventure said pulling up alongside the riverboat. Securing a line he climbed aboard and gave Arch a big, two-armed, bear hug.

"Easy there, Bon Bon," Arch said, "If you break me you won't get paid."

"Your name is Bon Bon?" Jennifer asked. She had come down to see the love of her life off.

"Yes, ma'am. It's a pet name I've picked up somewhere in my past. I have always been partial to it over my given name."

"May I ask or don't I want to know?" Jennifer inquired.

"It's Bonaventure, ma'am," Bon Bon replied.

"I see your point, Bon Bon."

"Who is this lovely lady?" Bon Bon asked.

"She's spoken for, Bon Bon," Menerva said stepping out from the crowd that had gathered around them.

"Menerva," Bon Bon said with an inhale of breath as he took a step back toward the railing after taking a moment before recognizing her in her cleaned-up state.

"She's part of our party, Bon Bon and taking this

voyage on the riverboat with us," said Arch. "She's, Mr. Templeton's companion.

"She's also been promised, Mr. Bonaventure," said Ben joining the group. Menerva looked at her father and swore that if it was in her abilities she'd?

"Ben you, old goat. The last I heard you was dead," Bon Bon exclaimed. "Is this a family gathering then? Can I expect to say hello to Chantel too?"

"She's home still running the bar," Ben said.

"Does, mother know what you've gone and done?" Menerva whispered having moved by her father's side.

"I'll take care of your mother besides I have no doubt that she'll approve," Ben said.

"May I inquire who this fella is?" Menerva whispered.

"When I get back we'll talk," Ben said walking toward the gangway.

"Let's be off then," Tommy said. "We'll catch up with you gals before the ship lands at Greensville," he added.

"This is truly to be a speed run then?" Bon Bon questioned. "Climb aboard and fasten your seat belts. The old Miss is about to witness something spectacular."

With Tommy, Ben, and Arch aboard Bon Bon cast off and pushed the ignition button to fire up the engine. Nothing happened. Bon Bon grinned and pushed the button again and once again there came no roar from the unmuffled engine. Drifting slowly away from the riverboat and out into the Mississippi Bon Bon crawled over the seat, through and over his belted-in passengers, and onto the back deck of his boat. Opening the engine compartment he began to look for the problem. "If that's all the faster Bon Bon's boat goes we will have completed our voyage all the way to Saint Paul and be back in New Orleans in time to greet them when they finally arrive," Jennifer said laughing along with all those standing around within earshot that were watching the show.

"I heard that, missy," Bon Bon shouted from the back deck of his boat.

"Try it now, Archie," Bon Bon said. Arch reached over and pressed the ignition button. The engine roared to life. Over its thump, thump, thumping, came the cheers emitted from those onboard the riverboat. Bon Bon closed the engine compartment's cover, stood on the rear deck of his speedboat, and bowed to the crowd standing along the riverboat's railing blowing Jennifer a kiss, and with Arch, Ben, and Tommy waving their goodbyes crawled back into the driver's seat, and headed downriver toward New Orleans in a burst of showoff speed.

Bon Bon's boat seemed to fly down the river on the outgoing tide. Even with their several stops for fuel they managed to arrive in New Orleans before Midnight. "Do you have a place to stay for the night, Bon Bon?" Arch asked. "I've got plenty of room at my place."

"Mighty kind, but I got a place," Bon Bon answered.

"Meet you back here then at?" Arch questioned.

"After three no later than five in the afternoon if you want to catch your riverboat before it reaches Greenville," Bon Bon said.

"I'll see the three of you back here right before five then," Ben said walking away and disappearing in the shadows along the wharf.

"I've called a cab," Tommy said to Arch. "It should be here momentarily."

The cab arrived and dropped Arch and Tommy back at Arch's place. "See you in the morning," Arch said heading for his bedroom.

"In the morning it is," Tommy answered going into his room.

# CHAPTER TWENTY-EIGHT

**"What the hell?"** A loud voice in the bedroom shouted waking Tommy up.

"I got another one in this other bedroom, too," someone else shouted from the direction of Arches bedroom.

"Get up and get out," an elderly man wearing a hard hat said.

"What the hell is going on?" Tommy asked crawling out of bed walking past the man in his underwear and into Arch's room where he found another man wearing a hard hat with his hands in the air.

"Arch?" Tommy asked as he and the other man walked in.

"These two gentlemen are about to explain why the hell they are in my apartment and they have one minute before I start shooting," Arch said pointing his 9mm automatic at the two men.

"The city has condemned this whole block and this morning we are going to level it to the ground through a series of imploding explosions. We're here checking to make sure this apartment and the rest of the building is clear." Arch lowered his gun and set it on the nightstand.

"The city has a restraining order preventing them from doing that," Arch said, "and I should know I'm the lawyer who saw it through."

"It was lifted four days ago," the elderly man said. "After which we were told to tear it down."

"Who lifted it?"

"You'd have to call city hall for that information."

"What about all my things?"

"We were told that anything of importance or value had already been removed."

"My gun is still here, and my clothes, and everything else I own as you can see so you must have been misinformed," Arch said just as two police officers arrived in the bedroom's doorway.

"Is there a problem? We received a call that two intruders are trespassing on this condemned property," one of the officers said.

"I'm Archibald Ponnard, officer and this is my apartment."

"Not anymore, Mr. Ponnard. It is city property and you are trespassing. Didn't you see the sign on the door?"

"We got in late last night, officer and all we wanted to do was get some sleep. I did see a sign and tore it off the door to read it when I got up. I figured it was one of those advertising flyers that get stuck on it every once and awhile. It's out there in the living room somewhere."

"We're sorry for unknowingly trespassing. We are

only here for a few hours and will be going back upriver around five," Tommy said.

"How much time can I have to gather up a few of my things before you blow the rest of it to smithereens?"

"We can give you an hour, no more," the elderly man with the hard hat said.

"We'll be out in an hour then, officers," Tommy assured the two policemen.

"We'll be back to see that you are," one of the officers replied following his partner out.

"Don't touch any of the wires that you may find or disturb any of the charges on your way out. If you do they could go off prematurely," the older man warned before leaving with the others.

"Get dressed, Arch and I'll help you round up your things. Do you have any garbage bags or bags of any kind, boxes, anything that we can put your stuff in?"

"There won't be that much, clothes mostly. I'll round up the containers, but after you're dressed I want you to go to Bell's first and retrieve those pies. I promised the girls we'd bring them and I don't want to break that promise or Jenny will never forgive me. I can't do anything to stop the demolition now there isn't enough time to submit all the paperwork. I'd need at least twenty-four hours to do that, but when I get back there will be hell to pay I can assure you of that."

Tommy dressed and hurried over to Bell's. He ordered four complete frozen pies putting them into the two freezer bags that they had brought with them from the riverboat to transport them back in. Once they cleared out of the apartment they could find some ice and a cooler to put the bagged pies into to make sure they stayed frozen.

On his way back Tommy noticed that the streets in the area were completely deserted. *They must be clearing the area for the demolition that's about to happen*, he thought. Looking down the block he noticed a gas company truck parked in the middle of the street. Quickly he set down the pies in the shade of a building's wall and started running. Reaching the street level door of Arch's apartment he opened the door nearly tearing it from its hinges and ran up the stairs to the apartment.

"Arch," Tommy yelled and started coughing because of the gas that was in the air and getting thicker. Trying not to breathe he ran through the apartment looking for Arch noticing that all the doors and windows were closed. *When I left I swear that everything had been open because of the heat.* Entering the bedroom he noticed Arch's feet still bare on the floor on the other side of his bed. Running over Tommy grabbed Arch's feet and drug him out into the living room. Then using a fireman's carry he hefted Arch across his back and hurried as fast as he could down the stairs carrying his friend.

Out of the building and across the street he went carrying Arch. When Tommy reached the protection of the building against which he had left the bags of pies he lowered Arch onto the sidewalk and checked his breathing. *He's breathing, but I need to try to clear his lungs.* Slapping Arch lightly to liven his senses he started giving him artificial respiration. Suddenly the noise of a huge blast filled the air causing the ground beneath them to shake. Tommy quickly rolled Arch onto his side facing slightly down and up against the building wall and protecting both their heads by leaning in toward the building's wall above Arch's face and head. Small particles of brick and other debris rained down upon and around them as they huddled, pressed there against the wall. "Who's making all the god damned noise?" Arch groggily asked.

"Stay where you are, just as you are, Arch," Tommy shouted and in the process leaning his knees up against the wall he pinned Arch in place.

"Who hit me? Did you hit me, old buddy? Why the hell did you hit me?" Arch asked freeing one arm and rubbing the back of his neck while coughing a cough that sounded as if he were going to cough up a lung.

"I slapped you to get you breathing, but I didn't hit you," Tommy answered.

"Someone sure the hell did. I was in the bedroom getting dressed when pow right in the back of the neck. Next thing I know here I am lying outside, on the sidewalk, and pressed tight up against this wall. Why do you have me pressed up against this wall, old buddy?"

"To keep you safe Tommy answered noticing that the debris had stopped falling. "I think it's safe for you to get up now," Tommy said standing up and releasing Arch. Arch started to sit up, but stopped. Then a bit more slowly he continued to sit up after realizing that the pain in his head meant that it was still attached to his body. After a few minutes of catching his breath Tommy helped him to his feet. "Still a little wobbly their, ol buddy," Tommy said as he had to grab him in order to steady him. "Just lean on me for a bit until you feel your equilibrium return."

"What happened?' Arch asked.

"When I returned with the pies I found the apartment filling up with gas. You were unconscious so I carried you over here figuring the gas was going to explode prematurely and if it did it was going to set off the other explosives that the city had set and I was right. Sorry about having to leave your things, but it was you I cared about and not them," Tommy said.

"There was nothing there that I can't replace. The biggest lose is the memories some of those items held," Arch replied rubbing the back of his neck.

"Why don't we get out of here and find us a cab. We'll have to find somewhere to get you new moccasins for your feet, a shirt, a cooler, and some ice for these pies," Tommy suggested grabbing the two bags of frozen pies as the pair with Arch leaning on Tommy started making their way to *Bell's* to call a cab.

"Don't forget a drink. I need one of those right now much worse than a pair of moccasins," Arch said.

"I'll see what I can do," Tommy replied thinking, *He's going to be alright.*

"Don't you think that we should stick around and let the police know that our bodies aren't lying beneath that pile of rubble?"

"No and I'll explain why later. Let's go," Tommy said leading the way to *Bell's.*

# CHAPTER TWENTY-NINE

**Tommy and Arch sat** inside *Bell's* for a couple of hours then they caught a cab that dropped them off at the mall. Tommy had managed to talk *Bell's* into selling him a cooler filled with ice to keep the pies in, which meant one less stop they had to make.

At a shop inside the mall Arch purchased a pair of comfortable boat shoes that he could wear without socks and a shirt. They made one more stop at a shop inside the mall and when they were done Arch said, "We still have three more hours to kill before we need to think about heading back to the boat. What say we head over to city hall, and see if we can find out who lifted that restraining order? I'm dieing to know."

They caught a cab that took them to city hall where Tommy waited while Arch ran inside. When he returned he had a puzzled look on his face. "What did you find out, Arch?"

"They said that the restraining order was lifted by request of the Ponnard Law Firm the original filer of the request. When I asked who had signed it they told me that Archibald Ponnard had."

"Did you?"

"Of course not," Arch replied.

"You weren't in one of your hangover states and did it without remembering?"

"When Jennifer hands me things to sign I have always made it a habit to at least read the heading. If I had seen that what I was signing had anything to do with my restraining order I wouldn't have signed it until I read the whole thing first."

# CHAPTER THIRTY

**"Now where to?"** Tommy asked.

"I'm done," Arch answered.

"You said that you once went to a party at Freddies' house so I'm taking it that you must know where he lives?"

"I do."

"Let's swing by the club and see if he's in the area and if not we'll give him a call or did you leave your phone in your apartment?"

"I have it. If I hadn't had my shorts on when that bastard hit me I'd really have been in trouble, but as it turned out I did so I have my phone and my wallet."

"Are you sure someone actually hit you or do you think someone did and passed out because of the gas? Gas can give you an awful headache."

"You may have a point because I don't remember hearing anyone come up the stairs into the apartment. I just don't know."

Tommy and Arch had the cab circle the block once and then stop in front of the fencing that surrounded the pile of rubble that was once *Lucifer's*. There was no sign of Freddie or anyone else for that matter so Arch called him from his cell phone. The connection was made, but no one said anything. Finally Arch said, "Freddie is that you, talk to me. Freddie this is Arch, Freddie?" and the connection went dead. "That's funny. Someone answered the phone, but they didn't say a word. Oh what the hell," Arch said giving the cab driver Freddies' address.

"Stop the cab! Stop the cab!" Tommy shouted and the cabbie pulled over. "Look, Arch in the cemetery over there. Do you recognize any of those people?"

"It looks like the crowd that usually hangs out at *Lucifer's*," Arch said.

"That's what I thought," Tommy said getting out of the cab. "Please wait for us," he said to the cabbie.

Crossing the street Tommy and Arch joined the mourners. "Glad you could make it, Arch," one of the mourners said.

"Gloria who died?" Arch asked.

"Where have you been? It's been all over the news," Gloria said.

"I've been out of town for almost a week and I'm only back for a few hours so who died?"

"Freddie," Gloria said.

"I just got done trying to call him. What happened?"

"He was so distraught over not being able to get a loan from anyone once they found out that he didn't have insurance on the club and that he was ass-hole over a tea kettle in debt that he poisoned himself."

"Do you happen to know what kind of poison?" Tommy asked. Gloria looked at Tommy as if she hadn't seen him before.

"It's okay, Gloria. This is Tommy Templeton an old uni chum of mine."

"They said it was arsenic," Gloria said.

"Give Taffy my condolences and let her know that I was here. Tell her that when I get back in town in at least another month from now that if she needs anything that she should call the law offices and ask for me. I'm sorry, but we have to go. We have a boat to catch," Arch said leaving the mourner's march and heading back to the waiting cab.

The cab dropped the two men at the wharf and they walked down to where the boat was moored. Bon Bon was in the boat lying on the rear seat dozing. "Leave him," Arch said. "There's a bar just across the street from where the cab dropped us off. Let's go have a drink and wait for Ben to arrive."

The two men entered the bar, ordered, and took a seat by the window from where they could watch Bon Bon's boat. An hour passed and at the end of it they watched a car pull up down on the wharf blocking their view of Bon Bon and his boat. Tommy got up and walked over to the bar returning with a sawed off shotgun. "Let's go, Arch. Bon Bon's in trouble."

Across the street and down to where Bon Bon's boat was moored they ran and from the look of things they arrived just in time. Bon Bon's face was bruised and he was bleeding at the mouth. One man was holding him, while the other was working him over. So intent were they that they didn't notice Arch and Tommy until Tommy crammed the barrels of the shotgun over the back of the beaters head and quickly raising it up toward the man that had been holding Bon Bon stuck the barrels in his face. "Go ahead give me an excuse," Tommy said. It took Bon Bon a moment to regain his composure then he turned and decked the man that had been holding him.

"Stay down and put your hands behind your head," Arch said.

"You go join your buddy and put your hands behind your head too," Tommy said after reviving the man he had cold-cocked with the shotgun.

"What's up, Bon Bon?" Arch asked as Bon Bon was in the process of frisking the two men and taking their guns from them.

"Seems that these low lifes wanted to know where old Ben was and didn't believe me when I told them that I didn't know."

"How much rope do you have onboard, Bon Bon?" Tommy asked.

"What do you have in mind?"

"A little body surfing."

"Then I've got more than enough."

"Give one of those guns to Arch, throw the other into the boat, get your rope, and start tying'" Tommy said. "God I hate assholes like you," he added looking at the two low lifes.

Gags?" Bon Bon asked.

"Let them scream the fish will love the music and it may shave a few days off their time in hell, but I doubt it," Tommy said as Bon Bon started tying the two men up.

"We'll tell you anything you want to know if you let us go," one of the men said.

The other man nodded his head vehemently in agreement. "That goes for me too," he said.

"I hope that you're kin of Tarzan's," Tommy said. "Everything else we want to know we already know."

"Archie I could use a little help carrying these low lifes over to the edge of the dock," Bon Bon said. Arch stuck the pistol into the back waistband of his shorts and helped Bon Bon move the trussed up men into a sitting position on the edge of the dock with their feet and hands tied.

While they were moving them Ben showed up in a cab. "Be with you in a moment, Ben. If you want you can start carrying those boxes over to and load them aboard the boat," Tommy said.

"You all havin' some sort of party?" Ben asked carrying a box to the boat.

"Do you recognize either of these two men, Ben?" Bon Bon asked. "They came here asking for you and started working me over when I told them I had no idea where you were."

"They must be hard a hearing. No one knew where I been," Ben answered.

"Any comment, boys before we wash the scum out of your ears," Tommy said.

"Since you already know the answer to everything the answer no," the man that seemed to be the leader of the two answered.

"If and that's a big if you do survive your body surfing experience I want you to give a message to your employer," Tommy said leaning in from behind him and talking in a lowered voice. "Tell him that I know who he is, but I haven't figured out just what his game is. I know that he's already killed two people and tried several times to kill a third. He failed and will continue to fail as long as I'm around and I ain't leaving until he's behind bars. You two got that? Not that it matters anyway now that I think about it.

"The rest of you ready yet?" Tommy asked in a loud voice.

"About as ready as we're gonna be," Bon Bon said.

"Then let's get on with this," Tommy said cutting the two men's hands free and joining everyone else in the boat.

Bon Bon fired up the engines and said, "Say when?"

"When!" Tommy shouted and Bon Bon threw the engines into high gear. The two low lifes splashed into old Miss' feet first resurfacing and started simultaneously skimming across the top of the water with their bodies turning over and over and even bouncing into the air a few times behind the speeding boat.

"Any gator holes on our way?" Tommy asked Bon Bon making sure Old Ben heard.

"Quarter mile up," Bon Bon replied. Tommy looked at Old Ben who nodded his agreement. "Slow down when you're just inside it and we'll cut them loose."

"Gottcha, Mr. Templeton," Bon Bon said smiling a hearty smile.

# CHAPTER THIRTY-ONE

**The rest of the** trip back to the riverboat was made in virtual silence. It was also a bit slower and bumpier than the high flying trip downriver that had been made with the current. Bon Bon pulled alongside the riverboat sometime around seven. The captain having kept an eye out for them stopped the riverboat to allow them to board. "He did that 'cause he don't want any a the shine falling into the river," Ben commented when he saw the riverboat stop.

The first thing unloaded was a mid-sized gator. "Have shotgun will have gator for dinner," Tommy had said when they had entered the gator hole. Finding a place to store it created a quandary at first, but then Arch suggested tying it onto the rear deck with some of the rope that hadn't been eaten by the gators, which had worked out perfectly.

Next went the pies, "Straight to refrigeration," Arch said. "To be served with the gator tonight and no snitching. I'll be measuring the crusts and adding them together expecting to get the correct circumference," he said to the steward.

"Does everyone at your table get a slice?" The captain asked.

"Of course," Arch said.

"Then the officers and myself, and that's to include the chefs would all like you to dine at our table this evening, Mr. Ponnard, Mr. Templeton, Ben, and Mr. Bon Bon if he's staying."

"It'd be a great pleasure, captain," Bon Bon replied, "But my lady is expecting me."

"Understood," the captain replied, "and the rest of you?"

"We gladly accept, captain," Arch said. "It'll mean smaller slices for everyone though."

"A smaller slice is better than no slice," the captain returned.

"Don't forget, captain that there are two more members to our party that will be accompanying us."

"I haven't forgotten," Mr. Templeton Captain Lyle assured him.

Finally six boxes of swamp shine were lifted to the deck of the riverboat with great care. "There's one more," Bon Bon said bending to get it.

"Leave it, Bon Bon," Ben said. "It's for services rendered."

"Thank you, Ben. With each sip I'll be wishing you the best. I'll be off then. Until next time, fellas. It's been fun," Bon Bon said untying his boat, firing it up, and waving goodbye as he headed downriver with it having fired on the first push of the ignition switch.

The girls were just waking up when Tommy and Arch entered the cabin. "I thought I heard that loud engine of Bon Bon's speedboat," Jennifer said as she and Menerva came out into the living area at the same time to see who had just come in. "Welcome back, honey," Jennifer said giving Arch a kiss and a hug.

"I'm glad you're back safe, Tommy," Menerva said giving Tommy a hug.

"How was the trip?" Menerva asked.

"Fast, furious, and rather uneventful actually except for the fact that Arch is now one of the homeless," Tommy said.

"What are you talking about?" Jennifer asked.

"You know that I've been fighting the city to keep them from demolishing my building? Well someone in the office lifted the restraining order and the city wasted no time demolishing it."

"It was as if they were waiting with their bulldozers and dump trucks," Tommy added.

"What happened to all your things?"

"They went the way of the dump or wherever they take the refuse and debris afterwards," Arch said. "When we get back I'll get to the bottom of it and then there will be hell to pay."

"Is that a shotgun on top of that box of shine?" Menerva asked.

"It's for your father to use at his shotgun wedding." Tommy quipped. "Actually it was to provide us with tonight's dinner and you only get one guess as to what it is that we're having," Tommy said.

"It better be a big slice of mud pie from Bell's," said Jennifer with her hands on her hips. "It was the only reason that I let this big lug go."

"Sorry about the mud pie," Arch started to say.

"You didn't get it. That was the only reason that I let you go I told you that. We don't care about the shine, but the mud pie, come on."

"We did get it, but the captain and the chefs were so insulted when they saw it that we had to throw it overboard."

"You what?"

"To make up for it the captain has invited us to dine at his table this evening," said Tommy playing along.

"It's not the same," Jennifer said walking back into the bedroom, pouting. "I was so looking forward to a slice of mud pie for breakfast, too," she added walking over to the bed and lying back down.

"Give us time to shower, shave, and change and we'll all go to breakfast, together," Arch said following Jennifer into the bedroom carrying his case of shine. "Call the galley."

"I'm way ahead of you, buddy," Tommy assured him.

"What are we having for dinner and what are you going to do with that thing," Menerva asked pointing to the shotgun.

"I'll put the shotgun on the shelf in the closet and the shells in this drawer," Tommy said showing her which drawer.

"As for dinner we are having gator thus the shotgun and your father."

"I sense that you're trip didn't go as smoothly as you've made it out to be?" Menerva asked.

"Ah, the soothsayer in action, but you're correct although some of it was actually fun. Arch losing his apartment though was not fun and it was a really neat place. We were in Bell's getting the pies when they set off the explosion. The sad news is that we got to pay our respects to Freddie before they stuck him in the ground."

"But, but Arch talked to him on the phone just as we left port. He can't be dead. He wasn't that old. How did he die?"

"Arsenic poisoning or so they say. The story is that he was despondent over losing *Lucifer's* and not being able to secure a loan to rebuild because of all the people that he owed money too so he took his own life."

"Not Freddie."

"On that point you and I are in total agreement, Menerva."

"How was Vicksburg?" Tommy asked coming out of the bathroom after his shower.

"Amazing. The cemetery and memorials were sad, beautiful, and depressing all at the same time. Jennifer and I did some shopping in the upscale shops. We bought you guys something, but you'll have to wait for it until bedtime.

"Tommy before you left you said that you wanted to sleep in the same bed in order to help me loose the foreboding that has been troubling me."

"I did and still do. Is it still troubling you?"

"As a matter of fact it isn't. Ever since I found out that

my father has promised me in marriage to whoever it is it has dissipated. It's gone. Now that I'm to be married to someone else I don't think that we should further our relationship by sharing the same bed."

"I understand, Menerva, but aren't indentured marriages a thing of the past. I'm sure that your father although well intentioned can't really force you to marry someone you don't want to."

"It's a family thing. You'd probably have to be connected to the South and indoctrinated in Creole tradition to understand."

"We're heading down the two of you coming?" Arch shouted from the living room.

"Don't let the door hit you in the ass, buddy," Tommy said as he and Menerva walked right past him and out the door.

# CHAPTER THIRTY-TWO

**"Compliments of the galley,"** the steward said placing a large, heart shaped piece of mud pie down in front of Jennifer.

"Steward," Arch said taking up the plate almost immediately and handing it back to him. "This isn't what we ordered," he said putting the engagement ring he had bought in New Orleans in the center of the slice of mud pie.

"Sorry, sir," the steward said starting to take the plate back to the galley.

"Wait, wait. Steward, wait," Jennifer almost shouted in a panic. "Was that a piece of mud pie?" she asked of whoever knew the answer.

"Yes, ma'am it is," the steward answered.

"From the galley?"

"Yes, ma'am." Jennifer caught the hint of a smile on Arch's face.

"Made in the galley or served from the galley?"

"Served, ma'am," the steward replied.

"Then bring it back here immediately your very life depends on it."

"And I'd like to change my order," Menerva said as the steward set the plate back down. It took Jennifer a moment before she asked.

"What's this on top of my mud pie?" Picking up the ring she looked at it, looked at Arch, and started to cry.

"Does that mean, yes?" Arch asked.

"Yes, yes, yes, a thousand times, yes," Jennifer replied leaning over and throwing her arms around Arch dropping the ring in the process and if Menerva hadn't acted quickly her mud pie along with it.

"Don't anyone move I saw it drop," the steward who had been standing back enjoying the moment with the foursome said dropping to his knees. "Got it," he said getting up and handing the ring to Arch who put it on Jennifer's extended finger.

"I believe it's safer here," he said.

"I do agree," Jennifer replied.

The steward left and returned with a slice of pie for Menerva and ham and eggs for the boys. "I should give you a swift kick for lying to me about throwing the pie overboard," Jennifer said, "but under the circumstances." She put her fork down, leaned over, and kissed Arch again.

"You know that aboard a ship the captain has the power to marry folks and I'll bet that if he asked Mr. Ponnard would be treated to one that any real person of royal blood would be envious of," Tommy commented.

"We'll sleep on it," said Arch.

"So what do you girls have planned for today?" Tommy asked. "Take your time answering. I don't want you to choke on your pie." Jennifer and Menerva started to laugh then started to choke on their pie with Tommy and Arch rushing to their aid.

"Thank you, Mr. Templeton, but I wish you'd make up your mind. First you save my life and now you are trying to kill me," Menerva said.

"And that goes ditto for me," added Jennifer shaking her finger at him.

"The reason I've waited this long is because at first I thought the two of you were worth saving, but now that I've gotten to know you better I've changed my mind," Tommy said throwing his hands up in the air making everyone laugh again and thankfully this time no one had pie in their mouths.

"To answer your question today we are stopping in Greensville. It is one of the largest cities in Mississippi and home to the Delta Blues Festival so make sure you have your dancin' shoes on," Jennifer said.

"I thought the dancing was going to take place tomorrow when we stop in Memphis the real *Home of the Blues*?" asked Arch.

"In Memphis I want to take the *Graceland* tour, spend some time in the Mud Island Theme Park, and eat some BBQ. I have this need to know if the BBQ Tommy shared with us was the best this side of Heaven like old Ben has stated," Jennifer said, "or not."

"Women? Why are you always the pessimists?" Tommy asked.

"It's just our nature," Jennifer answered

# CHAPTER THIRTY-THREE

**A day in Greensville** turned out to be a perfectly relaxing experience. A bit of shopping, a bit of bar hopping that included a dance or three, and all without thoughts of yesterday, tomorrow, or the future. Jennifer couldn't take her eyes off the ring that graced her left hand and wouldn't let herself get more than six inches from Arch at any one time.

"Have either of you called your parents yet and told them the good news?" Menerva asked.

"I have and my mother was ecstatic," Jennifer said.

"I didn't get to talk with my parents they were out of state attending a funeral of one of their close friends."

"Did you know the friend that died?" Menerva asked.

"Malcom couldn't recall them having mentioned the man's name. He did say that it was a man though. I asked Malcom to have them call me when they got the chance."

That evening back aboard the riverboat the foursome was sitting out on the sundeck watching the sun set on the river behind the ship when Ben appeared and pulled up a chair. "Evening everyone, daughter," he greeted taking the paper bag wrapped jar from Arch when it was passed his way.

"This new batch is better and more potent than the last case," Tommy said.

"That's because these seven cases were all that's left. They be what I called my emergency stash and they been resting for a good five years. When I gets back I'm gonna have to hole up for a few months and brew up another dozen or so batches. You fellas more than welcome to come help out and sample the results as we go."

"I don't have anything planned as of right now and if nothing turns up on the resume postings that I've had time to send I just might take you up on your offer, Ben," Tommy said.

"Don't forget to bring that scatter gun of yours just in case we run into any revenuers," Ben said smiling.

"When is the next best time to go fishing?" Arch asked changing the subject.

"Soon we be passing the junction with the Arkansas River and then it's Memphis. For some reason the fishies don't like the water around Memphis. If you want to go fishin' there we has to go somewhere out of the city. I know of a few small lakes in the area that has some dandy Big Mouth Bass in them."

"I'm sorry, Ben but once we hit Memphis the boys are all ours. Your daughter and I have already made plans that will keep them busy."

"I hear that there are congratulations in order for the two of you," Ben said nodding to Jennifer and Arch.

"You are correct," Jennifer said leaning over and holding out her hand for Ben to see the ring.

"Mighty nice, mighty nice."

"Would you like to see my ring, father?" Menerva asked leaning over and holding out her hand. Ben looked first at Tommy who shrugged and then looked at his daughter's hand.

"I see no ring, daughter. You ain't gone and lost it has you?"

"You don't see it because there isn't one to see. We need to talk, father."

"Not until I has a chance to talk with your mother," Ben replied.

"And when will that be?"

"I called her and I really did. I'm waiting for her to return the call."

"I can tell when you're lying, father and this is one of those times."

"Opps, gotta go the captain be a callin'," Ben said rushing off, but not before leaning over the back of Tommy's chair and whispering, "We needs to talk, son."

# CHAPTER THIRTY-FOUR

**That night Tommy found** that he couldn't sleep so he decided to get some fresh air and take a nighttime tour of the ship. Careful not to wake Menerva he slipped on his sandals, grabbed his shorts and a shirt, and slipped out of the bedroom.

Tommy saw that the Sky Lounge under its dimmed, night-running lighting had a few customers getting an early start on the day or refusing to let go of the one just past. The Paddlewheel Lounge held the same scenario when viewed through its deck side windows. Continuing his descent Tommy passed through the dinning room and ended up on the main deck. He walked back toward the paddlewheel standing for a while listening to its rhythmic churning of the Mississippi. "Lovely sound isn't it?" a voice behind him said. Turning around Tommy saw through the dark what looked like a tough-looking, big boned, but lean, red-headed woman standing there. "Name's Frankie, but most people just call me Red," she said introducing herself.

"Tommy," Tommy returned sticking out his hand.

"Sorry," Red said not shaking Tommy's outstretched

hand. "It's a taboo I have. One of those oddities that makes people refer to me as being odd."

"Understood we all have one or another of them. Where are you from," Tommy asked.

"New Orleans. Always heard of these trips and seen the boats come and go, but never was able to afford one. Things changed and suddenly I found that I could afford one so here I am," Red said.

"I'm here as sort of a graduation present to myself," Tommy said.

"You're with that Ponnard group aren't you?"

"They're with me actually. Do you know Arch Ponnard?"

"Seen him in court a couple of times," said Red.

"You with the court system?"

"You might say that. Nice meeting you, Mr. Templeton," Red said leaving Tommy standing there alone with the feeling that he was lucky to be still alive.

"You meet the strangest people walking around the decks in the dark of night," a familiar voice from out of the dark said stopping Tommy from continuing his night trek and bringing him out of his thoughts. Tommy hadn't left the spot at the rear of the riverboat and turning around saw old Ben standing in the deep shadows of the deck.

"Evening, Ben," he greeted.

"Seen you talking to that miscreant back here by the paddlewheel and thought that you might be needing some assistance," Ben said.

"You do get around," Tommy said.

"Had your back, son," Ben said nodding toward

the large Bowie Knife hanging from his belt. "Can't be too careful at night. Lot's of floaters start their floatin' after dark."

"So you know her that Red person?"

"She is what they call among other things a bounty hunter and from what I hear a damned good one too."

"She looked tough enough," Tommy said. Ben nodded his head.

"Hate to have to go up against that woman it might not end so well," Tommy said.

"What you doing up this time a night?" Ben asked.

"Couldn't sleep."

"That gator hole business bothering you?"

"Not in the least. I've already forgotten it. No it's what happened in the city, while you were getting your last cases of shine. There was what I'm perceiving as another attempt on Arch's life. Like the first and the others they still aren't making any sense. They have me wondering if I'm not looking at a string of natural occurrences of which I am turning them into something that they really aren't." Ben just nodded his understanding.

"I talked to Chantel. Told her that I've promised Menerva to a fella."

"I'll bet that went over big," Tommy said.

"First she liked the idea said it was about time. Said that she'd like a grandchild before she's too old and feeble to hold one. Then I told her who it was I promised her too."

"And what did she have to say about that?" Tommy asked.

"Do you know how to lift curses, son?" Ben returned.

"As a matter of fact I do," Tommy said. "Got your jar handy?" Ben handed Tommy the jar of shine he had been working on. Tommy took a sip and handed the jar back to Ben, spit the sip into his right hand, rubbed his left hand into his right, and placed them on top of the bandanna that Ben always wore on top of his head. "Got a match," Tommy asked.

"That I don't, son."

"No matter I'll do it the unnatural way," Tommy replied closing his eyes and when he raised his hands a bit higher over Ben's head his bandanna came alight.

"Shit! What you playing at, son," Ben shouted tearing the bandanna off his head and throwing it onto the deck of the ship.

"Don't," Tommy said throwing his arm across Ben's chest to prevent him from stomping out the fiery bandanna. "Pick it up. It won't burn you and throw it overboard into the Mississippi," Tommy said. Ben did what Tommy told him to do. When the bandanna hit the waters of the Mississippi a ray of green light shot up from it straight into the heavens above. "You are now free of any and all curses that have ever been put upon you, Ben," Tommy said. Ben looked at him suspiciously and stepped back into the shadows. Taking a long sip from his jar he handed it to Tommy who also took a long sip.

"Do you want Menerva?" Ben asked.

"I do, but I need permission so to speak," Tommy replied. Just then his cell phone buzzed and kept buzzing.

"Who from?" Ben asked.

"There was this woman, a real witch that was living in a coven. It's hard to explain. The coven was relocated, but since I wasn't officially a member I was left here, alone." Tommy's cell phone kept on buzzing. "Excuse me, Ben. Someone has just texted me and something tells me that I should answer it." Looking at his phone he added, "In fact there are three text messages. Let's see ah, the first one is from Menerva. She wants to know where I am."

"See what you'd be getting yourself into," Ben said chuckling. "Them womens are all the same."

"I'm back by the paddlewheel of the ship preparing to jump," Tommy texted back. His phone rang in the next instant. "Hello!" Tommy said. "How did you? She wants to talk to you," Tommy said handing Ben the phone. After hanging up and handing the phone back to Tommy, Ben said.

"You're gonna have to do that curse lifting again or does it cover all the curses I receive in the future too?"

"Just the ones in the past I'm afraid, but I'll talk to her and get her to lift this one."

"Who's them other text messages from?" Ben asked suddenly interested.

"Let's see. This one is just a pair of bells. Looks kinda like wedding bells with a smiley face after them and it's from."

"You all right, son? You just turned white as that moon overhead," he said glancing up at the moon. "Here sit yourself down," Ben said pulling up a stool and guiding Tommy onto it. Handing him his jar of shine he pulled another stool from out of the dark and sat down facing Tommy. "You alright, son?" Ben asked again taking another look up at the moon. He had never seen it look like that with a ring of stars around it. It held him in somewhat of a trance giving him a feeling of peace and tranquility that he had never experienced in all his years. "Would you look at that," he said indicating the moon with its ring of stars.

"I thought that this is where I'd find the pair of you. What are you starring at, father?" Menerva asked appearing from out of the darkness and following her father's gaze. "I noticed that on my way here. It's an omen I believe." Tommy interrupted her explanation by handing her his phone. "A pair of wedding bells followed by a smiley face. Who are you sending that too one of your friends?" She asked handing Tommy his phone back. Tommy took it and without saying a word pushed the button that showed who the message was sent from and handed it back to Menerva. She looked at it."

"Not you too, daughter? Here sit down on this here stool," Ben said guiding Menerva to his stool. "Any more of these shenanigans and I'll soon be sitting on the deck," he said retrieving another stool from out of the darkness.

"Either of you want to explain what the hell is going on?" Ben asked, "And why the two of you look like you've just seen a ghost."

"You've talked to mother haven't you?" Menerva asked changing the subject knowing that he had from the text message on Tommy's phone which was confirmed by the ring of stars around the Moon.

"I have, but Tommy here has already released me from the curse that she put on me," Ben assured his daughter. Menerva smiled.

"I thought I could smell the burnt hairs from an old dog," she said looking at her father.

"The two of you really do deserve each other you both know that," Ben said.

"So she really must have liked your choice of the man you've picked to be my lifetime partner. What else did she have to say?"

While Ben and Menerva were having their discussion Tommy checked the third text. "Dad we approve give her the ring." The text message was from Cricket, Phoenix, and Willow Witten and followed by a smiley face.

*My Daughters and Willow*, Tommy thought lapsing into a dream like state recalling the time Willow told him that she was pregnant with twin daughters.

Ben had been watching Tommy a little afeared for him with all that was taking place and when he looked as if he had started a journey down the path from which there would be no retrieving him he asked breaking the spell and bringing Tommy back to reality. "That the third one?" Tommy nodded and handed the phone to him. "Permission granted?" Ben asked after reading the text message.

"Permission granted," Tommy replied.

"Permission for what?" Menerva asked.

"This calls for a drink welcome to the family, son," Ben said taking a sip and passing the jar to his daughter who turned up her nose at him. "When you hear what we are gonna be a tellin' you, you're gonna want some and having one before that one will help that one produce the effect you'll be expecting," Ben said. "Remember only a sip." Menerva took the jar from her father and took a drink wrinkling up her nose afterwards.

"Where have the two of you been?" Arch asked as Tommy and Menerva entered the cabin. Menerva walked over to Jennifer and showed her, her ring.

"We've been stool sitting out on the stern of the ship by the paddlewheel talking with Ben and sipping shine," Tommy answered.

"Since?"

"About one or so," Tommy said.

"All night?"

"You shouldn't have gone to bed so early."

"It'll be the last time I can tell you that," Arch replied.

"We are going to bed now and would you order each of us one of those Bloody Mary, hangover specials? Just leave them on the tray by the door."

"What about Memphis?"

"Still on, old buddy," Tommy said walking into the bedroom followed by Menerva who waved her ring at Arch as she passed.

"Was that what I think it was?"

"Yes, dear. It seems that your influence has brought about two miracles on this trip," Jennifer said.

"What was the first?" Arch asked knowing full well what she was referring to.

"I'll let you take me to breakfast. I think that there is still a piece or two of Bell's mud pie left if those rascals in the galley haven't eaten it all and while we are feeding each other I'll explain it all to you."

"Keep going I like it so far," Arch said interrupting. "I'll whisper the answer in your ear," Jennifer said attaching herself to Arch's arm, kissing his cheek, and leading him toward the door.

# CHAPTER THIRTY-FIVE

**Memphis was the most** fun so far of all the cities they had visited thus far. The foursome were already in an elevated mood so Graceland followed by the monorail ride from the cities center to the Mud Island Theme Park with the entertainment there made it a maddening, great day.

"The BBQ was rather disappointing. It was okay and very tasty, but I expected more," complained Jennifer after they had returned to the riverboat.

"I'll see if I can get the chefs to have a Memphis BBQ Night at dinner one of these nights and have them use my recipe again," Tommy said trying to appease her disappointment.

Sitting on the balcony too weary and too full the foursome sat in silence reflecting on what had all transpired in the last few days. "I was just wondering if our killer has left the ship," commented Jennifer. "We haven't had a murder in how many days? If I recall correctly there hasn't been one since you guys went with Bon Bon and took that side trip to New Orleans. Now there's a thought. Maybe you should ask at the desk if anyone has left the ship, Tommy?"

"What does our friendly and recently engaged soothsayer have to say? Look in your crystal ball for us, Menerva?" Arch asked. Menerva looked at Tommy who shook his head, no.

"Really? What could it hurt?" Menerva asked.

"Ya what could it hurt?" Arch repeated.

"All right everyone hold hands and close your eyes," Menerva said.

"If I start to fall asleep and am about to miss the good parts kick me would you, honey," Arch said.

"Time to get serious, Arch. You know what happens when you fool around with my powers," Menerva said bringing everyone in line as she started to hum and chant in a low voice. She continued on for several minutes and then stopped. No one moved for several more minutes.

"Are we through?" Jennifer asked before opening her eyes. When she did she looked first at Arch and then at? "Where did they go?" Jennifer asked. No reply came from Arch. Reaching over and shaking his chair, she shouted, "Arch! Wake up."

"What? What happened?"

"Nothing that I can tell. When I opened my eyes, Tommy and Menerva were gone."

Menerva had conjured up an image of the two dead men and waited for another image to replace them. What she saw told her that there would be more murders to come and then she saw? Suddenly she left her chair and ran. Tommy felt the change and opened his eyes just in time to see Menerva disappear into the cabin. Leaving his chair he chased after her out the cabin room's entry door and found her waiting for him in the corridor outside. "Is this what it's going to be like married to you?" Menerva asked.

"I thought that you could handle it," Tommy said. "You know what it's like when you have a special gift given to you by the Dark One?"

"You've used your gift before I knew you."

"Before now my gifts, plural were always hazy at best and after receiving them I would take an educated guess filling in the blanks to come up with an answer that was pertinent to the situation at hand," Tommy said. "Isn't that how you go about your soothsaying by filling in the blanks? You must be an awfully good guesser too because you've said that you've never been wrong. Maybe your guessing hasn't been so much guessing but a real part of your gift one that you've just never admitted to."

"That may be, but now it's as if I'm actually there living it in full color cinemascope with all the emotions running through me at the same time there's no more haziness or guessing. I've never been able to do that before. Wait! I have. It was at the Ponnard's when I grabbed your wrist. Is that why it happened again just now because we were connected and through your powers my abilities were enhanced?"

"I sense things in a special way I don't see them. Take the ceiling at *Lucifer's*. When I looked up at it my eyes were drawn to certain spots that my senses told me had recently been weakened by a man made force. My senses told me to get everyone out of there. Just now you foresaw in one rush what is taking part in our lives right now and on into the future. It is what we can do and hopefully will continue to do whenever its really needed."

"I saw that the killer isn't done yet," Menerva said.

"If that's what you saw, but we will and can stop him by working together," Tommy assured her as Menerva stepped into his arms.

"Hold me. If you are going to spend your life solving crimes and I'm going to be there backing you up when needed I'm going to need a lot of holding," Menerva said snuggling even tighter into Tommy's arms.

# CHAPTER THIRTY-SIX

**"Something strange happened** to me the other night, the night I asked Menerva to marry me that I haven't told you about," Tommy said to Arch as the two of them sat with Ben cane pole lines in the water, sipping shine, while the riverboat was docked at New Madrid, Missouri. The girls said that they needed a day to themselves and left with the tour bus.

"Something strange is always happening to you so what happened this time?"

"I met a woman. Not your ordinary woman either. It is someone that Ben said he is acquainted with."

"It was that bounty hunter that goes by the name of Frankie Le Cock," Ben said.

"Red? She's one of the passengers on this voyage?" Arch asked seemingly agitated.

"When I asked her if she knew you she said not personally, but that she'd seen you in court."

"She certainly has. I've had her on the witness stand more than once. Her methods of running criminals to ground leaves a lot of room for a good lawyer to work with."

"She knew who I was though," Tommy said. "She made the mistake of using my full name when she left. I had only given her my first name when we introduced ourselves."

"If I know Frankie Le Cock that was no mistake. You know if she's onboard she might be after the same person that we are and in that case it might be wise to get to know her better. That may be why she was introducing herself? She was setting the stage for a future sharing of information. Or?"

"Or what, Arch?"

"What Arch is about to say is that there are things about the Red that are only whispered in the back rooms of New Orleans' Opium Dens," Ben said.

"Such as?" Tommy asked.

"There are rumors adrift that if you want someone killed she's the one that will take on the job," said Arch. "She's been suspected of having done that more than a dozen times, but if the two murders we've had onboard this trip are hers she has covered her tracks better than most."

"So what you two are saying is that she might not be after someone, but she might be that someone we're after?" Arch and Ben both shook their heads to the affirmative.

"Ben I have a job for you since you're in with the elite of the company. I want you to find out everything you can about her reservation. When it was made, who made it, who paid for it, anything the company can tell you," Tommy said.

"That's a pretty tall order for an ordinary deck hand, but I might be able to accommodate you," Ben answered smiling.

"Are you sure that there are fish in this river?" Arch asked. "I haven't had so much as a nibble."

# CHAPTER THIRTY-SEVEN

**"The girls aren't back** yet. I see that the tour bus has returned and left again and they weren't on it," Tommy said starting to worry.

"Jennifer said something about taking in a show. I've tried to text her, but I haven't gotten an answer," Arch said. A knock on the door when answered revealed the presence of Captain Lyle.

"We are ready to move on up river," he said. "All the passengers are accounted for with the exception of your two ladies or have we just missed them coming back onboard?"

"We were just discussing the fact that they aren't back yet and wondering what we should do. We've tried calling and sending them a text message, but haven't gotten a response," Arch said.

"I can delay our departure for another hour, but if they aren't back by then I'll have no choice but to leave without them."

"The riverboat's next landing is at Cape Girardeau and that's still in Missouri on this same side of the Mississippi right, captain?" Tommy asked.

"Correct, Mr. Templeton."

"Then if the girls aren't back Arch and I will go ashore to wait for them and catch back up with you at Cape Girardeau. If we aren't going to make the rendezvous we will call the desk and let them know." Captain Lyle nodded and left.

"Grab a jacket and those pistols you took off that hoodlum. You still have them don't you?"

"I do," Arch answered heading for his bedroom to retrieve the jacket and the hardware.

"To satisfy my curiosity have you told Jennifer or anyone else that you have them?" Tommy asked when he returned.

"Only you know about their existence, ol buddy."

"Good keep it that way," Tommy said.

"Get them and we'll go wait for the girls down by the gangway. If and when they either do or don't show up we'll know what course to follow," Tommy said.

"I'm sorry, gentlemen," Captain Lyle said joining Arch and Tommy at the railing just before the hour had passed. "I have to cast off."

"Then we shall be leaving you, captain and catch up with you at Cape Girardeau," Arch said.

"What now?" arch asked walking down the gangplank.

"We find a place to sit and we wait for another hour," Tommy replied.

"And if they aren't here by then?"

"Then one of us goes into town and the other one stays here just in case."

The second hour had just about passed them by when an older, faded red, pickup truck driven by a middle aged, local man approached the dock. In the front seat alongside him were the two missing women. The pickup truck stopped and Menerva and Jennifer got out as did the driver. "Where's the ship?" Jennifer asked as Arch and Tommy walked over to them.

"It left two hours ago. You're late and Captain Lyle couldn't wait any longer," Arch said.

"What happened?" Tommy asked sensing something.

"The strangest thing," Menerva started. "This is, Burt by the way. He was nice enough to give us a ride."

"Howdy," Burt said shaking Tommy's and Arch's hands.

"Anyway we went to the show and the film kept breaking which caused us to miss the tour bus. We were wondering how we were going to get back when a cab pulled up."

"Funny thing about that cab," Burt offered. "New Madrid doesn't have a cab service."

"We told the cabbie who was a strange, foreign looking man that we wanted to go to the riverboat landing. He said actually now that I think about it he didn't really say anything, but just nodded. We got in and he took off."

"Before we knew it we were in the countryside heading in the wrong direction," Jennifer continued. "We tried to get the cabbie to turn back around, but he didn't pay any attention to us. He just kept driving further into the countryside.

"All of a sudden the cab swerved and ran into the

ditch rolling over on its side. Menerva and I were laying on top of each other up against the door on the low side of the cab. There was water in the ditch and since we had, had the windows down it started to come into the cab as soon as we landed in it and needless to say we both got wet. The driver managed to crawl out his window and we figured he'd help us, but when he reached the road he took off running."

"We yelled at him to stop and come back, but he didn't," Menerva said.

"We managed to stand up and reach the open window on the up side of the cab. I helped Menerva get out and she stood on the door balancing herself there and helped me out. You should have seen us. It was hilarious," Jennifer said chuckling at the memory. "We managed to get out and up onto the road and while we were standing there wondering if we should start hoofing it back toward town Burt came driving down the road. We flagged him down and he was gracious enough to give us a ride back here."

"So now that the riverboat has left what are we going to do?" Jennifer asked.

"Catch back up to it and reboard it when it docks at Cape Girardeau," Tommy said.

"That's around sixty miles from here up I-55," said Burt.

"You wouldn't be going that way would you?" Jennifer asked Burt.

"No, Miss Jennifer, but we do have a motel that I can drive you folks to. You can stay there the night and catch the bus in the morning. It should get you to Cape Girardeau while the riverboat is still there before it leaves."

"We'd be much obliged, Burt," Arch said.

# CHAPTER THIRTY-EIGHT

**After offering Burt** a fifty for his time and trouble, which he refused to accept until the girls insisted, he left. Checking with the manager of the motel to make sure the bus did stop there and confirming the time it stopped the foursome checked in and were given two rooms at the far end of the second floor. Arch and Jennifer took the room on the end, while Tommy and Menerva took the room next to it.

Tommy sat bolt upright in bed waking Menerva up. "Call the desk and tell them to get the fire department over here right now," Tommy said to Menerva as he was getting dressed. Running out the door he went to and started banging on the door to Arch and Jennifer's room. "Arch open the door," Tommy yelled.

"No one at the desk answers," Menerva shouted from the doorway to their room.

"Then get dressed and go down there and hurry," Tommy shouted.

"Arch god damn it open the door," Tommy yelled again while banging on the door of the room. It was then that Tommy noticed that the door was a metal fire door. *Funny*, he thought stepping back so that he could get a view of his room's door, which was an ordinary wood door.

"Hold on, hold on. I'm coming," a voice inside said. The doorknob rattled, but the door didn't open. "The door is locked and I can't get it open," Arch said.

"Unlock it and hurry," Tommy shouted.

"I'm headed for the office," Menerva said running for the stairs. Tommy watched her go and waited to hear the click of a door unlocking. "I've tried the lock and it's unlocked, but the door still won't open," Arch said from inside his room. Tommy looked at the door and saw several small burn marks on the metal fire door. *It's been welded shut. The doors been welded to its metal frame. Now who would want to?* Something inside his head clicked. *At the top of the stairs there was a fire extinguisher and a fire axe.*

Tommy ran down the hallway to the fire box. It was empty. There was no extinguisher and no axe. Running back to his room he walked out onto his balcony. *The balconies are close enough so that they could,* and then he noticed the bars covering the outside of Arch's door to the patio, and the heavy chain and lock securing it shut on its outside. Tommy also noticed the flames that were rapidly climbing the outside corner of the building.

Returning to the hallway and the door to Arch's room, Tommy yelled, "Arch!"

"We're here," Arch yelled back.

"Do you have your pistol?"

"Yes!"

"Get it and come to the door," Tommy instructed.

"Are you there?" Tommy asked hearing coughing from inside the room. *Smoke*.

"Ya."

"I want you to put the barrel of your pistol against the crack of the door on the side that opens. I want you to put your fingers on the top of the door and where the bottom of your elbow touches the door I want you to fire one shot right there."

"Bang!"

"Down an inch and fire one more."

"Bang!"

"Down half-an-inch and fire one more."

"Bang!"

"Now I want you to measure with the tip of your finger down to the bottom of your elbow from where that last shot went in."

"Got the spot," Arch replied coughing some more as the smoke began to thicken in his room. He could see the flames along the outer wall making their way up the wall of their room.

"Same scenario fire one shot."

"Bang!

"Down half-an-inch and fire one more."

"Bang!

"Down another half-an-inch and fire one more," Tommy instructed.

"Bang!"

"Now hold the door knob open and stand back. I'm going to give the door a kick and a shoulder," Tommy yelled kicking the door with all his might. It didn't budge. Trying to shoulder it he got the same result.

"I'm back," Menerva said appearing at Tommy's side.

"Someone has welded the door shut and we need to get it open. On three we both kick," Tommy instructed. "Arch you still holding the knob open?"

"Still holding, buddy."

"Three!" and they both kicked as hard as they could. The door didn't move.

"Arch! You and Jennifer sit down on the floor with your backs along the wall on the side of the door that opens not the side that the hinges are on," Tommy shouted. The smoke in the hallway was getting thicker as well and Tommy could feel the heat from the fire raging in the floor beneath them. "Menerva I want you to put both your hands on the top of my head," Tommy instructed stretching his arms along the seam of the door. "I want you to chant with me over and over and don't stop until the door opens up. It might help if you close your eyes and mean what you're chanting. Flesh from metal in days gone dark now into the light I've power over thee release those within. Got it?"

"I think so," Menerva said.

"Then here we go. Flesh from metal in days gone dark now into the light I've power over thee release those within. Flesh from metal in days gone dark now into the light I've power over thee release those within. Flesh from metal in days gone dark now into the light I've power over thee release those within." Suddenly as if the door had been hit with a wrecking ball it flew inward crashing against the far wall taking its metal jam along with its hinges and parts of the wall along with it.

Smoke billowed form Arch's room and flames were visible in the bathroom and along the outside wall. "Arch! Jennifer!" Tommy shouted entering the room. Barely able to see he found Arch and Jennifer sitting there on the floor along the outer wall beside the doorway. "Menerva give me a hand." Menerva stepped into the room. "Jennifer's right here. Drag her outside and toward the stairway." Menerva grabbed Jennifer under her arms and drug her out the door with Tommy dragging Arch along right behind her.

Coughing and hacking Arch and Jennifer slowly recovered enough to make it down the stairs and out to the grass strip between the motel and the highway under their own power. From their vantage point they could see that the whole end of the motel that they had been in completely ablaze and burning ferociously. Several other occupants of the motel had after moving their vehicles further away from the motel joined the foursome on the grass.

A single fire truck arrived and started throwing water upon the flames. The night manager showed up and Tommy walked over to him. "Did the people beneath us get out okay?" he asked the night manager.

"You were the only ones in that entire wing," he answered. "I don't understand it. We just remodeled that wing upstairs and down we even added fire doors on some of the rooms."

"Did you put bars on some of the patio doors as well?" Tommy asked.

"Bars? What are you talking about?" the manager asked.

"Nothing forget I asked," Tommy said.

"I do have one more question though, please. Why did we get the upstairs rooms when the entire first floor was empty?"

"Sometimes we get a tour bus that just shows up late in the evening. So as not to disturb the other occupants we put the early arrivals on the second floor on the far ends and those that show up late on the first floor and near the stairs on the second. There's less banging, clomping, and general noise that way for those that arrive early."

"Makes sense," Tommy said. "Thank you.

"We will need another room for the night now that ours has been consumed by the fire."

"Come to the office and I'll see what I have," the night manager said. "That goes for anyone else here too. If you want a new room come along to the office with this gentleman," the night manager announced loud enough for all those gathered on the grass strip to hear.

# CHAPTER THIRTY-NINE

**After a restless rest** of the night the foursome were waiting at the entrance to the motel when the bus showed up early the following morning. Paying the fare they got onboard and were seated in the very back of the bus as it pulled away from the motel.

The bus didn't take the main highway, but stuck to the back roads following the Mississippi as it made its way toward the next small town. "Look! There's the cab that kidnapped us. It's still in the ditch," exclaimed Jennifer as the bus passed the cab.

"Stop the bus! Stop the bus!" Tommy shouted making his way as best he could up the aisle. The bus driver stopped, but his look showed his contempt at having done so. "You will stay here and wait for me or my friend back there will put a bullet through the back of your head," Tommy whispered to the driver before exiting the bus.

Walking back to the cab Tommy slid down the bank of the ditch and opened the cab door propping it open with a stick that he had picked up on his way. Checking the glove compartment first he took everything that was inside it stuffing it into his pockets. Looking under the seat he found nothing. Leaving the front seat he leaned over the windshield and entered the vehicle's VIN number on his phone. Propping open the back door he looked around. *It's strange that this cab doesn't have displayed a picture of the driver with its permit license and number,* he thought. Finding nothing there he popped open the trunk and searched it too finding nothing of interest.

Returning to the bus Tommy said, "Thank you driver for waiting. It really was important and my friend wouldn't have shot you I was only kidding." *And besides he's all out of bullets,* Tommy chuckled to himself on the way back to his seat.

"What did you find?" Arch asked.

"I cleaned out the glove compartment. Here go through what I found," Tommy said emptying his pockets and handing the material to Arch. "It just looks like a bunch of old maps."

"They are and they're city maps of Monroe, Louisiana."

"I'll bet that's where the cab will be from too. I copied the VIN number."

"Read it to me. I have a friend that I can text and he'll find out all about the vehicle for us," Arch said. Tommy read the number and Arch sent the text.

"I feel so safe sitting here alongside you two sleuths," said Jennifer hugging Arch's arm.

"I have taken everything into consideration since the first day that I came to New Orleans and I've come to a conclusion. Rather I've formed a hypothesis," Tommy said.

"Before you enlighten us tell me about what happened last night," asked Jennifer.

"I have a few questions that I would like to ask too," Menerva said.

"I'll include the hotel in my hypothesis," Tommy said to Jennifer.

"When I'm through I will do my best to answer any questions that you may still have," Tommy said looking at Menerva.

"Someone has been trying to kill one or all of us and I don't have a clue as to why. First I thought it was all of us, but the more things have happened the more I have been able to narrow it down to just one maybe two of us," Tommy said looking at Jennifer and Arch. "Whoever it is doesn't seem to care that in the process they kill a few or hundreds more as long as they get the person or persons that they are after. What I've observed is that when they do succeed the death of that person or persons has to look like an accident. That fact is very important to the killer and I'm sure it is a vital clue in knowing the reason why, which will lead us to the who.

"When I talked to Freddie at the club that night he told me that he had just had some work done on the ceiling and roof of the club. I think that whoever did the work sabotaged the roof so that it would fail when given the command to do so. I'm sure that if they went through the debris they'd find evidence of explosive materials in it."

"Why didn't the roof fall when we were in the club if it was set to do so on command?" Jennifer asked.

"I suspect that the minute explosions were staged to

only weaken the roof and allow gravity to do the rest," Tommy answered. "While we were there I thought I heard a strange noise above me and that must have been the explosions weakening the roof. Looking up there I really didn't see anything, but I had this feeling."

"We know about your feelings don't we?" Menerva said looking from Jennifer to Arch for confirmation. They both nodded their heads.

"And to that all I can say is thank goodness for someone's miscalculation on how long it takes gravity to work.

"Next we have the poisoning at *Oak Alley*. My intuition told me that there was a great danger in the fresh tray of pâté sandwiches that were put out just as we approached the table. I watched them being put out even though the tray that was already there had only a few sandwiches taken from it. I thought that by knocking the tray to the ground all the sandwiches would be thrown away, which they were all save the one and I have to take some of the blame for that man's death in that I didn't do a better job of making sure that all the sandwiches were uneatable. The man must have picked one up that I didn't soil badly enough."

"You can't have known that, that would happen," Jennifer offered.

"So far the incidents didn't point at any one person," Tommy continued after smiling a thank you smile at Jennifer, "but that was about to change. In Baton Rogue we all went to the Cajun Heritage Museum where Arch had his near death experience in the Grist Mill. Was that just stupidity? Sorry, buddy or a planned accident? I think it was planned and that the warning tape and sign had been removed on purpose and from what Arch has told us was lured into that room. This made me wonder about just what was happening.

"The next death was the man on the bridge at the *Rosewood* Plantation. Arch you commented to the fact that, that man was dressed almost exactly like yourself and at the time he was murdered he was one person behind Jennifer. Even Jennifer said that when she saw the man in the water she thought that it was you and I believe that it was because of the clothing that he was wearing. At first I wondered if they might have been after Jennifer, but now I believe that our killer made the same mistake and thought the man was you Arch because of the clothing he was wearing. Then I had this thought was it Arch they were after or was that man killed just to throw me off when in fact he was after somebody else?

"Then we went back to New Orleans for more swamp shine. We didn't tell you girls, but Arch was almost killed when there was a gas leak in the apartment that caused a premature explosion." Jennifer looked at Arch.

"Why didn't you tell me?" she asked.

"It wasn't that big of a deal," Arch replied, "besides Tommy got me out in time."

"Thank you, Tommy for saving my big lugs ass yet once again," said Jennifer.

"You are more than welcome, Jennifer. I would miss the big lug myself if anything should actually happened to him.

"Arch I have a question that has bothered me about that incident. I want you to think back and tell me that when I left for Bell's if all the windows and French doors were open? They were weren't they? We did open them all before we crawled into bed that night to cool down your apartment?"

"We did open them," Arch replied after taking a moment to think about it.

"Did you close them after I left for Bell's?"

"No I didn't have time. I was to busy packing up my things. Why?"

"I noticed that they were all closed when I pulled you out of the apartment."

"That means that I didn't imagine someone knocking me unconscious. It really happened."

"It sure looks that way," Tommy said.

"To add to our mystery I don't think that Freddie's' death was a suicide. I think that he was murdered because he said something to the wrong person after remembering something suspicious or strange about the work that he had hired done on the club's ceiling and roof."

"That makes three deaths so far. Who and why is this person doing this?" Jennifer asked.

"Now we come to the kidnapping, your rescue, and the motel fire," Tommy said. "I think that our killer isn't after Menerva, or myself. All of the evidence points to the killer being after Arch and last night's fire proved that to me. First if the killer wanted Jennifer or Menerva dead the cab accident would have been much worse and right now they'd both be dead. It was the perfect opportunity to kill either of them, but whoever didn't and I've asked myself why not and came up with the answer. They were kidnapped to get us off the riverboat. They were rescued and driven back to us so that we could be taken to that motel."

"What you're saying is that the taxi driver and Burt were all in on it?" Jennifer asked.

"Is it possible that the cabbie was Burt in disguise?" Tommy asked looking at Menerva and Jennifer.

"Now that you mention it, it could have been," Menerva replied.

"Then he must have had his truck hidden up the road somewhere," added Jennifer.

"Then after we arrived at the motel we were assigned rooms far away from anyone else and I'd be willing to bet that if we went back our night manager wouldn't be anywhere to be found. He wasn't answering the bell before we left. I tried. It also wouldn't surprise me if Burt and the night manager are both reported missing in the near future and later found dead having both been murdered."

"Whoever is doing this must really be deranged," Jennifer said.

"I am now sure that the killer is after Arch because of the fact that Menerva's and my motel room door is made of wood, but Arch's and Jennifer's was an easily secured metal door in a metal frame. Your room also had bars covering the door that led onto the patio. When I checked on using the patio as an escape route I saw that it had been chained and the chain padlocked from the outside, which prevented you from escaping through it."

"I noticed that too 'cause I tried to open it," Arch said.

"So who wants you dead so badly that they are following you up the Mississippi and attempting to take your life and making it look like an accident at every opportunity?" Tommy asked.

"No one that I can think of. Everyone loves me you all know that. I'm a Teddy Bear."

"Think about it seriously and get back to me will you, buddy please it's important. Someone out there really wants you dead. Here's something to make you think. I have gotten this feeling that if they can't kill you accidentally then they are going to settle for Jennifer so if you want to protect her, think."

"You make quite the case there Mr. Templeton," Arch replied.

# CHAPTER FORTY

**The foursome arrived** in Cape Girardeau shortly after eleven o'clock and were back in their cabin by noon. Having showered and changed they headed for the dining room. Everyone ordered and sat back. "I'm glad to see that you ladies and gentlemen have caught up with us. What was the problem that prevented your reboarding the ship in New Madrid?" Captain Lyle asked looking at the girls.

"The show ran late because of an old film that kept breaking," Menerva said.

"The show was so interesting and with everything that was going on we forgot to watch the time and missed the bus back," added Jennifer.

"You should have called and we would have come to get you," Captain Lyle said.

"Really? I wish we had known that," Jennifer said.

"Well we are glad that you made it to Cape Girardeau."

"We did however get to see some of the countryside from a different viewpoint as we came back by bus that took us along the river," Jennifer said.

"I had my doubts about joining my friend here on

this voyage, captain, but never in my life have I had so many once in a lifetime experiences," commented Arch.

"Not to toot the company's horn, Mr. Ponnard, but there is always the return trip downriver from Saint Paul to New Orleans. I'm sure that if you all joined us on that trip back you could add to those experiences."

"A wonderful suggestion and one I hadn't thought about, but now it'll be one we may all consider, captain. It would be a sort of honeymoon cruise," Arch said looking at Jennifer who gave him the 'Are you crazy' look back.

After lunch Arch and Jennifer headed up to the Sky Lounge for a few afternoon toddies. Menerva stayed with Tommy at the table sitting back and just relaxing. "Tommy now that we are alone and there aren't any people around. I have a few questions."

"Go ahead ask," Tommy said as if he already knew what was coming.

"The motel fire? You knew about it just as it started. How?"

"It's my internal warning system. I knew about the fire just as I knew about the ceiling of the club. It's one of my warlock gifts."

"And the door of Arch's room? It hit the wall opposite it so hard that it almost took out the wall and at the very least it had to have left an impression in the wall."

"I've been waiting for you to ask me about that one. I've been trapped before and a witch showed me how to free myself. I thought I'd try it on Arch's door and it worked. If you hadn't helped by adding your powers to mine the door might not have hit that wall quite so hard."

"Was that witch Willow?" Menerva asked.

"It was. Now I need to find your father. He was going to try and find something out for me. Want to tag along?"

"I'll pass."

"Still haven't achieved enough of the forgiving nature that inherently comes with the powers you've acquired. Want to know a little secret? It will come and when it does you won't be able to resist it," Tommy said standing up. "See you later."

Tommy went to the desk, and asked the whereabouts of old Ben. He was told that they'd check and let him know that he was looking for him. *I might as well go join the rest of the group*, Tommy thought to himself and headed for the Sky Lounge.

# CHAPTER FORTY-ONE

**Opening the door to** the inside of the Sky Lounge Tommy was hit by an uproar of noise. It was a large group of passengers that had gathered around one of the tables and were obviously enjoying something going on at it. As Tommy approached the group he saw Jennifer and Menerva standing with the others around the table, but he didn't see Arch until he was standing next to the two of them.

Arch was seated at the table opposite another man. Each of them had twelve shot glasses in front of them. Each man in turn would take a shot glass down its contents and set the empty glass upside down in the center of the table or as far as they could reach toward the center of the table with the crowd counting aloud the number of shots that had been taken. It was Arch's turn to down shot number ten. As he reached for the shot glass Tommy reached his hand across the table blocking Arch from taking his shot. "Excuse me, gentlemen," he said. "I think in all fairness and to make this contest a bit more interesting I'd like the glasses numbered ten to switch sides of the table. Is that alright with you, Arch?"

"Whatever, Mr. Templeton," Arch answered.

"And you, sir?"

"Name's Frank and no it isn't alright with me."

"Then how about switching sides of the table taking each others seats to finish off the game?"

"Still not alright with me," Frank said.

"You don't mind then?" Tommy asked taking Frank's number ten and sniffing it. "Sir are you a drinking man?" Tommy asked a man he was standing next to.

"I am," the man said.

"Would you toss this back and tell me what you think?" Tommy asked. The man looked at Tommy. "For fifty dollars," Tommy added. The man took the shot glass and tossed it down. "What did you think?"

"It's water," the man said in a surprised voice.

"Steward call your mates and have this man and his accomplice held until they can be turned over to law enforcement officials when we reach our next port. They are con men and I think that their presence onboard doesn't board well for the lines reputation." Frank and a man wearing a waiter's jacket were ushered away.

"How did you know that man Frank wasn't playing fair?" Arch asked.

"When you throw down a shot of vodka your face naturally reacts differently than when you throw down a shot of water. Something I just noticed. You can add that to the rest of those peculiararities you're always accusing me of having," Tommy explained.

"Thanks, buddy. I guess then that his five hundred

dollars is mine," Arch said picking up the man's five hundred dollars from the center of the table along with his five hundred dollar bet.

"The man had to be a fool anyway. I've seen you drink and there is no way that you could have lost. Hell even I would have bet on you," Tommy said. "And I don't bet as you well know." Arch nodded.

The crowd drifted away and Tommy suggested that they all go outside and sit. When they were in a deck chair with a tall glass dripping in cold sweat in their hands Arches being one of the special Bloody Mary concoctions that the ship provided. "You know Arch that what you did in there was a very foolish thing. You obviously haven't been paying attention to what I've been telling you."

"What have you been telling me that I've missed?" Arch replied.

"Someone is trying to kill you, you dumb bastard. Any one of those people in there could have slipped a little something into one of those shots and we wouldn't be having this conversation."

"I hate to interrupt, but you said it had to look like an accident. Just how was an accident going to happen with all those people standing around?"

"Dope you, get you outside, and watch as you fall overboard, and drown for starters, and that's just off the top of my head. Whoever our villain is may be getting desperate. We are now in day number eleven near the halfway point of this voyage and getting further and further away from Louisiana. There are some people that for the right amount of money wouldn't mind spending a length of time in prison for killing someone and this villain of ours obviously has plenty of money to pay someone to do that."

"I get your point, buddy and I promise to be more careful from now on," Arch said.

"And just to be on the safe side from now on all our food and drinks should be made in quantity. No individual servings drinks from pitchers and food from tureens or like our gator something that we all share."

"So we can all die together?" Menerva asked.

"I can't think of anyone else in this world that I'd rather die with than you, love, and Jennifer, and of course Arch," Tommy said.

A steward appeared. "We have located old Ben, sir. He is on the bow of the main deck waiting for you," he informed Tommy.

"Time to go and while I'm gone the three of you at least make an attempt at behaving yourselves."

# CHAPTER FORTY-TWO

**Tommy found Ben sitting** in a deck chair on the port side of the bow with his back to the rail. "Got your prisoners trussed, bound, and locked in the storage room there. Seems they snuck aboard at our last stop and aren't part of this cruise. I'm guarding 'em so that no one sets 'em free before the law takes 'em away."

"That means you have your Bowie Knife handy, I hope?"

"Better than that, son got it and my pint sized blunderbuss too," Ben said reaching behind himself and bringing out a foot long, old time pistol that looked like a miniature blunderbuss. Tommy nodded his approval.

"Did our con men have any identification on them?" Tommy asked.

"Nothing but a wad of cash. A big wad on both of 'em," Ben said.

"So you think that they came onboard at New Madrid. Where do you figure they spent the night?"

"Probably just been moving from place to place."

"If that were so wouldn't you have noticed or

heard them. You heard me the other night," Tommy reminded Ben.

"True, but this here is a big ship and I don't see everything old eyes and all you know?"

"They may be old, but I think that they're sharper than the day you envisioned your first bottle of shine.

"Have you found out anything about what I asked you to find out for me?"

"This old deck hand pulled a few strings and found out that Red's reservation was made at the same time as yours was and paid for by the same person that paid for yours."

"I paid for my own reservation and I made it six months ahead of time," Tommy said.

"That isn't what I was told. They told me that, that Ponnard fella paid for it."

"Ah, the cabin upgrade," Tommy said remembering.

"Another question, Ben. After the riverboat left New Madrid did you see Frankie Le Cock onboard?"

"Been keeping an eye on her for you and yes she sailed with us."

"You saw her then?" Tommy asked trying to make sure.

"That's what I said, son. I seen her with these here sharp, old eyes of mine."

"Thanks, Ben. I just wanted to be sure there was no insult intended," Tommy said in the way of an apology.

"Is there anything else that happened on the way from New Madrid to the Cape that I would be interested in?"

"Just the usual, pirates, whores, and con men," Ben said offering Tommy a big smile with his comment.

# CHAPTER FORTY-THREE

**"Captain! Got a minute?"** Arch asked catching Captain Lyle in the hallway. The riverboat had docked at Chester, Illinois, but the foursome had decided that they had, had enough of tours and adventures onshore and would spend the day in anticipation of tomorrow's stop in Saint Louis by staying aboard.

"I do, Mr. Ponnard. What can I do for you?" Captain Lyle asked.

"By now I'm sure that you've heard of my engagement?"

"I have and that of Ben's daughter to Mr. Templeton. In fact we've had several others on this trip also."

"I have been told that if I asked you with the authority given a captain you might perform a marriage ceremony aboard the ship."

"It would be my pleasure, Mr. Ponnard," Captain Lyle said.

"It will be a double ceremony," Arch said. "And include everyone onboard as our guests."

"I understand, but might I add that when word gets out that we will be holding a wedding ceremony onboard there may be several other couples that might like to join in with their matrimonial and it will be hard to say no to them joining in."

"I don't see any reason the ceremony can't include everyone that wants to get hitched," Arch said.

"Thank you for that. Tomorrow we will be in Saint Louis and while we are there I will make the necessary calls and have all the supplies for a multiple wedding delivered to the ship. I will personally see that it is one that royalty would be proud of. When we leave Saint Louis we have no stops scheduled for that day. It is to be a day of just cruising the Mississippi and it would be the perfect time to hold the weddings if that fits your time table."

"That would fit perfectly, captain," Arch replied.

"I'll get the process started then."

"We're all set people," Arch said rejoining the group. "I just ran into Captain Lyle in the hallway and when I asked he said that he'd be happy to perform a double wedding the day after tomorrow, which he estimates may turn out to be a multiple wedding because he said that there have been several other couples that have become engaged on this voyage and if they want to join in the ceremony he wouldn't be able to say no to them. The day after tomorrow is a day the riverboat has no scheduled stops and will be just cruising Old Miss so he thinks that it would be the perfect day for a wedding. And for your information Mr. Smarty you were right he said that it would be a wedding that even royalty would approve of."

"I've changed my mind," Jennifer said. "I feel like celebrating Arch's news. Tomorrow we will be in Saint

Louis and it will be a busy day. We'll have wedding dresses and tuxes to buy and if there's time a site or two to see so let's go out and celebrate the good news today.

"Really, Jenn?" Menerva asked. "I've really been looking forward to a day of doing nothing but laying back. Can't we celebrate onboard? We'll order up a couple bottles of champagne and maybe some strawberries dipped in melted chocolate to go along with the champagne. What say?"

"You are right maybe we should stay onboard. If we go ashore we risk the chance of something happening that will spoil our time in Saint Louis tomorrow and the wedding the day after," Jennifer admitted looking a little disappointed.

That night at dinner the captain provided a special meal in celebration of the upcoming weddings, which he announced to all those gathered in the dining room at the time. "If you see the captain thank him for tonight's dinner it completely made my day," Jennifer said as she sat with the others on their balcony afterwards sippin' shine.

# CHAPTER FORTY-FOUR

**"Ladies and gentlemen,"** the first mate's voice came over the riverboat's speaker system. "We have discovered that we are a crew member short this morning. I must apologize, but this will delay our landing in Saint Louis. We will be holding our position on the river while we go in search of him. Don't be alarmed our holding here will only be temporary."

"Arch go get your handgun and give it to me right now," Tommy said.

"Why?"

"Go get it right now," Tommy insisted. Arch went and when he returned he had a strange look on his face. "What's wrong?" Tommy asked.

"The gun I took from that miscreant wasn't where I put it, but this one was," he said handing Tommy his 9mm automatic. "This is my pistol the one that I left on the nightstand in my apartment back in New Orleans. I thought that I had lost it in the fire and explosion of my old apartment."

"Jennifer! Menerva!" Tommy called and they joined Arch and him in the main room.

"We have a problem and I want us to drop what we are doing and to search this entire cabin. I want us to search the ceilings for loose panels, turn on all the lights and look for shadows beyond their covers and shades, check the floors under loose carpets for loose floor boards, pull out all the drawers and search behind and under them as well as their contents, search inside the cabinets for something attached to them out of sight when the drawers are out. Take the beds apart remove the mattresses and if they have been cut or have zippered covers take them off and search under or in them, look behind the pictures on the walls I want us to look everywhere. Check the bathrooms remove drawers, look in the tanks I want a complete search of every inch of this apartment."

"What are we looking for?" Jennifer asked.

"Anything that doesn't belong there," Tommy said. "I'll start out here and if you find something holler out, but don't touch it."

It took the four of them two hours of searching without coming up with anything that didn't belong there. "Okay did you find a pistol or bullets for one?" Tommy asked. Blank looks shown on the faces all the other occupants of the cabin.

"Your shotgun is still on the shelf, but I didn't find any shells for it," Menerva said.

"The reason I called for this search was to make sure there wasn't anything left in our cabin by the intruder."

"Someone was in here without one of us being here with them weren't they?" Jennifer asked.

"Yes," Tommy said. "And since our cabin is likely to be the first one searched after they find the body I wanted to make sure that there is nothing here that doesn't belong.

"I have to step out for a minute and I'd ask that you all stay in the cabin," Tommy asked. Tommy first called the desk to find Ben's whereabouts. Leaving the cabin he went down to the main deck and knocked on the door to the engine room.

"I've got a problem, Ben," Tommy said when Ben opened the door.

"Only one? Ain't you lucky," Ben replied returning to what he was doing. When he turned his back to him Tommy noticed the bandage on the back and top of his head.

"What happened to your head?"

"Someone snuck up on me while I was guarding those fellows and smacked me good. I never saw 'em or heard 'em and to top it off they let them fellas out and now the captain's gone missing too."

"I suspected it might be him," Tommy said. "You know that when they find his body he's going to have several bullets in him?"

"You know something I don't? You suspect them con men done it?" Ben asked.

"Not sure at this point," Tommy answered.

"So what be your problem, son?"

"I have to hide something that I don't want the police to find," Tommy said.

"That shotgun be that something?"

"No something smaller."

"Fit in there?" Ben asked pointing to a barrel that was sitting on a stand in the corner, with a spicket in it.

"What's in the barrel?" Tommy asked.

"Oil."

"They'll search in there for sure. I would," Tommy said.

"Will it fit in here? This is the brace for the paddlewheel and it has adjustable arms that have these spaces covered by access panels that are secured with removable screws." Tommy reached into his pocket and took out the automatic.

"See if it will fit." He said handing the automatic to Ben. Ben took the gun and looked at Tommy.

"It will fit nicely," Ben said after holding the gun up to the side of the brace. Giving the automatic back to Tommy he started removing the screws.

"I know you're wondering?"

"Don't need to know, son. Family trusts family."

"I know you don't, but when they find the body this is going to be in all likelihood the murder weapon. It was planted in our room up top and I need to un-plant it until the right time comes along, which may or may not be for some time." Ben removed the cover for the empty space and turned to have Tommy hand the automatic back to him. "Got a clean rag?" Ben nodded stepped over to and took one from a stack on the shelf that ran along the back wall of the engine room. "Wipe your prints off it and leave the rag around it so it won't rattle in the cavity," Tommy suggested.

"Gottcha," Ben said taking the automatic from Tommy, wiping it down, and after placing it in the open cavity making sure that it was in there snuggly he replaced the cover along with its screws.

"Thanks, Ben. If and when the time comes I may ask you to retrieve it for me."

"Before you go you should know that I seen Frankie Le Cock prowling around early this morning about the time they figure that the captain went missing."

"You didn't happen to hear a big fish dropping back into the Sippy?" Tommy asked.

"A man's gotta sleep sometime," Ben answered.

"Thanks again, Ben for solving my problem."

"That's what family does for family."

Shortly after noon the State Police who had joined in the search recovered Captain Lyle's body from the river.

# CHAPTER FORTY-FIVE

**Within half-an-hour** of the recovery of Captain Lyle's body the F.B.I. took control of the riverboat. They set up headquarters in the Paddlewheel Lounge and started questioning all the passengers. Leading the team was an old veteran and a legend in the agency, Agent Danny Lee.

To expedite the questioning of the nearly two hundred passengers and crew three questioning stations were established. Agent Lee was at the principle station to which anyone from the other two stations with questionable alibis were shuffled. Agent Lee sat along the wall his back to the silenced paddlewheel with his eyes closed listening to the questions and answers being asked and given at the two other stations that were located along the wall to his left and the other along the front of the bar on his right.

"You wish to see me, Agent Lee?" Arch asked.

"Have a seat, Mr. Ponnard. You are Archibald Ponnard with a residence on Bourbon Street in New Orleans?"

"I was, yes."

"Was? Explain 'was' to me."

"My residence has been demolished since I've been on this voyage by the city of New Orleans with the permission of a person or persons unknown who lifted an injunction I had against the city forbidding them to do so without my permission."

"But you did live there?"

"I did, Agent Lee."

"Recently we have had several inquiries about you, your past, and anything else we had on you?"

"Really by whom?" Arch asked.

"Have you ever heard of the law firm of Harold, Harold, Gibbons, and Ashworth?"

"Not that I recall. I don't think that I ever ran into them in a courtroom. Are they the ones making the inquiry?"

"Yes.

"Moving on. Where were you this morning between the hours of midnight and three o'clock?"

"Sitting on the private balcony of the owner's suite located on the top floor of this vessel enjoying the sights and sounds of the mighty Mississippi," Arch answered leaving out the fact that they were all sippin' shine which was illegal in the eyes of the F.B.I.

"Were you alone?"

"I'm never alone, Agent Lee. My friends won't let me be alone you see they think that someone is trying to kill me and won't unless it looks like an accident, but that'll be hard to do if they are all where I am all the time."

"Very interesting. Were these friends with you this morning on the balcony?"

"You bet all of them."

"Do you own a 9mm automatic?"

"Not any more," Arch answered.

"Why not? You have a permit for one and if you sell it or dispose of it in any way the law requires that you are to notify the issuer of that permit."

"I am aware of my responsibilities as a gun owner, Agent Lee."

"Where is that firearm at this moment?"

"Not a god damn clue. The last time I saw it, it was on the bed stand of my apartment. That by the way is the same apartment that the city of New Orleans has demolished. They have it now as far as I know. They destroyed it along with all the rest of my possessions when they tried to kill me in the process of that demolishment. Everything I owned except what I had brought along with me on this cruise was destroyed and taken god only knows."

"That is not what we have been told," Agent Lee said.

"May I ask by whom you were given that information?"

"Do you mind if we search your cabin, Mr. Ponnard?"

"As long as I or one other of my friends are present with every agent you send to do the searching, no I don't mind." Agent Danny Lee raised his hand and signaled two other agents over to his table.

"These agents will go with you to your cabin at which time they will search it."

"Did you not hear me? For each one of them I require one of my party to be with them or my permission isn't given."

"Who do you want to take with you?" Agent Lee asked.

"Tommy Templeton."

"He's up next so after I interview him the two of you can go with my agents. Just wait over there by the door."

"Thank you, Agent Lee," Arch said walking over to the door to wait with the two F.B.I. agents.

"One of you fellas wouldn't mind going over to the bar there and getting me a double whiskey would you?" Arch asked his companions getting looks for which he had no explanation.

# CHAPTER FORTY-SIX

**"Have a seat,** Mr. Templeton," Agent Lee said when Tommy appeared before him. "Where were you between midnight and three o'clock this morning?"

"Sitting on the balcony of our cabin along with its three other occupants."

"During that time did any of you leave?"

"Leave where exactly?"

"The cabin?"

"No, no one left the cabin until we all came down for a late breakfast about ten or there abouts."

"How can you be so sure?"

"I am a very light sleeper."

"I see," replied Agent Danny Lee.

"Do you own a firearm, Mr. Templeton?"

"I have one, yes. I recently borrowed it from a bartender in New Orleans."

"Where is it now?"

"On the shelf of the closet in my bedroom."

"Back in, in Massachusetts?" Agent Lee asked referring to the file in front of him.

"No it's here in the closet of this bedroom. I haven't

been back to Massachusetts since I left to start on this voyage and if you've been paying attention I did say New Orleans, bartender, and recently."

"Why would you want to borrow a shotgun and bring it along on a cruise ship?"

"There is more to cruise ships then meets the eye, Agent Lee. There's gator hunting for example. You don't catch gators with a hook attached to a cane pole." Agent Lee shook his head.

"You have a permit for hunting gators?"

"I have a guide that takes care of those things for me so I didn't know if one is or isn't required besides I have no shells for the shotgun and we already ate that gator and man was it delicious. Have you ever had a deliciously cooked gator, Agent Lee?"

"Can't say that I've had the pleasure."

"You've missed out then, Agent Lee."

"Your friend seems to think that someone is trying to murder him. Do you share his opinion?"

"Most assuredly. In fact I am the one who has pointed it out to him after saving his life from his assassin's attempts several times."

"I see and you can detail these events to me?"

"I can and in minute detail each and every one of the attempts."

"Do you know who the assassin is?"

"Not a clue at this time, but I'm getting closer to finding out."

"Finding murders or an assassin is a job for the police

not for private individuals. It is dangerous. You could get yourself caught in the middle and end up dead."

"Like Captain Lyle?" Agent Danny Lee visibly perked up.

"Who told you that Captain Lyle is dead?"

"I like yourself am a sleuth with extraordinary powers of deduction. When I say that someone is trying to kill my best friend or that Captain Lyle was shot twice in the chest and once in the head after first being bludgeoned unconscious and then thrown overboard I know what I'm talking about. And after saying that you'd like the devil to have the authority to lock me up, but you can't because I have a three person alibi, you don't have a murder weapon, or the slightest motive as to why I would kill a man that was about to marry me in two days and make me one of the happiest men on this planet."

"I may want to talk to you again, Mr. Templeton. Don't leave the ship," Agent Danny lee warned.

"'If the fall don't get you the mud at the bottom of the river or the gators will', a quote from a friend of mine so I'll be here," Tommy said. "That's a clue by the way and I know that I am to join my best friend and your two associates in a search of our cabin so I'll say goodbye for now."

When Tommy had left the lounge with Arch and the two F.B.I. agents and was clearly out of earshot Agent Lee turned to his assistant and said," I want you to get me a DNA Sample from our Mr. Templeton and his three roommates and I want a background check on all four of them, A.S.A.P. and I want a couple of divers to search the mud at the bottom of this river for the murder weapon if that's even possible."

Tommy and Arch returned to their cabin with the two F.B.I. agents who began searching it with Jennifer following right behind them cleaning up the mess they were making. "How did it go, buddy?" Arch asked as they stood watching the agents search.

"You first since you went first," Tommy countered.

"Agent Lee didn't learn anything from me, but I learned a few things from him. He knew that I had a 9mm registered in my name and accused me of having it onboard this ship. I also found out that a law firm has been making inquiries including several to the F.B.I. about me."

"Now that could be very interesting," Tommy said. "Did he give you the name of the law firm?"

"He did and it didn't ring a bell, but on the way back here the light came on."

"And?"

"It is the firm my father's partner started after they split up a long time ago, before I was born," Arch said.

"Do you know why they split up?"

"I've no idea."

"We're finished your cabin is clean," one of the F.B.I. agents that had been searching it said. "We've gotten a call and have been asked to take DNA swabs from each of the four of you. Do you have any objections?" Menerva looked at Tommy with that I'm worried look.

"We don't have any objections, agent," Tommy said.

The agents took the swabs and left. "Tommy what about?" Menerva asked.

"I'm human just like the rest of you besides the F.B.I. already has a DNA sample from me on file. I had to submit one when I submitted an application to join them before I left uni.

"What about you? Are there any secrets in your DNA that you want to tell me about before the F.B.I. does?"

"The only thing you need to know is that I love you and I don't think that my DNA is going to tell them that."

"You never know. They discover new techniques every day," Tommy quipped leaning over and giving her a kiss on the cheek.

"Arch I want you to call a private eye that you know you can trust one that is unaffiliated with your father or your family. I want you to have him find out what caused the breakup between your father and his partner. I also want you to have him or an unaffiliated someone else would be even better to find out why this law firm is making its inquiries. Can you do that?"

"I'll get right on it," Arch said. "Making the first call now," he added giving Tommy the thumbs up.

"You girls haven't been called down to be questioned yet have you?" Tommy asked.

"No and I'm feeling a little left out," said Jennifer. "I've never had a good looking F.B.I. agent question me before. Plenty of them have come into the office and they've all been good looking too."

"Well I wouldn't exactly call Agent Danny Lee good looking, but after all his years in the service I imagine he's entitled to what the good lord has given him," Tommy said chuckling at his own joke.

"Don't worry, Jenn," Arch said having completed his two calls, "you are right here in the very heart of the investigation and on a first hand get to know everything that I do basis."

"Tommy what did you learn when they interviewed you?" Arch asked.

"Not one thing new, but I gave Agent Danny Lee a few things to think about. Because of that I don't think that he is going to bother with you ladies until after he has the results of the background checks he has ordered on each of us. The DNA results he won't get back for at least a few days beyond that."

"What about Saint Louis and our wedding?" Jennifer asked.

"What about the voyage?" Menerva added.

"Delayed with our money back along with a 'we're sorry', and here is a gift certificate for a fully paid trip at some other time," Arch answered holding up the certificate.

# CHAPTER FORTY-SEVEN

**It was dinner time** and Jennifer was close to death from hunger. "Someone should stay here in case we have another break in," Arch said.

"Are you volunteering, honey?" asked Jennifer.

"There's no need for that now that the F.B.I. has searched the room and found nothing," Tommy said. "But if it bothers you, Arch I will lock the door personally and no one will be able to get in either through the door, the walls, the windows, the floor, or the patio door."

"You forgot sand through the keyhole, Rick," Arch mused.

"Or sand through the keyhole since we don't have a keyhole," Tommy added.

"How can you guarantee that?" Jennifer asked.

"Have you ever watched *Harry Potter*?" Tommy asked.

"I have," Jennifer answered.

"Then you should already know the answer. I thought you were starving?"

The dinning room was packed. "Come have a seat at our table," Agent Danny Lee offered the foursome as they stood looking around for one.

"Why thank you, Agent Lee we gladly accept your kind offer," Tommy said before anyone else could refuse.

"Over this way," Agent Lee said. "You four find somewhere else to eat," he said to the four lesser agents already sitting at the table. A waiter appeared immediately. "I've ordered already so go right ahead," Agent Lee said. Arch ordered for everyone and the waiter left.

"I tried ordering gator, but was told that unless the two hunters come up with another one that gator isn't on the menu. Can I ask who the other hunter is?"

"My father better known as old Ben. He's part of the crew and fishes a lot. He was the one that caught the first one and Tommy here sort of caught the other," Menerva said.

"So you must be Menerva and this other lady is Jennifer?"

"You are correct, Agent Lee," Arch said. "And Jennifer is engaged to me and Menerva is engaged to Tommy."

"If we are going to have a conversation I'd ask that you please skip the agent bit and just call me Danny."

"Okay, Danny," Jennifer said. "We were all the four of us supposed to get married the day after tomorrow by Captain Lyle. Have you found out who or why yet?"

"So you know it was the captain too?"

"We keep nothing from each other," said Tommy.

"I assume that, that also includes old Ben?" Agent Lee asked.

"He's not really part of the group. He's more what you'd call?"

"An informer I know. We've done some checking on him and found out that he's been checking on people for you as well as guiding your fishing and gator hunting and is a very close friend of Captain Lyle's."

"You've also made two calls after I talked with the two of you."

"You're tapping our calls?" Arch asked.

"As a lawyer you know that without a warrant that would be illegal, but we can keep track of who is calling you and whom you are calling without a warrant. And as I was saying the two calls you made were to some very interesting people."

"They were indeed and so is what they do," said Arch.

"May I ask?"

"That would be giving a secret away and one you don't seem to be interested in anyway even if it does tie into and may lead to the killer of Captain Lyle," Tommy said.

"You applied recently to be admitted to Quantico, Mr. Templeton."

"I did."

"And you were turned down because you lacked experience in your field."

"Correct again. Your information is very good, but it has nothing to do with this investigation."

"You were right about the mud by the way," Agent Lee said. "I didn't get it until after I got a report from the team of divers I sent down to search for the murder weapon."

"You should have asked old Ben. He would have told you about the bottom of the Mississippi," Menerva offered.

"The mud down there is so thick that if someone threw it overboard it will never be found."

"Stranger things have happened," Tommy said getting a strange look from Agent Lee.

"I have a feeling that there are things you're holding back from me, Mr. Templeton."

"This may help you out. The two con men who we figured were paid to and are the killers of Captain Lyle that you're not looking for at present you will probably find dead. You might start looking for them in Chester, Illinois where they got off the ship. When you find them if you ever do make sure you take lots of samples and to speed things up you might want to send a forensic team to the cabin of Frankie Le Cock to do there thing there too. You may get lucky and find evidence in her cabin that will link her to those two men," Tommy offered.

"You don't say," Agent Lee said pulling out his cell phone, getting up, and leaving the table.

"Is there anything else you'd like to share with me?" Danny Lee asked after returning to the table from making his call.

"Food, our orders are here," Tommy said seeing the waiters headed their way. "As a gesture of good faith I'll have to see if I can rustle you up some gator," Tommy offered. "By the way can you loan me some shells for my borrowed shotgun? It's a 12 gauge." This brought laughter from all those around the table.

# CHAPTER FORTY-EIGHT

**It was breakfast time** on the Mississippi. "Ladies and gentlemen the F.B.I. is going to allow us to continue on to and dock in Saint Louis," the first mate announced over the riverboat's internal speaker system. "You may leave the ship after having your fingers printed and a DNA swab taken. You can take nothing with you and must also surrender your driver's license. I have been informed that they are in the process of setting up a station to do this. It will be off to the side of the gangway's exit onboard the ship and you can go get the work done at your convenience before we arrive to save you time when we get there.

"If you want to leave the ship and discontinue the voyage you must let them know as they will then want more information before you leave. And on a sadder note while we are in Saint Louis we will be assigned a new captain to take us through to Saint Paul."

"That is awfully nice of you, Danny," Jennifer said. "Now with a new captain to marry us we can do the shopping in Saint Louis that we had intended to do yesterday."

"For the four of you I am foregoing the fingerprinting and DNA swabs."

"I wonder why?" commented Arch. "What's the catch? When the police are doing a nicety for someone there is always a catch."

"The catch is that I'm going to assign two agents to go with you when you leave the ship. They'll try not to interfere with your shopping and touring unless they have to. They are there more for your protection then as our watchdogs so please don't loose them."

"Thank you, Danny. We appreciate the gesture," Menerva said.

"I think you should also know that I've taken Frankie Le Cock into custody and she will be spending some time behind bars once we reach Saint Louis. There are a few questions we want her to clear up before we allow her to rejoin the ship and at this time she has lawyered up thus the jail time." Tommy got up and walked away from the table and out the door motioning for Agent Lee to follow him.

Once Agent Lee had followed him outside Tommy said, "You may want to check Frankie Le Cock's reservation and who paid for it. When you do find out and pull Mr. Ponnard's not his son my friend Arch's bank records and check his phone calls. What you find may or may not be of interest to you."

The engine coughed into life, the paddlewheel started churning the bloodied waters of the Mississippi, and the riverboat headed for Saint Louis. "What was that about?" Arch asked Tommy when he returned to the table.

"I wanted to know how much slack Danny was going to allow me if I came up with that gator."

"You couldn't ask that here?" Arch asked.

"You're a lawyer. Would you perjure yourself in front of witnesses?"

"Got it. Sorry, buddy," Arch said.

"Where are you going to get a gator? We're too far up the river for gators," Menerva asked.

"I've been thinking that maybe we should put off the wedding," Arch said without warning.

"Arch!" Jennifer almost shouted drawing the attention of people at the nearby tables.

"Captain Lyle said that he'd make some calls, do some special shopping, and have what he needed delivered to the ship when we were in Saint Louis. Now that he's dead I doubt if that will happen."

"I'll go ask the chefs and stewards in the galley and see if he's talked to them," Jennifer said jumping up from the table, heading for the galley at almost a run.

Her return was by no means as rambunctious. "Well?" Menerva asked.

"They said that Captain Lyle had talked to them, but that they have been told to stand down by the first mate. I asked why and they said that the first mate told them that the new captain might have a different opinion of performing a marriage onboard. They said that Captain Lyle was a rare breed. He was a romantic and was always looking for a way to make these voyages each and every one different and special in and of itself whereas most other captains pretty much stick to the printed schedule."

"I'm sorry, Jenn. I just had a feeling," Arch consoled.

"We could get married in Saint Louis," Menerva suggested. "After all we are going to have our two witnesses with us."

"Illinois might have other restrictions such as licenses, shots, blood tests, and a waiting period for example. Most states have them where ships on the other hand, which are ruled by maritime law usually don't have those same restrictions."

"Damn, damn, damn," Jennifer blurted out again drawing the attention of those seated at nearby tables.

On the way back to their cabin, Tommy asked Arch, "Did either of your calls call back?"

"Not yet," he replied.

When the foursome returned to the riverboat from their day in Saint Louis Arch excused himself. "I'm going to go talk to the new captain," he said and left.

"Good luck," Tommy said. "Now that the wedding isn't going to happen onboard have you girls thought about where you'd like to get married?"

"I always thought it would be romantic to be married in Paris, France," Jennifer said.

"I never thought that I'd ever get married so I haven't thought about it until you suggested the riverboat. I thought that was the most romantic suggestion I've ever heard," said Menerva.

"What a grump our new captain is. He even looks like Grumpy of the Seven Dwarfs with a white beard and all," Arch sputtered upon his return to the cabin displaying all the signs of having been upset after his talk with the new captain.

"I take it there won't be a wedding, tomorrow or at anytime aboard this ship?" Tommy asked.

"The man wouldn't even consider it," Arch replied.

# CHAPTER FORTY-NINE

**"I got a call** from the person checking on my father," Arch said. "He said that the breakup was caused over a woman. It seems that they were both after the same one."

"Did he say who the woman was?" Tommy asked.

"No! But there's something else."

"What?"

"Ever since he started making his inquiries he's been followed by some very unsavory characters that have worried him to the point that has him hiding out."

"That doesn't surprise me. Did you tell him that everyone associated with our investigation has been murdered?"

"What and scare him to death?"

"It may save his life, Arch."

"I'll call him back."

"Any word on the law firm inquiry?"

"Nothing yet," Arch replied.

Tommy went to his locked chest and took out a jar of shine. Relocking it he went out to the balcony and was about to sit down for a little contemplation time, but was interrupted from doing so by a knock at the front door.

Going to answer it he found Agent Lee standing there with several file folders in his hand.

"May I come in?" Danny Lee asked.

"Of course. Mi casa, su casa," Tommy said.

"Well, Agent Lee. Come to ask us more questions?" Arch asked entering the room.

"Arch I was just going to sit out on the balcony and I'm sure that Agent Lee would like some fresh air too. Would you care to join the two of us?"

On the way to the balcony, Agent Danny Lee noticed the paper bag in Tommy's hand. "When my agents searched this cabin not only did they find your shotgun, but several cases of what Mr. Ponnard here described as home brew. They wanted me to arrest the two of you for having it."

"It isn't against the law to home brew as long as you don't sell it," Arch said.

"But it is illegal to transport it across state lines especially in quantity," Agent Lee replied.

"So why didn't you arrest us for having it?" Arch asked having got his lawyer up.

"Because we found a case of the same stuff in Captain Lyle's cabin and it got me to wondering and when I wonder I make inquiries."

"Have a seat," Tommy said arriving out on the balcony. Everyone pulled up a deck chair sitting in somewhat of a half-circle. "I was coming out here to do a little contemplating along with a little sipping. This jar has in it what is known as swamp shine. It is a home brew that was given to Arch and me as a gift. Captain Lyle was given his case as a gift also and he happens to be a fan of the stuff as well as an off duty consumer."

"He and old Ben. I've checked on and questioned the old man. Seems he and Captain Lyle go back a long way. It was Captain Lyle that asked old Ben to come along on this voyage because you asked for a fishing guide."

"You have been doing your homework, Danny and all of what you've just said is correct.

"Captain Lyle and old Ben were running low on shine, which is the reason we took our side trip back to New Orleans. If we hadn't gone to retrieve more shine we'd never have known about Arch's apartment being demolished and subsequently there wouldn't have been another attempt on his life."

"We've also contacted Mr. Bonaventure and he has confirmed your story. When we questioned him he told us about the thugs that were after old Ben the ones you subdued and left on the dock as well as the cases of shine, the gator hole, and the Mud pies. Everything you've told me as far as I can ascertain has been the truth and the leads that you've given me have proven to be most interesting and helpful just how helpful only time will tell."

"Can I interrupt here and ask if Bon, Mr. Bonaventure needs a lawyer?" Arch asked of his old friend.

"Mr. Bonaventure is not in custody or being charged with transporting, etc. He's fine and sends his regards."

"Thank you for that," Arch said. Agent Lee smiled and nodded.

"Since you have been honest with me I am going to go one step further and share what we have so far with the two of you."

"Can we make that the four of us?" Menerva asked from the doorway.

"We didn't hear you come in," Arch said tilting his head back to let Jennifer give him a peck on the cheek.

"I don't see why not ladies please pull up a chair and join us." The girls pulled up a chair next to their betrotheds with Menerva leaning over and giving Tommy a peck on his cheek. Tommy in turn smiled back at her and took hold of her hand.

"Before we go on would you like to sample the swamp shine, Danny? It's a new jar and I have a feeling that I will be needing a sip or two and I offer it to you all in turn," Tommy said to Agent Lee.

"I really shouldn't but as part of my investigation I should not knowing exactly what I've left you five miscreants get away with," Danny Lee said taking the jar from Tommy.

"Just sip it," Menerva warned. "If you drink it we may have to put you to bed before you go back and that may cause a bit of concern among your associates." Agent Lee took a sip as instructed and passed the jar to Arch who did the same and so on.

"Wow! I see what you mean," Agent Lee said after a bit.

"This batch has been aged."

"No it hasn't, dear," Tommy said before Menerva gave her father up to the feds. She looked at him and he looked at her and they both smiled. "Truthfully this is a jar from the first case. I haven't gotten anywhere close to opening the case I'm letting age," Tommy added.

"What I've been carrying around with me is the background checks we've done on the four of you," Agent Lee said passing to each of the foursome their file. Jennifer reached over and snatched Arch's file from him before he had a chance to open it smiling at him afterwards. "Inside you won't find anything that really concerns the F.B.I. Growing up always is a challenge for most people and I must say that you four have done really well."

"Is that why you are willing to share them with us?" Jennifer asked handing Arch his folder back after she had quickly scanned it with her secretarial eyes.

"It was more to ease your minds as to where you and the F.B.I. stand in regards to each other."

"Thank you for that," Arch said once again. "The girls I think were a little more than worried than either Tommy or I."

"We have questioned and released, Frankie Le Cock. She finally decided it was in her best interests to co-operate with us. When the riverboat makes port in Hannibal she will be coming back onboard at least that is what we've been lead to believe."

"Thank's for the warning," Tommy said.

"You still think that she has something to do with these murders?"

"I'm almost certain that she is the murderer or is it murderess?" Tommy said

# CHAPTER FIFTY

**"I find that passing** through these locks to be just so exciting and today we have four or five of them to pass through Don't you agree, Mr.?" asked Alyssa of a fellow passenger aboard the riverboat.

"The name is Greg Winter. Maybe you've heard of me I'm quite famous in the sports world especially in track and field circles."

"What do you excel in, Greg?" Alyssa the beauty made of good makeup that had been previously discussed by our foursome in the dinning room when they first came onboard asked.

"Besides the layout position if you catch my meaning I'm a cyclist. I've come in third in the *Tour de France* twice."

"How wonderful for you," Alyssa said giving Greg her most flirty look.

"Would I be too forward in asking you to share a drink with me?" Greg asked.

"Your place or mine?" Alyssa returned.

It was day fifteen of their voyage the day that they were to be married and Jennifer was in an ugly mood. "I just want to sit here on the balcony and sulk," she said to Arch.

"The rest of us are going to take a dip in the pool and then let the sun dry us off. Are you sure you don't want to come with us?"

"I'm sure. Maybe later," Jennifer replied.

"If we're not by the pool check the nearest watering hole," Arch said leaving with Menerva and Tommy.

"These locks are a miracle of engineering. Just look at the size of some of the ships that pass through them," Arch said indicating the ship passing through the other lock across from theirs.

"They are indeed," answered Tommy who seemed to be further away than Jennifer.

"A penny for your thoughts, ol buddy."

"I was hoping you'd tell me what I was thinking. I can feel my mind working at solving our mystery and yet the reader board doesn't have one word on it."

"It'll come to you. Quit fighting it. Relax and let it come to you that's what I do when I'm having a problem involving something mysterious like thinking," Arch suggested.

"That was fast," Menerva said as Jennifer joined them.

"I was more miserable sitting there by myself so here I am."

"They say that misery likes company, but what it doesn't know is that when it's in my company it doesn't hang around long," Arch said giving her a peck on the cheek.

"Can I trust you girls to watch Arch and protect him

from himself, killers, and con men for the rest of the morning? I want to talk to old Ben if I can find him."

"He's safe in Menerva's hands, but not in mine," Jennifer replied in her old joyful tone.

Tommy found a phone, called the desk, and was told that Ben was in the chart room which is where Tommy found him engrossed in several charts, turning pages back and fourth. "What are you looking up, Ben?" Tommy asked.

"Checking the water depths around Hannibal where we'll be docking next. Haven't done any fishing lately and thought that I might try my hand once we're there."

"We're too far north for a chance at catching us a gator aren't we?"

"We are, son. We are."

"How's my daughter taking the wedding delay? Wasn't today supposed to be the day?"

"Far better then Jennifer," Tommy replied. "She goes from letting it go to cursing the world for the bad luck."

"I'm glad you brought up the subject, son," Ben said smiling at Tommy. "I heard something interesting in the galley this morning. It seems that our new captain was given specific orders that he was not to perform any weddings onboard this ship and Mr. Ponnard's in particular. It was part of his orders when he was assigned to complete this voyage."

"You wouldn't know by whom?"

"Somebody with influence at the main office. That's where his assignment and orders came from."

"That's very interesting, Ben," Tommy said.

"I heard that the F.B.I. questioned you?"

"They sure did and they wanted to know about where I got the shine from, how close Captain Lyle and I were, and if I'd seen or heard anything that could help them catch his killer. Of course I was mum on the shine. Told 'em I made it in my basement, but that I hadn't made any for a long time as I was trying to give up drinking."

"I'm sure they believed you," Tommy commented, chuckling.

"Captain Lyle and I was real close. How close are you to finding out who done it to him?"

"I think I know that Frankie Le Cock either killed the captain to prevent him from performing the two marriages today or those two con men were paid to do it. By the way those two con men are dead and Frankie Le Cock will be reboarding the boat when we land at Hannibal."

"Then I will have to keep a special eye on her, won't I?"

"Remember that she is extremely dangerous, Ben," Tommy warned.

"I'm dangerous too," Ben replied.

"By the way how's the back of your head?"

"Point taken, wise-ass, want to be son-in-law," Ben said smiling at Tommy.

"Not yet, but that too will change soon, Ben, soon."

# CHAPTER FIFTY-ONE

**"When we dock** check to see if you can see the ghost of Mark Twain somewhere in the crowd," mused Arch.

"Why would you be saying something like that, honey?" Jennifer asked.

"Well when Twain was living here the riverboats would dock bringing comedians, singers, gamblers, swindlers, etc., and since the passengers onboard this ship fit that bill I just figured his ghost would surely make an appearance. What say you soothsayer?"

"You don't need a soothsayer, Mr. Archibald Ponnard. What you need is a psychiatrist," Menerva replied.

"We shall see. All ashore that's going ashore so follow me. You know it was Mark Twain that immortalized riverboats in the minds of the American public, but did you know that for a brief period in his life he was actually a riverboat pilot himself?"

"You seem to be well versed on Mr. Twain, Arch. How come?"

"I was schooled in Louisiana and one of my teachers was a Twain nut."

It was day sixteen and the scheduled stop at Hannibal,

Missouri the boyhood home and museum of Samuel Langhorne Clemens better known by his pen name, Mark Twain, which was a riverboat term meaning two fathoms, (a depth of twelve feet).

Standing by the gangway was Agent Lee and several of his cohorts. "Aren't you afraid of mass desertions by letting all these people leave the ship?" Arch asked.

"It's not who's getting off, but who's getting on. Look to your two o'clock when you leave." Arch scanned the shoreline in the direction indicated by Agent Lee.

"I assume you are referring to that red-headed beauty out yonder?" Agent Lee nodded.

"Enjoy the tour," Agent Lee said.

"I wonder why we weren't assigned our F.B.I. protective entourage?" Jennifer remarked.

"At this point I think that Agent Lee would welcome another murder. He would appreciate something to work on. What he thought he had he now realizes that he hasn't got," Tommy said.

"You want to run that by us again this time in English," said Arch.

"He has suspects, but no proof," Tommy answered.

"Aren't we in the same boat?" Arch asked.

"We are, but we are working on getting some proof."

"I got all the proof I need in a jar wrapped in a paper bag back in our suite," stated Arch which made everyone chuckle.

The tour bus had returned and all the passengers had been accounted for. "What's on the schedule for tomorrow, girls?" Arch asked being in good spirits for when they had gone ashore they had enjoyed the tour and no one had tried to murder him.

"Tomorrow I am going to lock you in the bedroom and make you pay for that ghost business this morning," Jennifer said a bit too loudly as some of the people sitting at the surrounding tables in the dining room looked her way and either smiled or giggled. "During that entire tour your story had me looking for that damn ghost and the funny thing is I think I actually saw him."

"Come on, Jenn it was just a joke," Arch stated.

"No, I saw him too," Menerva said.

"So, did I," Tommy said adding his assurance to the sighting.

"How come I didn't see him?" Arch asked in a disappointing tone, which caused all the others to break out in laughter.

"Oh, I get it. It's make fun of good old Arch time isn't it?"

"What's good for the gander in the morning is good for the goose in the evening," Tommy said.

"Okay I guess I deserved that one," Arch admitted. "So what are we ordering tonight? I'm starving."

# CHAPTER FIFTY-TWO

**"This is the captain** speaking would Mr. Greg Winter please contact the desk as soon as possible," the captain announced over the ships speaker system.

"Haven't heard that one before," Arch said on his way to answer a knock at their door.

"Well, Agent Lee come on in," Arch said loud enough to bring everyone into the living area. "To what do we owe this visit?"

"You just heard the announcement?"

"We did and thought it odd," Arch replied.

"Last night we had a late passage through a lock."

"We know. We were all sitting out on the balcony enjoying the event," Arch said.

"This morning the captain got a call from the attendants at the lock who reported finding a body floating in that same lock. It was pretty beat up given that there were several more ships that passed through the same lock after we did, but just before the captain received the call Mr. Winter's wife reported that her husband was missing."

"I have a question," said Tommy. "Wouldn't a body

float out of the lock along with the ship when the gates are opened?"

"I asked the same question and normally you are right a body would float out with the ships passing through it and if not with that one the first one that followed it. In this particular instance it seems that when they found him and remember they didn't find him until it got light out he was hung up by his watch band on the side of the lock. Anyway this Greg Winter is a cyclist *the Tour de France* kind and I am told a noted personality in some circles. His wife said that he is also a womanizer, but has never spent the night out when she is accompanying him to an event or on a trip such as this one. She said that she controls the purse strings and he needs her support to support his athletic endeavors. Now the body may be from another ship or just someone from shore viewing the operation of the locks that may have accidentally fallen in, but in my experience one and one equals two. Unless Mr. Winter shows up alive and breathing that body will be his."

"Why are you telling us this and in person?" Tommy asked.

"I'm sticking to my part of our agreement," Agent Lee said. "The sharing of information agreement we have. We do have such an agreement don't we?"

"We do," confirmed Arch, "and thank you for keeping your end of it."

"My agents are going door to door checking and asking the passengers if and when they last remember seeing Mr. Winter. I'll let you know what they come up with, but the main reason I came 'round to inform you in person was to ask if you had any idea as to why he would have been a target?"

"None of us spoke with him or even knew who he was," Tommy said looking at the others for a contradiction. They all just shrugged and shook their heads. "All I can suggest is that you do what you do. Check his background and financials to see if you can come up with any link to any one else involved in this case."

"As soon as we're sure the body is he I'll do that," Agent Lee said.

Agent Lee left and soon after he was gone there was another knock on the door. This time it was Ben. "Can't stay," he said. "Just thought you should know that I seen Frankie Le Cock talking to the missing fella just as we were entering the lock."

"Thanks Ben," Tommy said after which Ben left.

"Well that fits. This is an unattached murder to throw us off the scent," stated Arch.

"I've a feeling that there is more to it than that," said Tommy.

"Breakfast? I'm starving. All this murder and mayhem is getting to me. I need some comfort food," Jennifer said.

"Or it could be that you're pregnant," suggested Menerva.

"Don't be silly. I take the pill," Jennifer replied.

Later that morning Agent Lee caught up with the foursome while they sat by the pool. "Hello again," he greeted. "Mind if I sit and chat?"

"Not at all," Tommy said.

"My agents during their investigation came up with a few things I thought might interest you. Plus I got a report from the medical examiner who confirmed that the body recovered from the lock was indeed our missing Mr. Winter."

"That was fast."

"Well his wife told us that he had broken his leg during one of his events and had it repaired with a metal splint. The medical examiner x-rayed his legs and sure enough there was the fracture and the metal splint. When he checked the serial number on it against the one that had been put in Mr. Winter they matched.

"It also appears that Mr. Winter spent yesterday afternoon in the company of a woman that he picked up as the ship was passing through one of the locks and you know what they say 'if it works why change it', which means that he may have been looking for another score and someone took objection to it."

"I don't suppose that anyone saw it happen?" Tommy asked.

"No, but a few of the passengers said that just before the ship entered the lock they saw him talking to a woman with red hair."

"It was Frankie Le Cock," Tommy informed Agent Lee.

"How do you know?"

"Our mutual informant informed us of the fact just after you left last time and we know that he knows who she is."

"And you didn't tell me."

"We knew you'd be back around and besides it doesn't prove that she murdered him."

"She didn't say anything about talking with him to my agents."

"You could arrest her for obstruction of an investigation and withholding information, but given the fact that he was a married man and all she'd only get is a slap on the wrist and a fine that someone else would be happy to pay," said Arch.

"Damn! You know and so do I that you're right. So what do I do?"

"You're the F.B.I. Agent and you're asking us?" Jennifer asked.

"Yes dammit I am? What I'd like to do is harass her a bit, but do we want her to know that she is being watched? Do we?"

"You are a good agent, Danny Lee and no we don't. We need to catch her in the act of actually doing something we can put her away for," Tommy said.

# CHAPTER FIFTY-THREE

**"It's time to head** down for dinner," Arch said.

"Can't we go later we are about to go through another lock and Menerva and I want to watch from down here. Went to get a different perspective than what we see up in our royal palace," Jennifer said as they stood on the main deck.

"You watch Tommy and I will be in the Magnolia Lounge when you're ready."

"It's been half-an-hour I think I'll go check on the girls and see what's up with them since they haven't joined us yet," Arch said.

"Watch your back and don't get too close to the railing," Tommy warned as Arch got up to go. After a minute or two Tommy had second thoughts and went to join his friends.

Exiting the vestibule on the main deck he looked along the railing and saw his friends up toward the bow. Walking toward them he heard someone behind him call his name. Turning around he saw Agent Lee walking toward him. "I need to talk to you alone and in private," Agent Lee said when he got within hearing distance.

"Now's?" Tommy cut his answer short, spinning around, and taking off running all in the same motion toward Arch and the girls. Halfway to them he saw a hooded figure emerge from the forward edge of the riverboat. In its raised hand Tommy recognized a leather sap. Unseen by the trio who were watching the workings of the lock the hooded figure's arm started downward striking Arch in the back of the neck. As the figure bent down in order to give Arch an additional push in the back something shot into the back of the hooded figure's knees bending it backward and crippling it to the deck.

Arch's waist had already cleared the railing when Tommy reached him. Throwing himself onto the back of his legs he grabbed for Arch's belt which stopped him from falling into the water between the riverboat and the side of the lock. "I got her," old Ben shouted behind Tommy.

Agent Lee arrived and helped Ben subdue the hooded Frankie Le Cock. "I need some help ladies," Tommy yelled. "One on each side of me, reach over and grab an arm, and help me lift him back onto the deck, but be careful not to tear his arm from their sockets," Tommy instructed.

Laying Arch down on the deck Tommy checked his pulse. "He's alive. Menerva go get some ice in a bag, a big bag. Jennifer watch him," Tommy said walking over to where, Agent Lee and old Ben had Frankie Le Cock subdued. They had removed the hood and the mask she had worn for her attack. "Getting rather desperate there, Red. Pressure being put on you for a result?" No answer emitted from Frankie's lips. Four F.B.I. agents that had been summoned by Danny Lee came around the corner.

"I want her feet cuffed and a chain from them to the cuffs on her wrists. I want her secured in the main deck toilet next to room 123. Check the room it should be vacant and make sure that its balcony door is locked and when you're through checking it make sure that the door to the room is locked. I want two of you watching the toilet room's door one standing outside the toilet room door itself and one at the foot of the stairs coming down from the deck above. When you get her into the toilet I want her strip searched. Leave the chains and cuffs on and cut away her clothing and leave her sitting completely naked on that toilet. Bag her clothing and anything else she has on her. If she makes even the slightest fuss or utters any sound at all gag her. I'll be checking on you so stay awake and alert," Agent Lee instructed.

"How's Arch doing?"

"I'm alive, but man what a headache. Apartment reminiscence all over again. What happened?" Arch said regaining his senses.

"You have successfully helped to catch the person that has been trying to kill you," Tommy said.

"Was it Frankie Le Cock?"

"It was and between old Ben and Mr. Templeton here we have her in custody," Agent Lee said. "I'd better go check to make sure they're handling her as I've instructed."

"We still need to talk," Agent Lee whispered to Tommy as he was leaving.

"I'll come find you later," Tommy replied.

"Ben you got her. Thanks for the help," Tommy said.

"I was in my usual room when my daughter and her friend showed up by the railing. I thought I'd come out and see what they were up to. I was about to open the door when Mr. Ponnard showed up so I hesitated. I decided to come out anyway and as I opened the door a dark figure ran past the door. I stepped out in time to see her sap Mr. Ponnard so I tackled her.'"

"Never had a doubt as to who it was did you, Ben?"

"Never," Ben answered.

"I owe you, and so does Arch."

"We all do, father," Menerva said walking over and giving him a hug.

"Stop by the cabin later, and we'll sit and sip some," Tommy said.

"Can't," Ben replied. "Me and my 'Mini' has got to watch the watchers and make sure Red doesn't get away."

"Just be careful and don't get caught in any cross fire," Tommy added before putting Arch's arm around his neck and helping him to the elevators and back to their cabin.

# CHAPTER FIFTY-FOUR

**Back in their cabin** Tommy made a call to the galley and ordered dinner brought up. News had already spread throughout the ship of the killer's capture and when their dinner was brought up the captain accompanied it. After thanking Tommy and everyone involved for their help in rather a dry manner, he left.

"What a dead fish," Arch said.

"I'm surprised he came at all," Tommy said. "He's probably under orders not to help us in any way so his appearance here was probably a personal choice putting his job maybe even his career at risk."

Dinner was consumed and Tommy offered to return the trays and utensils to the galley. "Does anyone want anything from the galley or bar while I'm down there?" he asked.

"More ice would be nice," Jennifer said.

"I'll bring some. I need to stop in and ask Agent Lee a few questions and check on Ben so if I seem to take longer than needed don't worry," Tommy said balancing the stack of trays etc., while passing through the open doorway and kissing Menerva as she held the door open.

Taking the elevator down to the first floor, Tommy checked in on Ben and asked the agents guarding Frankie the whereabouts of Agent Lee. Dropping the trays etc. off he took the elevator to the second deck and walked back to the Paddlewheel Lounge. "You wanted to see me, Agent Lee?"

"It's Danny," Agent Lee said.

"You wanted to see me, Danny? Was that better?"

"Much," Danny answered.

"I got the DNA results back today and I think you are going to find them very interesting. Come pull up a seat.

"First though I have to know."

"Know what?"

"How you knew and don't tell me that you didn't know. I've been around this job far too long not to know what I know. If you had reacted one mille-second later Mr. Ponnard would have been a goner so my question is how did you know to react the instant that you did?"

"How can I tell you the truth without telling you the truth," Tommy started. "In the bayous of Louisiana, Mississippi, and Florida live a people from an age that is part of the world we live in and yet not really a part of it. I am a child of one of those families."

"As is your fiancée?" Danny asked.

"What?" Tommy asked and Danny Lee handed him a folder marked Menerva Morgan along with one with his name on it.

Tommy opened the folders and compared the DNA

findings inside. "Seems the two of you are closely related," Danny Lee commented. "Almost as close as brother and sister."

"You wouldn't happen to have one on Ben or his wife would you?"

"We would on Ben," Danny Lee said shuffling through a stack of folders on his desk. "Ah here it is," he said handing a folder marked Ben Morgan to Tommy. Tommy opened the folder and compared it to the other two which showed that the DNA's weren't even close.

"I see that the results have you puzzled, but don't fret I have one here that's even more of a mystery," Danny Lee said handing Tommy two folders. One of the folders was marked Archibald Ponnard Jr. and the other was marked Archibald Ponnard Sr. Tommy opened the two folders and compared the results. Once again the DNA's weren't even close. Tommy sat there speechless his mind revolving at the speed of light.

"Do you have a DNA report on Arch's mother Anne Ponnard?"

"Is it important?"

"In solving the question that these last two folders have produced, yes.

"Have you received the background check, financials, and phone records on the Sr. Ponnard?"

"We're working on them. Somehow he found out that we were asking for them and is fighting us in court."

"Will the arrest of Frankie Le Cock and the connection we already have between them help?"

"It may speed things up a bit, but I'm not sure."

"Use it anyway even if it doesn't hurry things up. You might also want to bring Ponnard Sr. in for questioning. How long can you hold him?"

"Twenty-four hours."

"So the timing will be tricky and I'll leave that part up to you. What we need most is those other records and Anne Ponnard's DNA and if you can get it the DNA of Ben's wife Chantel I'd like that too, but she's something else grown in the swamps so be careful. Thanks for showing me these. Can we keep it for the time being just between the two of us?"

"Of course," Agent Danny Lee said.

Leaving the Paddlewheel Lounge Tommy went down to the galley and picked up a couple-three bags of ice. Taking the ice back to the cabin he gave one to Jennifer and put the others in the freezer of their cabin. "Menerva I'd like to talk to Ben and when I do I'd like you to be there. Are you up to doing that right now?"

"You sound mysterious, my warlock and I'm at your bidding," Menerva answered.

Tommy and Menerva took the elevator down to the main deck and collected Ben. Tommy led the way and they walked out to the bow of the ship. "Three stools and a jar of shine, Ben," Tommy said.

"Stools I have, but I don't have no shine down here. I figured that with what has gone on the F.B.I. would be searchin' so I took it to one of the upper decks."

"I'll go get a jar," Menerva said.

"Bring two and make it from the new case the good stuff," Tommy said.

"Be right back," Menerva said leaving.

"So what's up, son?" Ben asked.

"I've just seen something very interesting," Tommy said. Ben just sat there unperturbed. "It was an F.B.I. report on the DNA taken from me, you, and Menerva."

"Don't have a clue as to what you're talking about. Don't know nothing about all that modern mumbo jumbo stuff like DNA."

"I think you do and the report that I read says that Menrva and I are brother and sister. I thought about that and I realize that it can't be true. So I think back and recall some of things I learned while I was in High Cliff."

"Where is High Cliff?" Menerva asked returning. She handed a jar to Ben who opened it and drank about an inch of shine.

"Dad? What are you doing?" Menerva asked taking the jar away from him.

"To answer your question High Cliff was the coven I stayed in."

"That's where you met Willow?"

"Yes and it's where I learned that witches and warlocks have very deep blood lines. They are all related in one way or another. So when I see a DNA report that says you are my sister."

"I'm your sister? Tommy Templeton what are you trying to pull? Are you trying to dump me?"

"Whoa there, daughter," Ben said.

"Dad?"

"Tommy's not trying to dump you he's just looking for the truth. Sit down and take a drink of shine." Menerva sat down on a stool and sipped a little shine.

"The F.B.I.'s DNA report came back today. In it, it said that you and I are related so I wondered how that could be and came up with the deep blood lines theory. Now if that is true it means that Ben and Chantel must also be warlock and witch so I asked to see their DNA report. Danny didn't have one on Chantel, but he did have one on Ben and when I compared it to yours it shows that you are not a product of his loins."

"Dad?"

"Would you like to explain, Ben?" Tommy asked.

"Chantel and I tried to have a child of our own and after a time we went to the sawbones for help. They said that we could never have children because of one illness or other that each of us had when we were children ourselves.

"One day I was comin' back from my still and I came across this woman dying in the woods. She had a baby with her."

"Hand me that jar, Tommy," Menerva said taking a drink and handing the jar to her father.

"Well the woman died right there in my arms. I suppose the right thing to have done was take the baby to the authorities, but then it occurred to me that maybe the baby was sent to Chantel and me to care for. So I took the baby home and we raised her as our own.

"As you got older we discovered that you were a gifted child. As you grew older still you showed and taught your mother many things. Chantel isn't a witch and she doesn't have any special fortune telling powers. All she is, is what you taught her. The other thing she has is a real mother's love for you as do I a father's love. That's why she opposed your union with Tommy warlock here and why I seeing the other side of the coin wanted it. Just as you were meant for Chantel and me I can see that you and Tommy were meant to be together."

"That's why when we work together our powers are heightened like your visions and the motel door for example. I should have seen it earlier, but when I think of you I get all weird feeling, kinda warm and fuzzy," Tommy admitted. Menerva just sat there without saying a word. Suddenly she stood up and walked over to Ben who also stood up. "I love you, dad," she said starting to cry disappearing in Ben's arms. "And I love mom too," she added sobbing even harder.

Later that night Menerva snuggled even tighter into Tommy's arms than usual. "Thank you, Tommy. I love you," she said falling asleep.

# CHAPTER FIFTY-FIVE

**The next morning** lying in bed together, Tommy said. "I have something else to tell you about the F.B.I.'s DNA reports. This is not about you, but it concerns Arch and our investigation."

"What did you find out?"

"Arch's father isn't his real father."

"I knew it. I knew it. I could sense it when he asked me to see what I could do about having Arch go with you on this voyage. I thought that I could put a spell on you and Arch, but then when I met you in the foyer of the Ponnard House right after I knew that I was wrong in having told him that I could put a spell on the two of you. When I touched you I knew that it wasn't going to work."

"That's why you said to tell him that you were wrong," Tommy said.

"Later I knew why the spell wasn't going to work on you, but I never have been able to until now to figure out why the spell wouldn't have worked on Arch."

"And now you've gotten around all that and have found a way to really put a spell on me." Menerva just smiled and kissed Tommy.

"Have you told him yet?" Menerva asked.

"No and mum's the word. Agent Lee is checking on something for me and Arch still hasn't gotten an answer from one of his associates who is checking on why his father disbanded the firm he started out in. Until I get an answer to both of those questions we aren't saying anything to him."

# CHAPTER FIFTY-SIX

**The riverboat pulled into** the mooring in Davenport, Iowa and waiting for it were three unmarked cars and a dozen F.B.I. agents. "This is goodbye then," Agent Danny Lee said shaking each of the foursome's hands. "I have my killer and I'm taking her in."

"We still haven't found out who hired her so the case isn't really solved. Mr. Ponnard is still fighting us in court over the release of his information and until that's settled," Danny said throwing his hands in the air. "I'm hoping that once Frankie realizes that she isn't going to buy her way out of this one she will spill the beans on Mr. Big."

"I doubt that, that will happen," Tommy said. "In fact I expect Mr. Big to hire someone else to do what Frankie didn't."

"I've talked the captain into allowing an agent to stay aboard until the voyage is complete. She'll introduce herself sometime today. If you run into a problem she'll know how to get in contact with me. Good Luck."

"Good Luck to you too, Danny Lee," Arch said.

The foursome stood on the deck and watched as

Frankie, Red, Le Cock was loaded wearing chains into one of the cars. Several agents carried boxes and equipment from the Paddlewheel Lounge and loaded them into the other two cars. In a blink they were gone. "I never thought I'd say this," Arch admitted, "but I'm going to miss their presence."

"I'm sure it'll pass, Arch. your just a convict that has spent most of his life behind bars and now finds himself standing on the corner, outside, in the free world, waiting for a bus to take him from what has been his home and family for the past number of years."

"Take him where, Tommy?" Jennifer asked.

"That's the point he doesn't have a clue and is probably why some of them go right out and get themselves arrested and sent back."

"And what's this?" Tommy asked as a helicopter landed as near to the riverboat as possible. Watching the foursome saw two men carrying briefcases emerge from the helicopter and start walking toward the gangway. "Sorry fellas you just missed your cohorts," Arch said in jest, but not loud enough for them to hear over the noise from the helicopter.

"Well let's go get ready," Jennifer said. "We are still going ashore aren't we? This is a big city with lots to see and I want to see its art museum, its downtown, and taste some of its fare."

While the foursome were still in their cabin getting ready someone knocked on the door. "I'll get it," Tommy said. "It's probably the F.B.I. Agent they left onboard wanting to introduce herself." Opening the door Tommy found that it wasn't the F.B.I. Agent but the two men with briefcases from the helicopter. "Wait here a moment," Tommy said shutting the door and running into his bedroom where he took the shotgun from the closet and returned. Throwing the door open Tommy showed the two men the shotgun and told them to put their briefcases down and their hands up. "Okay now you," Tommy said indicating the man on his right. "Step inside and over to the right. Frisk him for a weapon, Arch," he said as Arch appeared from his room.

"You are, Archibald Ponnard the Junior?" the man still in the hallway asked.

"I am," Arch answered. "This one is clean," he added finishing his frisking of the first man.

"Okay you next inside and to the left," Tommy instructed after which Arch went about frisking him.

"He's clean as well," Arch said.

"Bring their briefcases in and set them out on the balcony," Tommy said.

"If I may I'd like to show you our business card?" The second man frisked said.

"Slowly," Tommy said. The man reached into the chest pocket of his suit coat, opening the lapel wide so Tommy could see what he was extracting and pulled out a long rich looking wallet, opened it, took out a business card, and handed it to Arch.

"It says they are from the law firm of Harold, Harold, Gibbons, and Ashworth."

"That's the one we have been trying to get information on," Tommy said.

"Can you put that shotgun down, please? We are here to inform Mr. Ponnard about the outcome of Mr. Harold Harold's will."

"Go ahead and put your hands down, but no quick moves," Tommy said lowering, but still holding onto the shotgun.

"May we have our briefcases, please?"

"And you are?" Tommy asked. "Arch go open the briefcases one at a time and when you do keep their open side facing away from you. Open them from behind so to speak."

"Gottcha," Arch replied going out onto the balcony.

"There have been several attempts on Mr. Ponnard's life recently. The last one was only yesterday and that assassin is on her way to federal prison today," Tommy related. "So you don't mind if we take a few precautions in light of that and never having seen either of you before."

"We understand," the two men said in unison.

"You haven't introduced yourselves as I've asked."

"And you are still pointing that shotgun at us."

"Not directly though and that can change very quickly," Tommy said.

"The briefcases are clean," Arch said setting them down in front of the two men.

"I am Harry Harold a member of the mentioned law firm and the deceased Mr. Harold's brother's son. This man next to me is Lester Gibbons another member of the aforementioned law firm. May I?" he asked reaching into his briefcase and taking a folder from it. "The papers in this folder explain in detail the terms of Harold's will.

The man never married and leaves his entire fortune some one hundred billion dollars worth to you."

"You must have the wrong Archibald Ponnard. Why would a man I've never met leave me that amount of money?" asked Arch.

"That is the sum worth after taxes and death penalties, etc. It includes a house, several businesses, this law firm, and well it's all detailed within that folder.

"There are papers to sign, which authorize the continual payment to those in your hire, and the running of the businesses. We are staying at the Hilton in Davenport, and you can call us at any hour or if you prefer we can return or meet you somewhere else, it's your call. We are at your service, Mr. Ponnard."

"Gentlemen, Mr. Ponnard will need a few hours to go over the papers in that folder so if you don't mind you can return here to this room at say three o'clock.

"I must warn you that other people who have offered to enhance the life of Mr. Ponnard have all been murdered very recently. If what you have told us is true and I have no reason to doubt you, Menerva?" Menerva came over. "Gentleman if you would be so kind as to take off your jackets roll up your sleeves, and hold your arms out for my fiancée here. All she is going to do is hold onto your wrists for a few minutes." The two lawyers looked at Tommy as if he were mad, but did as he instructed.

"If you gentlemen are going to stay with the firm you had better get used to some strange requests from this man as we are inseparable," Arch said.

"Nothing," Menerva said when she had finished taking vibes from the two gentlemen.

"Okay, gentlemen we shall see you again at three and would you bring two boxes of 12 gauge, double-o buckshot with you when you return, please?"

"Don't come back without them" Arch reaffirmed. "Even better make that four boxes."

The lawyers left and Arch looked at Tommy with a bewildered glaze over his eyes. "I'll get a jar of shine," Tommy said as Arch took the folder and headed out to the balcony.

"Did they say billions, one hundred of them?" Menerva asked.

"Yes."

"Jennifer you haven't said anything?" Tommy questioned.

"I suppose he'll want the ring back, now," she said.

"Why? Nothing has changed," Tommy replied.

"In our business you see it all the time. Money does change people." Jennifer looked at her watch, got up, and headed for the door. "The bus is leaving. I'm going to the art museum," she said.

"You'd better go with her, Menerva. Don't let her do anything stupid, stay with the tour groups, and don't go off by yourselves."

"I think we learned our lesson last time," she replied kissing Tommy and headed out the door after Jennifer.

Tommy went into his room, retrieved a jar of shine, and went out onto the balcony. Handing the jar to Arch, he said. "The girls have left on the tour bus. Is there anything I can do or get for you?"

"I just need to go through these papers so, no."

"And I need to sit and think," Tommy said taking a chair and leaving one empty between them.

At three o'clock the two lawyers returned. "Here are your four boxes of shotgun shells, Mr. Templeton," Lester Gibbons said handing them in a bag to Tommy who took out a box broke it open, broke the barrel of his double open, and loaded the two shells into it.

"Yes it wasn't loaded before, thank you," he said watching the surprised look on their faces. "I asked the F.B.I. for some shells, but they just laughed at me," he added. "So thank you for these."

"You have been checking up on me and I suspect on the girls too."

"You haven't given us much time," Harry Harold answered.

"Contact Agent Danny Lee, of the F.B.I. and tell him to give you anything he has on all of us. If he baulks tell him Tommy Templeton said no info, no gator. He'll understand and give you everything they have."

"Let's get on with the signing then, gentlemen," Arch said as the lawyers opened their briefcases with their eyes on Tommy who sat watching them with his shotgun resting across his knees.

The lawyers left and Arch took a deep breath. "Two things, Arch. Number one. You need to let Jennifer know that nothing has changed and if that isn't the case you need to tell me as soon or sooner than you know yourself."

"Nothing has changed, Tommy. We may have to relocate to Shreveport, but she shouldn't mind that as her parents live there."

"Good onto number two then. Tomorrow we are going to jump ship in a somewhat unorthodox fashion."

"Where are we going?"

"Somewhere we can't be found. I'll explain it to you all after the girls return."

# CHAPTER FIFTY-SEVEN

**When the girls returned** Jennifer was still in a funk. One look from Tommy told Arch that he had better do something, now. He followed her into the bedroom and shut the door. "Jenn we have to talk," he started. Jennifer started to cry and sat on the side of their bed. "Look I know that at times I've been a big baboon that never pays much attention to what others are saying, but I want you to not be like me and listen to what I'm now saying," Jennifer dabbed at her eyes and tried to get a hold on her emotions.

"It took this trip to get me to realize just how important you are to me." Jennifer stopped sobbing and with red eyes turned to face Arch. "I love you, Jenn, and I really, really want to marry you. This inheritance hasn't changed that. According to those lawyers we now have a big ass house with servants and caretakers. I have my own law firm and it and the house are located in Shreveport.

"When Bon Bon ran Tommy and I back to New Orleans and I was almost killed in my own apartment I woke up laying on the sidewalk pressed against a wall unable to move held there by Tommy's knees. All I could think about during the entire incident was you. Right then and there all I wanted was to be somewhere together with you and holding you. It was while I was lying there that I thought about what you had said about changing your mind about having a house, a home, a dog, and a husband. I knew that no matter what this life had to offer I never wanted to lose you and I made up my mind while I was lying there that at the very first opportunity I was going to ask you to marry me. Will you marry me, Jennifer?"

"I can't, Arch," Jennifer replied.

"Why on god's green earth can't you?" Arch shouted in surprise getting to his feet.

"Because I've already promised to marry the most wonderful man on god's green earth see," she said holding up her hand with Arch's ring on it. Arch bent over and swept her into his arms.

Tommy had left for a few moments to talk to Ben and when he returned everyone was in good spirits. "I'm starving. Isn't it time for us to be headed down to the dining room?" Jennifer asked. Tommy looked at Arch who gave him the thumbs up.

"Let's go. I'm ready," Tommy said and the foursome headed for the dining room.

# CHAPTER FIFTY-EIGHT

**"Hello I'm F.B.I. Agent** Darci Klassen," a middle aged, dark haired woman said. "Agent Lee instructed me to introduce myself to you and let you know that if you have anything for the F.B.I. or Agent Lee personally to let me know and I'll put you in contact with him."

"Care to join us for dinner, Agent Klassen?" Tommy asked.

"I've already eaten, but thank you I could go for a drink," she said sitting down.

"Which cabin are you in?" Arch asked.

"It's on the main deck just opposite the vestibule number 123," Agent Klassen replied.

"We will need to see you tomorrow morning, Agent Klassen. Would you make it a point to come to our cabin just before the ship docks in Dubuque. It is very important," Tommy said.

"I'll be there," Agent Klassen assured Tommy and left without having ordered her drink.

"Not quite the same as Agent Danny Lee," Tommy

noted aloud. "He was always willing to sit and possibly learn something that he didn't know."

"I don't think this agent has much pull within the organization," Arch commented. "She's just a lackey left here to spy on us."

"She's in for a big surprise then," Tommy said.

When the foursome returned to their cabin Tommy called everyone together for a conference. Everyone took a seat in the living area and Tommy outlined his plan. "We need a place to hide out for a few weeks until we can figure out how to trap the big man," Tommy said using Danny Lee's words. "So consider what I've said and we'll talk more in the morning."

# CHAPTER FIFTY-NINE

**The riverboat pulled into** the channel preparing to dock when Agent Klassen knocked on the cabin door. Tommy answered it, "Good morning, Agent Klassen. Come on in."

"I have something for you," she said handing Tommy a folder. "Agent Lee said to thank you your suggestion and that it paid dividends. He said to include the second folder and that you'd find the comparison most interesting.

"He also said that the subject about whom the folder is about has fled and said to be on your guard."

"Yes it's about that warning I have asked you here to meet with us. Excuse me," Tommy said going to the door to answer another knock.

"Good morning, Ben."

"Where should I set these?" Ben asked giving Agent Klassen a questioning look as he set three cases of swamp shine down.

"This is Agent Klassen Agent Lee's right hand woman," Tommy said.

"Where'd you get three cases from?"

"Agent Lee thought that Captain Lyle's case would be safer with me," Ben said.

"Obviously he doesn't know you like we do," Tommy said with a smile.

"I'll be back. I have a couple of bags to go along with those."

"Knives and firearms?" Tommy asked.

"In the bags and I feel awfully naked."

"Go get the bags, Ben."

"Getting back to agent Lee's warning. I have considered the facts and we have decided to desert this ship. We will be leaving all of our things behind and ask that you gather them up and ship them by freight with the F.B.I.'s seal of approval, as the shipment will contain illegal alcohol and personal firearms. If you have any questions concerning the shipping of these items I suggest that you ask Agent Lee who will explain things to you.

"You also need to inform Agent Lee that he should gather his team and go to Baton Rouge and in two weeks time he should call this number." Tommy handed Agent Klassen a piece of paper with a cell number written on it. "Tell him that, that phone will only be turned on for one hour, at gator time, two weeks from tomorrow. He'll understand what I mean. Until that time we in fear of our lives and unable to trust the F.B.I. to protect us and will attempt to disappear from the face of the earth," Tommy said opening the door to allow Ben in.

"Is that it, Ben?"

"All I own in the world," Ben replied.

"Good luck, Agent Klassen," Tommy said following Ben who was followed by the others out the door closing it behind them and leaving Agent Klassen standing in the cabin scratching her head.

# CHAPTER SIXTY

**The cab** they had arranged for was waiting for them. "Airport please and hurry we have a flight to catch and we are already late. There's an extra fifty in it for you if you get us there in time," Tommy said.

Having survived the jostling from the cab ride to the airport as the cabbie darted in and out of traffic like a man possessed the foursome arrived at the airport and went straight to the airline counter. After a short wait in line they reached the counter. "You have four reservations for Templeton to New Orleans?" Tommy asked.

"Yes, sir," the attendant said taking care of Tommy.

"I'm thirsty," Arch said to the attendant from where he stood beside Tommy. "Where is the bar?"

The attendant gave them directions after processing their tickets and off they went with Arch leading, but instead of going to the bar the foursome split up went out different doors, grabbed different cabs, and headed for the small plane airstrip that was located in its own area behind the main terminal. Tommy hung back stopping long enough to purchase a burner phone before leaving the terminal.

On his way to the small plane airstrip Tommy took out the folder that Agent Klassen had given him. The folder contained the information on Mr. Ponnard Sr. that they had been trying to get. Tommy scanned the papers noting the areas highlighted by Agent Lee. *Nothing new,* Tommy thought. *It's just as I suspected.*

Opening the second folder marked, 'DNA: Archibald, Jr.' he found another report and a note: 'We found that we already had Anne Ponnard's DNA so I am sending it along. Things are getting interesting, signed: Danny Lee'. Tommy compared the two reports. *So Anne is Arch's actual mother. As you say Danny things are getting interesting.*

"We would like to fly to Baton Rouge and we're in a hurry and able to pay," Arch said to the woman in the small plane terminal. The flight left twenty minutes later.

"I hope all that was worth it?" Arch asked.

"Do any of you think you were followed?" Tommy asked.

The 'I didn't see anyone suspicious' came from everyone.

"Now down to business. Someplace to hide is first on the agenda," Tommy said.

"How about Bon Bon's?" Arch asked.

"The F.B.I. already know about him so they will check him out, thoroughly," Ben offered.

"We need to go see Chantel," Menerva said. "She will know a place and a preacher that is trustworthy.

"Maybe, daughter, but I has my doubts that she'll help any of us out," Ben said.

"We don't have anyone else," Menerva said.

"There are people I could ask, but any one of them would sell us out for a price," Arch said.

"We'll try Chantel first then," Tommy said.

The plane landed and Jennifer went to the rent-a-car counter where she rented a car. "And make sure you get the insurance that covers it if the car is stolen," Arch said. "We are going to leave it and it may never be seen again."

# CHAPTER SIXTY-ONE

**Arch drove** the rent-a-car around the outskirts of Baton Rouge taking every back alley that he remembered circling several blocks three or four times trying to make sure that they weren't being followed. After a reasonable effort and satisfied that no one was following them Arch parked the rent-a-car in *Mel's Used Cars* lot. Tommy and Arch went inside, while the others waited in the rent-a-car. "Howdy, Mel," Arch greeted. "Tommy this is Mel." Mel stood up and shook Tommy's hand. "Mel has been a client of mine, more times than he'd liked to admit," Arch said smiling at Mel.

"Ain't that the truth," Mel affirmed.

"We're here to buy, Mel on credit without any paperwork and," Arch leaned across the desk and into Mel's face. "If it isn't the most reliable, the most unnoticeable car I've ever driven, and I don't care if you have to sand blast it first, next time you're in court I'll be sitting across the aisle on the plaintiff's side of the courtroom and I know all your dirty laundry which will only mean that the outcome as far as you're concerned won't be pretty. Get my drift?" Mel shook his head to the affirmative and Arch taking a step back continued, "And later when the problem I'm having is over say within a month's time I'm going to send you a check for three times what the car you're providing us with is selling for. Can you help me?"

"Sounds like you're in a bit of a mess, Arch. Is this fella the cause of the problem 'cause if he is I can have some of the boys make him disappear." Mel said trying to help.

"This man is a friend, my best friend, and he is the only reason I'm still alive and talking to you today. Hands off him or he'll do you worse than you've ever imagined anyone could be done and I know don't I that you have not only imagined but tried out more than a few innovations of your own so hands off him and all my friends. Now can you help me or not?"

"Just trying to be helpful," Mel said looking at Tommy adding. "He don't look like a killer."

"Would you like to find out?" Arch asked. "Which eye can you do without?" Mel walked out from behind his desk taking a set of keys from a board filled with keys that were hanging on the wall behind him. Walking over to the door, he opened it, and stepped out onto the deck that ran across the front of his office. He handed Arch the keys and said. "See that pale green Chevy two rows in she'll fit what you're asking for. Owned by a little old lady." Arch looked at his past client. "That's the god's honest truth, Arch. I swear," Mel said.

"You do me right, Mel and when this is all over I'll set you up in your own major dealership.

"Tommy," Arch said tossing Tommy the keys. Tommy walked down the steps from the deck toward the rent-a-car. "Menerva care to go for a short drive?" he asked loud enough for her to hear. Menerva got out of the rent-a-car and walked over to where he was standing. The two of them then walked to the pale green Chevy, got in, and drove away.

"Was that Menerva? Thee, Menerva?" Mel asked.

"Yes, Mel she's Tommy's fiancée." If Arch had turned his head to look at Mel at that moment he would have seen the look of a man who was suddenly filled with terror.

"He can really do those things you said?"

"We came here in a rent-a-car from the airport, Mel. Here is the paperwork. I want you to have one of your men drop it off back at the airport a man that can disappear and leave no trace with the cops and F.B.I. watching his every move and Mel, don't touch or mess with the car just have it delivered and make sure you wipe the whole thing down inside and out first."

"What kind of trouble are you in, man?"

"The kind of trouble that either gets you killed or taken on a long vacation behind federal concrete and steel," Arch answered. Mel looked at his lawyer and offered, "It happens to all of us every now and then when we try to do something right for someone, doesn't it?" Arch didn't answer him.

"The car is okay," Tommy said returning from his test run and stopping by the rent-a-car to pick up Jennifer and Ben.

"Be seeing you, Mel and remember major dealership, I promise," Arch said getting into the car beside everyone else.

# CHAPTER SIXTY-TWO

**Tommy parked** the pale green Chevy in the alley behind *Grumpy's*. Menerva got out, walked over to the delivery door, and banged several times on it. She knew there was a surveillance camera above the door so she looked up at it. A few seconds passed and Chappie the barman opened the door. "I have an entourage with me. Let them all in," Menerva said stepping past him. When Chappie saw Ben he blocked his way. "Let him in Chappie. I said everyone," Menerva said re-emphasizing her instruction.

"I have my orders, Miss Menerva," Chappie said.

"I'll be responsible for him. Let him in." Chappie looked at Ben and after giving him a warning look stepped aside.

"No hard feelings, Ben," he said in a way of apology.

"You're still a good man on the door, Chappie," Ben said stepping past him.

"Hello, Chantel," Ben greeted walking into the kitchen of the living quarters that were located behind the barroom.

"You! I've told Chappie to never let you in this establishment ever again."

"Come on out to the dining room your daughter wants to ask you for a favor," Ben said turning and walking out to the dinning room where he took a seat at the dinning room table along with the rest of the group. Chantel followed him out and stopped dead in her tracks when she saw who else was sitting at the table.

"Daughter," Chantel greeted walking over to the empty chair at the table.

"Mother," Menerva greeted.

"So are you married to that, that yet?"

"Soon, mother and we all hope that you'll be there," Menerva replied holding up her hand so her mother could see the ring.

"Not very big is it?" Chantel said sitting down. "I'd of thought his kind could conjure up something twice that size at least and even then it'd be small.

"So why do I have the pleasure of the soon-to-be Ponnard's, my ex husband, my daughter, and this creature's presence at my dining room table?" Tommy sat there and smiled at Chantel's reference.

"Chantel," he replied to her dry wit.

"Mom, Mr. Ponnard is being hunted by someone that is trying to kill him."

"I wish them luck," Chantel said.

"I know you don't mean that, mom.

"Because of this killer trying to get to him it has put

all of us in danger so we all need a safe place to hide, including me."

"And they need a preacher. One that can be trusted to keep his mouth shut," Ben added.

"No," Chantel said. "I won't help."

"I've told Menerva everything. I've been shown the what do you call it?" Ben asked.

"D.N.A.," Menerva answered.

"She knows everything including how she happens to be calling you her mother. I know and so does everyone else sitting at this table," Tommy said.

"We all know, Chantel," Jennifer said and it makes no difference to Menerva. She still is and will always be your daughter."

"And I will never love you less than I've loved you all those years before I knew," Menerva added. "Father has told me your secret and I am so grateful that it was the two of you that found me and raised me. I couldn't have asked for anyone better to do that. Right now though I, we all need your help. Help us, please." Tommy could see tears in Chantel's eyes. She dabbed at them with a bandanna while sitting quietly thinking.

"I don't really think that you're some creature," Chantel said looking at Tommy. "I just don't want to lose my daughter."

"I understand, Chantel and I will never in any way try to change her feelings toward you or destroy your place as her mother in her life."

"Ben remember the *River House*?" Chantel asked turning to him.

"I thought that it was consumed by the swamp," Ben replied.

"I've been there recently and it's in a livable state. It would be the perfect place to hide you all and a wonderful place to hold a wedding provided not too many people are invited. I'd a thought that you'd of known about that place seeing it's just down the road from your still?"

"Haven't been that way in a while. The last batch was a big one so there's been no need," Ben replied.

"Thank you, mother," Menerva said getting up and giving her mother a hug from behind.

"Time to go then folks, we don't want to be discovered here," Arch said bringing everyone to their feet.

"We were never here, but we will be in touch, Chantel and don't forget about the preacher. He's an important piece to finding the person that is hiring these assassins," Tommy said giving Chantel a hug to which she did not resist before he and the others departed.

"I'll have Chappie run you out a truck load of supplies just after daybreak tomorrow. It'll be enough to last the four of you say 'bout two weeks."

"Tell him to be very careful and insure that he isn't being followed," Tommy said.

"Thank you, mother," Menerva said giving her mother a hug.

# CHAPTER SIXTY-THREE

**"Is the *River House*** the place in the swamp where you used to take me fishing," Menerva asked her father as they got back into the car.

"The very same, daughter," Ben replied.

"Then you're all going to love it there," Menerva exclaimed.

Once everyone was back in the pale green Chevy Tommy asked everyone to shut off their cell phones and hand them to him. One by one he removed the Sim cards from their phones and handed the Sim cards back. "You can put them in your new phones once all this is over," he said. "I'm going to destroy these phones so that no one will be able to trace their GPS signals."

"I have a better idea. Father where is the nearest truck stop?" Menerva asked.

"What a grand idea, daughter," Ben replied.

Ben's instructions took Tommy to a twenty-four hour trucker's stop. There he took the phones from Tommy including his and left the car. When he returned he said. "That will confuse the hell out of them for awhile.

"Now son-in-law to be drive back to the road and turn

right." Ben's instructions took Tommy down a seldom used road that ran through the middle of the swamp. "Pull off here," Ben said. Tommy stopped the car.

"Where? I don't see a road. All I see is swamp. There's water everywhere," Tommy replied.

"Trust my father, Tommy," Menerva said.

"Everyone get out," Ben said. Tommy got out of the car along with everyone else. "See that rock?"

"I see the rock," Tommy replied. "It looks just like a rock is supposed to look like."

"Is this what I'm getting? If it's a wise ass for a son-in-law I might have second thoughts. Look across the road and just ahead of us, wise-ass see that rock?"

"I see the other rock," Tommy said not making a comment although he wanted to.

"What's so special about that rock?" Ben asked.

"It's a whole lot bigger than the other one and it looks like it has recently been painted by some High School, 'Class of 2019'."

"Every year the graduating class of Cajun High School comes out here and puts another coat of paint on that rock. It's a school tradition, done at midnight, under a Full Moon. It's a superstition that they say brings the graduating members of that class good luck in their future endeavors. When you comes upon those two rocks you need to turn between them staying closer to the painted rock. When you turn you'll find yourself on an underwater concrete roadway that was built long before you were born. If you stay between the trees on either side of the road you'll soon be out of the water and onto dry land that's hidden behind the trees over there. Trust me, son," Ben said slapping Tommy lightly on the back.

Everyone got back into the car and Tommy turned where Ben had told him to turn expecting to drive right into the swamp. Instead he found that he was indeed driving on something solid. The water covered roadway ran straight for three or four car lengths and then veered to the left. "That little turn makes the trees on the side of the road look like a natural part of the swamp and hides the fact that there's a roadway over here," Ben said.

At the end of another two blocks the roadway rose above the water of the swamp and onto the forest floor. The road through the forest was covered by all kinds of debris and occasionally someone had to get out to remove a larger piece of it so they could get past. "Natural cover helps hide the concrete underneath," Ben said. Straight through the forest Tommy drove the pale green Chevy with the swamp running on both sides of the raised roadbed for about another half-a-mile. "There she is," Ben said.

"There what is?" Tommy asked unable to see anything but the forest and the swamp.

"The *River House* you're new home. Drive on a bit further," Ben instructed. "Now turn to the left and pull under that overhanging limb. Be ready to stop or you'll hit the back wall which is made up of solid tree trunks." Tommy did as he was told. "You are now parked in your garage which you can't see into from the roadway.

"The house is through there," Ben pointed to an opening between the wall of tree trunks that made up the sides of the garage. Everyone got out and Menerva led the way.

Walking through the opening brought everyone within twenty feet of a door in the outer wall on the side of a house. "This house was once a houseboat that had been overgrown and camouflaged by the surrounding forest. We added to it and fixed it up some. I had no idea it was still in a livable condition. Chantel must be keeping up on the repairs," Ben said.

"This old place has a front porch, a dock down by the water, and an inside that as I recall is like living in a cabin in the North Woods. It has bedrooms upstairs and down and toilets on both levels that open to the swamp some distance below so don't go drinking or swimming in the swamp," Menerva instructed.

"'sides there's gators and a lot of them in that there swamp and they are huge as I recall. If they don't get you hepatitis or some kin of it will," Ben added.

"There are showers, but they work only when there is sufficient rainwater in the catch barrels. I'm sure that when Chappie shows up tomorrow he will bring plenty of drinking water enough to use for cooking or drinking when needed," Menerva said.

"First thing we should do is open the place up so it airs out good include the mattresses by bringing 'em outside. They should be military grade and are supposed to withstand the humidity, but a good soaking in the Sun's rays with a touch of soap and water doesn't hurt them either. There are sleeping bags in the cupboards upstairs and they should be stored in airtight containers so they're good to go. That's about it," said Ben.

"Are you leaving us, father?" Menerva asked recognizing the nuances in his voice.

"I'm heading for the still. If I leave now I should make it before dark."

"Be careful," Menerva cautioned.

"There's two cases of shine in the corner of the outside wall right over there under the floorboards, left of the fireplace. It should be real good as it's been aging for nearly a century," Ben said walking out the door.

# CHAPTER SIXTY-FOUR

**Tommy and Arch** took turns keeping watch throughout that first night. The following morning Tommy's attention was drawn to headlights penetrating the darkness of the swamp. He watched as the lights came closer following the raised roadway. When the vehicle got close enough Menerva announced, "It's Chappie." She had heard the truck when it turned off the back road and started splashing through the waters of the swamp. Waking the others they had joined Tommy watching the headlights approach.

Backing in behind the pale green Chevy Chappie literally all but dumped his load and left apologizing for doing so, but not wanting his absence from his regular routine to be of a length that might cause suspicion.

"Thank you, Chappie that's good thinking and thank Chantel too for all the goodies. We'll be in touch," Tommy said watching Chappie pull back onto the raised forest roadway and turn left away from the main road.

"Where is he going? He turned the wrong way," Tommy asked.

"Didn't you notice that his load was double stacked

and after he dumped the top and most of what was under it onto our driveway there was still half a truck bed of boxes left unloaded?" Menerva asked.

"I did, but I was so grateful for all this," he said indicating with a sweep of his hand the supplies Chappie had unloaded, "that I didn't question the stuff he had left on the truck."

"I imagine what was left was for dad. This road takes you close to the still. Chappie will drop what's left there and take another road back to town. He was born out here in these woods and knows them like the back of his hand. He and my father used to be quite close and have spent a lot of time together out here in this swamp and forest."

"I wouldn't have guessed that by the way he treated him at the bar yesterday," Tommy said picking up a box and heading for the back door of the *River House*.

"What you saw was a gesture of love and concern for his old friend and his friend's wife," Menerva said picking up a box and following him.

"Believe it or not I understand that," Tommy replied.

Tommy, Menerva, and Arch carried the boxes in and set them on the kitchen floor where Jennifer opened them and started storing the cans and jars of vegetables, meat, gallon jugs of water, bottles of wine and beer, snacks and everything else Chantel thought that they might want or need during there stay.

Opening one box she was surprised to find boxes of ammunition, holsters, and a half-dozen automatic pistols. Pushing the box aside she opened another. When Arch came in she directed his attention to it. "I imagine that

Chantel intended those for all of us. I've never shot a gun before and if I'm to carry one around with me I'll need some instructions," Jennifer said.

"Are we talking guns?" Menerva asked setting down the box she was carrying.

"Your mother thought of everything," Jennifer said. "There are flashlights, batteries, guns, and a lot of other things that I would have never thought of."

"I hope that includes a few packages of socks and underwear," Arch said.

"As a matter of fact it does," Jennifer replied.

"When you teach Jennifer about the firearms only dry fire the guns, Arch. Did you hear that Tommy?" Tommy nodded. "I'll allow her to fire one to get the feel of it, but do it while standing inside the garage, from one side to the other. You'd be surprised how far noise travels in this swamp. It bounces around and only a real swamp rat would be able to tell you its origin, but let's not take any chances the trees and their openings that make up the garage should muffle most of the noise," Menerva warned.

"It's the same with light that's why I had you shut the shutters before we lit the lanterns last night. Not wanting to offend anyone, but no shouting, keep talking to a minimum when you're outside, and when you do, do it in a quiet voice," she said.

"As to why my mother knew what to send in these boxes this is where my mother and father were living after they were married and at the time they found me. It wasn't until later that we moved into Baton Rouge. In less than a year after moving into the city my father bought the bar and we moved into the apartment behind the barroom."

During the first week the foursome spent at the *River House* Tommy asked the forgiveness of the others for the time that he spent away from them. He spent that time wandering the forest around the *River House*, sitting on the dock with a cane pole in his hands and a jar of swamp shine by his side, or spread out in the Sun atop a large rock all the while thinking.

"Have you girls thought about where you'd like to have the wedding? Is there any clearing and moving around that you want Arch and I to do?" he asked one day.

"As a matter of fact we have been planning," Jennifer said. "We thought we'd have it in the afternoon. The sun coming through the trees at that time of day will give the scene a special ambiance. We will stand in front of the dock and use the porch and the front yard to seat people on. If you guys wanted you could figure out how to string vines and some of that wonderful moss around to help add to the ambiance."

"I figured that I'd ask Chantel to bring a cake, champagne, a spread of sandwiches, etc. I'll ask and leave the particulars up to her," Menerva said.

"We'd like to go into town and pick up a few things. White ribbon to make bows with, wedding dresses, shoes, and order the wedding flowers," Jennifer said.

"I'll have the F.B.I. pick up the flowers and bring them out with them as they should be here before anyone else shows up," Tommy said. "I also think it would be a good thing to ask Chantel and your mother, Jennifer to go along with the two of you when you pick out your dresses. I'll have the F.B.I. escort Jennifer's parents down to *Grumpy's* and maybe Chantel could put them up for the few days that they're here. I'd feel a whole lot better knowing that they're safe with her. Do you think she'd agree to that?"

"I can ask, but I don't see why not. She may even have a few ideas of her own," Menerva answered.

"Okay then at first light tomorrow we'll go into Baton Rouge and make a few calls."

# CHAPTER SIXTY-FIVE

**Tommy parked** the pale green Chevy in the alley and Chappie let them in. "Chappie do you ever sleep?" Tommy asked.

"I've learned to sleep standing up and take little snoozes in-between customers," he replied. "Chantel is in the barroom."

"Hello, mom," Menerva greeted giving her mother a hug.

"You should be careful coming here. There have been strangers asking about you all," Chantel warned. "Tommy a friend of yours stopped by too. He left something for you." Chantel walked over behind the bar and laid two towel wrapped items on top of the bar. "He said that you might be needing them."

"Did he say anything else?" Tommy asked. Chantel shook her head. "Hilton bath towels. I wonder if the F.B.I. is paying for them?"

"He was an F.B.I. Agent?" Chantel asked.

"And a friend, Chantel so not to worry," Tommy said in an insistent tone.

"He just asked if I had seen Menerva or you? I said, no."

"Do you have a large paper bag and a piece of paper?" Tommy asked Chappie who provided them for him.

"Mother can Jennifer and I impose on your hospitality and use the shower. It's been a week and?" Chantel started to laugh remembering her days in the *River House*.

"Of course, daughter," she said. After Menerva set Jennifer up she returned to the barroom.

"Mother while we're waiting for Jennifer I have some questions to ask you," Menerva started. Chantel when asked was delighted that she could help and agreed to everything including putting up Jennifer's parents. "We do have a guest room that hardly ever gets used. It'll be a pleasure to have some new faces around for awhile," she said.

Menerva showered next and Jennifer called her parents to arranged things with them. She also warned them to be careful telling them about the big man and their F.B.I. escort.

# CHAPTER SIXTY-SIX

**Their business** in Baton Rogue accomplished the group left the bar. Tommy drove around making sure they weren't being followed between stops which they left to make on their way back to the *River House*. He always parked in the alleys and they entered the businesses through their back doors.

"Fast food how long has it been?" Arch asked sitting in the pale green Chevy that was parked in the shadows beneath an overpass that supported the traffic flowing along above it on Sherwood Forest Boulevard. The foursome were all sitting in that pale green Chevy and were chowing down on burgers, fries, and cokes purchased from a back-alley burger joint.

"I do have to admit that it is nice to have someone else do the cooking for a change," Jennifer said.

"And there are no dishes for us guys to do," Tommy added chuckling as he chewed.

Back at the *River House* their purchases were unloaded and since it was late in the day they settled in for the night. "I'd like to go over the invitations with everyone," Menerva said.

"That's what we forgot to pick up today, the invitations," exclaimed Jennifer who was sitting with the others on the floor in front of a fire that was burning in the fireplace.

"Not to worry I am good for something," Arch said getting up and walking over to a cabinet, removing a bag, and pulling from it two stationary boxes. "Will these do?" he asked handing them to Jennifer.

"When did you get these?"

"When the two of you were arguing about how wide of a ribbon to buy. I spotted them and thought they'd fit the bill so I just added them to our purchase."

"You are remarkable," said Menerva.

"And he's all mine," Jennifer said reaching over hugging and kissing her fiancée.

"Okay before the two of you get too involved let's get back to the list of who we are going to invite," Tommy said.

"Chantel and Ben, Dorothy and Ray, Anne and Mr. Ponnard, Sr., Chappie and Agent Lee and that woman agent, Klassen and who else?" asked Jennifer.

"I want to invite my new partners, Harry, Lester, and Derek," Arch said.

"Don't forget Bon Bon," reminded, Menerva.

"And his missus," Tommy said making everyone smile.

"I can't wait to meet her," said Menerva.

"I have and she's a Cajun ball of fire. She's the only woman to have ever tamed old Bon Bon. She'll lighten up the wedding for sure," Arch said.

The next morning the boys were up early and gone before the girls got up. "What are the boys up to?

They've been out in the swamp the entire morning?" Jennifer asked.

"Tommy said something about setting up the battery-powered flood-lights that we bought at the hardware store. Tommy said they were going to light up the entire swamp."

Returning to the *River House* for lunch Tommy informed the girls. "Tomorrow we'll set up the flood lights around the perimeter of the *River House* and tomorrow night for a minute or two we'll throw the switch and check our work to see if we'll need to make any adjustments. The lights will all point outward and illuminate everything around the *River House*, the garage, and sections of the raised roadway, but not the house or the garage proper. We want to be able to see out of those buildings and blinding any intruders in the process."

"We've finished the invitations today," Jennifer said.

"Then in three days we will go back into town to buy dresses, order the flowers, etc., and I will meet with Agent Lee to let him know what we are up to."

"My parents are supposed to be coming down in two days from now and you haven't contacted Agent Lee to request an escort?" Jennifer said.

"It's all been taken care of Jennifer. I sent Danny Lee one of his towels back in a paper bag with an unsigned message inside thanking him for old Betsy and requesting the escort. I had Chappie have someone drop it off at the Hilton. I also reminded Agent Lee of gator time."

# CHAPTER SIXTY-SEVEN

**The lights around** *River House* and the garage were installed and that night Tommy installed the remote that controlled all the lights half-way up the railing to the second floor. "I wasn't sure where to put it and figured that this was a central point to our movements in the house. If we are attacked and every fiber of my being tells me that once we mail those invitations out that we will be then this is as good a place as any."

"But no one knows where we are and to get here we are going to put hoods over their heads and load them all on a van with darkened windows that will bring them here." Jennifer said.

"Your parents, Chantel, and the F.B.I. will all be coming here on their own. Only Arch's parents, the lawyers, and the Bon Bon's will be coming in the van driven by Chappie. Anyone of those not coming with him I will be telling the route to this place and they might be a spy themselves or inadvertently give our location away. If I am right there will be an attempt to finish Arch off along with you possibly before the wedding takes place."

"What happens if they fail or no attempt happens?" Arch asked.

"Mr. Big wouldn't have gone through all the previous trouble if your death wasn't very important to his plans. He kept trying before and he isn't going to stop now. He will try again you can bank on that."

"Okay so are we ready with the lights? Turn the lanterns down to dim and here we go, presto," Tommy said hitting the remote's 'On' button. The *River House* stayed almost dark except for the dim glow given off by the lanterns, but the surrounding area outside the *River House* lit up as if it were high noon in the dessert. Tommy walked out the front door and surveyed the swamp. "I'm good to go up front, Arch," he shouted.

"We're good to go back here too," Arch shouted back." Tommy re-entered the house and hit the off switch and the area outside went night again.

"That was amazing," stated, Menerva. "I could see through the swamp almost to the road."

"Remember that the light does not penetrate the trees. If someone is hiding behind one you won't be able to see them. The trick is that when the lights first come on to open your field of vision and notice any movement like someone taking cover behind a tree or stepping into a shadow. Shoot the ones caught out in the open first, but remember where you saw the movement and when they step out shoot them too."

"All right everyone get your weapons and go outside, down the stairs, and take up a position on either side of the porch. I want you to make it a kneeling position. I'm going to turn the lights back on for just a minute and as soon as they come on I want you to shoot the two men that are at this moment hurriedly paddling a canoe toward the dock."

"You're kidding, right?" Arch asked getting his automatic.

"No, Arch something we've brought into the *River House* has been bugged. They know we're here. When I turned on the lights I saw them on the fringe of the floods. I've been watching the shadows on the water and they are just about to reach the dock so everyone outside and take up your positions, quickly. Yell when you're ready."

It took but a few seconds and Arch yelled, "We're ready." Tommy flipped the switch. Two men in full camouflage, paddling a canoe, were almost to the dock, and died in a hail of automatic gunfire. Tommy after hitting the switch had run out onto the porch with his shotgun at the ready. Seeing an empty canoe he ran down the stairs and out onto the dock. The water beyond the dock was in turmoil. It was a scene he had witnessed on his trip back from New Orleans on Bon Bon's boat after they had entered the gator hole with the two hoodlums in tow.

Grabbing the canoe as the frothing water pushed it into the dock he pulled it backwards up onto the shore with the bow on dry land.

"Arch go get a can of fuel for the lamps and turn out the lights," Tommy said.

When Arch returned Tommy dowsed the empty

canoe in lamp fuel and pushed it back into the waters of the swamp. "Menerva," he called. Menerva stepped beside him and took hold of his outstretched hand. When the canoe had floated a sufficiently safe distance into the swamp Tommy and Menerva closed their eyes. Tommy spoke the words of an ancient chant and the canoe burst into flames and sank.

"Someday you are going to have to show me how you do that," Arch said.

"Mr. Big will try again, but it won't be at night. I doubt if he'll try another attack through the swamp either, not after this one failed so badly, which means that he'll be coming at us down the road and if he's smart it'll be from both directions at the same time."

# CHAPTER SIXTY-EIGHT

**It was early** in the morning when Ben showed up. "You folks ought to be a bit quieter in your night time activities. Keep that up and the neighbors will start to complain."

"Good morning, Ben you are just the man I want to talk to," Tommy said.

"If you feed me first you won't have to torture me to get me to tell you all my dark and dirty secrets, son," Ben said.

"It just so happens that you couldn't have timed it better. Let's step into the kitchen," Tommy said leading the way.

"We need another plate," Tommy said entering the kitchen with Ben walking in right behind him.

"Morning, dad," Menerva said stepping away from the stove and giving him a hug.

"I love to be loved, but I hate my food being burnt even more," Ben said with a smile.

"Just for that you'll be getting raw bacon with two, fresh, just cracked eggs on top or would you rather settle for a little burnt?"

"Anyway you're serving it, daughter is the way I like

it," Ben replied getting him a peck on the cheek before she returned to her cooking.

"We had an attempt on our lives last night as you probably heard," Tommy said. "I expect them to try again and this time from the road and more likely it'll be from both directions at once."

"I'd be more afraid of one of them air-o-planes dropping a bomb on this place in the middle of the day," Ben said.

"No I don't think our Mr. Big would take that chance. Planes are too easy to track and trace."

"How about one of those mini, remote controlled things? They make 'em big enough to carry a bomb don't they?"

"They're noisy and too easy to shoot down especially one that big. If they would have used one of them first it might have worked, but now that we know they know where we are I doubt if they'll try it. They will have to use men and those men will be well paid," Tommy said.

"Today I'm going to cut down two large trees and drop them across the road on either side of us far enough away so that if they have anything mounted on their trucks or whatever it won't be able to be part of their game. I'll need a place to hide the pale green Chevy. Can you suggest a place, Ben? And when the time comes I'll need to be shown the way back to Baton Rouge using the back roads."

Tommy cut his trees, hid the Chevy, and as night fell the foursome took turns in pairs watching for intruders, but none showed up. "Mr. Big must need time to recruit," Arch suggested in the morning. Everyone had breakfast and left for Baton Rouge, as planned.

# CHAPTER SIXTY-NINE

**Jennifer and Menerva met** their mothers at *Grumpy's* and took a cab into town. Arch, Ben, and Tommy invited Jennifer's father, Ray along with them and headed into town in the pale green Chevy in search of some dynamite. What they came back with was even better, remotely detonated, claymore mines. "You just have to know the right people," said Ben expecting some appreciation, but only got a shaking of heads from everyone.

The women returned and were getting dinner ready in the living quarters behind the barroom when Tommy turned on his burner phone. It rang almost immediately. "*Grumpy's* now," he said and turned the phone off.

Ten minutes later Agent Danny Lee walked into *Grumpy's*. "What can I get you to drink, Danny Lee?" Tommy asked.

"Whiskey, a double, no ice. And for your information I shouldn't be drinking with you. Do have any idea the wild goose chase you sent us on with those dismantled cell phones, which by the way was a brilliant idea."

"It was meant to throw the bad guys off. We figured

they might have a way of tracking their GPS signals. I can't take the credit for that one though it was Menerva's idea."

"I see that the two of you are complimenting each other."

"More and more as time advances," Tommy said.

"I have a question, Danny Lee why would you be tracking the signals from our phones?"

"Agent Klassen discovered it while checking on someone else. As soon as we saw that Mr. Ponnard and Miss Curtis were headed out of town she and a couple other agents took out after them."

"Again I have to ask why?"

"What is this? Why the concern over our tracking Mr. Ponnard's cell phone?"

"A suspicion," Tommy answered. "And you've mentioned Arch's cell phone, but not mine, why?"

"Klassen couldn't find a signal from yours or Miss Morgan's phones."

"What explanation did you come up with?"

"Klassen said that you and Miss Morgan must have gotten rid of your phones because you were up to something. She thought that you might possibly be following Mr. Ponnard and Miss Curtis to see who was following them in the hopes of catching them."

"So you sent agents to get in the way?"

"Klassen suggested that if her assumption was correct you might be needing some backup so I sent her to try and catch up with the GPS signal and offer any assistance needed."

"One more question. The agents that went along with Agent Klassen did you send them?"

"I left that up to Klassen it was her detail."

"Thank you, Danny Lee," Tommy said.

"Oh before I forget. Returning the towel with a note inside the bag was cute. How did you know where I was?"

"The towels bore the Hilton's monogram," Tommy said. Danny Lee just shook his head.

"So what's up now?" Agent Danny Lee asked.

"For two weeks we've been hold up at a house in the swamp and last night we were attacked."

"Anyone hurt?"

"Just the bad guys. The gators loved 'em," Tommy replied to which Danny Lee just shook his head.

"We mailed the wedding invitations out today and here is one for you and one for Agent Klassen."

"Klassen? Why Klassen?"

"After putting her through the fear of getting busted by shipping illegal substances I figured we owe her."

"You owe her more than that. I told her while she was onboard the ship she should go through Frankie Le Cock's room again. She did and she found a pistol with the serial numbers filed off. We had forensics run the ballistics and it turns out that, that gun was used in several gangland killings and it gets even better. We can place Frankie Le Cock in the vicinity of all but one of them. She isn't going to see the light of day ever again."

"Really, interesting. Have you offered her a deal?"

"Yes, but she's more afraid of Mr. Big than she is of spending the rest of her life in prison. She kept saying that she'd been set up." Tommy didn't say a word for a few minutes as thoughts were arranging themselves inside his head.

"Thanks for my shotgun by the way," he finally said. "And I want you to know that your disguise worked. No one here suspected you of being F.B.I."

"Is that right? I must be losing my touch. I know what the problem is my raincoat is at the cleaners," Tommy Lee said bringing laughter to everyone.

"Speaking of weapons how are you fixed for guns?"

"We have the house rigged with flood lights and the road blocked with fallen trees. We have my shotgun, a few automatics, and today we picked up a few claymores."

"I wasn't sure so I brought along a few Uzis. They're in the trunk of my car," Danny Lee said.

"Here's a list of the people we've invited to the wedding," Tommy said handing the list to Danny Lee and laying out their plans. "Of course you are invited to come spend the time between now and then out in the swamp with the rest of us fighting the bad guys."

"If I do would you guarantee me one meal of gator? Ever since you mentioned that and I don't know why, but my mouth has been hankering to try some."

"I can do you one better follow me," Tommy said leading Danny Lee behind the bar and into Chantel's dinning room where there upon her table sat a gator with his back split open and ready to eat.

# CHAPTER SEVENTY

**The foursome returned to** *River House* and continued their nighttime vigil. The next morning Chappie showed up bringing Agent Lee and two other agents to take over night time surveillance duties allowing, Tommy, Arch, Menerva, and Jennifer to sleep through the night so that they could prepare the *River House* for the upcoming wedding during the daylight hours.

Finally the day arrived and as soon as it was light out, Tommy, Arch, Ben, and Danny Lee headed for the raised roadway to cut away enough of the tree on that side of the roadway to allow the cars and the van that would be coming to get through.

While they were in the process of removing a good portion of the tree by cutting it with a chainsaw into foot long sections and then rolling those sections one at a time to the side of the road and out of the way Agent Klassen along with two more agents sitting in the back seat of a Suburban arrived at the scene. "We'll have the opening cleared away in about ten minutes," Tommy told them after walking up to the Suburban and greeting them. "Did you have any trouble finding the roadway?"

"No, Mr. Templeton no trouble at all," Agent Klassen replied.

"I see that you brought the flowers with you, thank you," Tommy said noticing that the back of the Suburban was filled to capacity with them.

"Did she say how she found the place?" Danny Lee asked waving to Agent Klassen and the other two agents when Tommy returned to where they were working on the tree.

"I didn't ask, why?"

"I didn't know how to get here. I got here because that fellow Chappie is it? He picked us up at the hotel and brought us here. It was dark out when he picked us up and not being familiar with the roads in this area I was always lost. It was as if someone had put a hood over my head. Klassen was supposed to call me for directions and I was going to ask you to relay them to her and she didn't call me. Did she call you?"

"Maybe she called, *Grumpy's* and asked?" Arch said.

"I don't think *Grumpy's* would give the directions to the pope if he asked," Tommy replied. Arch had to chuckle when he thought about the pope calling *Grumpy's*.

Tommy had ever since Danny Lee had left his shotgun for him at *Grumpy's* carried it with him everywhere he went it was never far from his reach. Now he picked it up from the stump he had laid it on, cocked it, and without anyone seeing it carried it alongside his leg, out of sight over to where Ben was clearing the bit larger than small stuff from the roadway. "Ben," Tommy whispered, "without being seen by the agents in the Suburban when

I turn around to head back I want you to lift up my shirt and take the automatic from the holster at my back. Then I want you to nonchalantly take up a position behind the Suburban from where you can cover the doors on the passenger side from behind. Do it nonchalantly, but be ready, and shoot to kill."

Next Tommy stepped between Agent Lee and Arch making sure that they both saw the shotgun. "Easy," he warned. "No sudden moves just be ready. I've a feeling something is terribly wrong here. Arch as soon as Agent Klassen or one of the other two agents step out of the Suburban I want you to hit the ground behind what's left of this tree."

"Gottcha," Arch replied.

No one in the Suburban made a move to get out so Tommy, Arch, and Danny Lee kept working. When they were finished, Tommy signaled them with his right arm while keeping his shotgun resting behind him against his right buttocks. "All clear come on through," he shouted.

Agent Klassen started the Suburban and when she did the rear and all the side windows rolled down. As the Suburban moved forward toward the opening in the tree Tommy saw a gun barrel being raised by her and the agent in the seat behind her. Arch saw them too and threw himself down upon the roadway, rolling down the slight embankment toward the edge of the swamp lessening his chance of being hit by a bullet.

Tommy already had his hand on the shotgun and as he brought it up level he fired at almost point blank range. Ben saw Tommy raise the shotgun and fired at the same time that he did. He fired two shots through the back window of the suburban that took out the other agent that was sitting in the back on the passenger side.

Agent Danny Lee found himself out of position for a kill shot when Tommy fired nevertheless he drew his weapon and shot twice into the windshield with the bullets only creating large star clusters in the glass.

When Tommy fired Agent Klassen floored the gas pedal of the Suburban spinning its back wheels and kicking up forest debris and wood chips from cutting a passageway through the fallen tree. The wheels finally found the necessary traction and the Suburban went tearing off down the roadway. As the Suburban roared past him Danny Lee dropped to one knee and started firing at the tires and kept on firing until his clip was empty. While he was in the process of changing clips the Suburban slid sideways on the roadway, flipped, and rolled over. Over and over several times it rolled coming to rest with the edge of its roof and the passenger side crumpled against a tree on the edge of the swamp. If it hadn't been for that tree being there it would have continued on rolling into the swamp itself.

Tommy and Danny Lee had both reloaded and ran down the roadway toward the overturned Suburban. Cautiously they peered into the wreckage keeping their guns pointed in the direction of any possible attacker, just in case.

The agent in the back on the passenger side was dead having taken a bullet in the back of the head from

Ben's automatic. The other agent sitting next to him was unrecognizable having taken the brunt of two barrels of double-00 from Tommy's shotgun. Agent Klassen was bleeding from double-00 grazings along her temple, top, and back of her head. Pulling her from her seat Danny Lee laid her on the roadway and inspected her head. "She has a few holes in the side of her head so I can't tell just how bad she is. She needs to be rushed to a hospital."

"No, leave me," Agent Klassen said in a raspy voice grabbing hold of Danny Lee's arm preventing him from getting up and making a call or leaving her. "It's better to die here then in a hospital bed."

"The doctors may be able to save you if we get you there in time," Danny Lee said.

"That's not what she meant, Agent Lee. Remember Frankie Le Cock's response," Tommy said reminding him of her choice.

"Who hired you?" Agent Lee questioned. "You have to tell me, Agent Klassen," he added. Agent Klassen looked up at him and did her best to smile.

"Just leave me lay here and go away," she said in a weakened voice. Agent Lee stood up and stepped back to where Tommy, Arch, and Ben were standing. "Ben, gather up all their weapons and see what you can do about making this massive hunk of metal invisible or in the least like its been here awhile," Tommy said. Ben nodded and went to work.

"Agent Lee what do you want to do with these bodies?" Arch asked.

"Danny these two agents with Agent Klassen. Are

these the same two agents that went with her when she went chasing after Arch's cell phone?" Tommy asked interrupting and preventing Danny Lee from answering Arch's question.

"One of them is, but not the other. Why? Is it important?"

"Where is the other one? Don't tell me he's one of those men that have been watching our back at night?"

"No the two that have been watching our backs are men I've worked with for many years. They are what you might call senior agents like myself and can be trusted to the max. I don't know where that other agent is right at this moment."

"Call your office and have him arrested and locked up on conspiracy charges. Have them call you when they have him. I'm sure he's been bought as well," Tommy insisted.

"Arch let's see what we can do about salvaging those flowers. I imagine they're a mess," Tommy said. Arch walked over and looked at Agent Klassen. He started to kneel down when Danny Lee grabbed his shoulder and pulled him back. "What if she has a knife or another gun? I haven't searched her yet," Danny Lee said bending down to check for a pulse in front of him.

"Well?" Arch asked over his shoulder.

"She's dead. Go help Tommy with the flowers. I'll frisk her and then I'm going to go back to the house and retrieve my two senior agents and have the bodies loaded? We'll have to use your car and we'll need directions. I'll send one of them back with these bodies to the morgue."

"I thought I saw a plastic tarp in one of the cupboards to put underneath the bodies to protect the seats. You might even consider taking the seat out and Danny Lee senior or not don't go in there without having your weapon in your hand," Tommy warned. "After you retrieve the tarp send the girls out to help with the flowers. I'm sure they'll be better at it then Arch and I are. We seem to be making more of a mess than anything else."

Arch standing next to Tommy suddenly reached in and took one of the flowers from an arrangement. Walking over to where Agent Klassen lay in the roadway he laid the flower across her chest.

"I'll just don't understand," he remarked bowing his head.

# CHAPTER SEVENTY-ONE

**"Do me a favor,** Arch. I've seldom asked you for a favor, but this one is so very, very important."

"What is it, Tommy?" Arch replied.

"Hug me," Tommy said.

"What?" Arch asked surprised.

"Hug me," Tommy repeated.

"Okay if that's what you want." Arch moved to hug Tommy and felt something cold on his chest. "What the hell?" he said backing away.

"That cold feeling could have been a knife. If it had been by now you could already be dead," Tommy said opening his hand to show Arch the squirt bottle filled with ice water in it.

"What's the point that you are obviously trying to make?" Arch asked.

"I want you to promise me that you won't get any closer than arms length to anyone today until after midnight. The only exclusions are Jennifer, Menerva, and me. I don't want you to hug anyone, the preacher, your mother, your father, Jennifer's or Menerva's kinfolk, no one. Stand back like this," Tommy took a step back, "and shake their hand, kiss their hand, but keep your head up and your eyes open, and stay that arms length distance between you and them. Promise me that you'll do this your life may depend on it. It'll be the hardest with your parents, but you have to do it for me and most of all for Jennifer."

"I promise," Arch replied.

"There's one more thing. I want you to always be aware of the person standing next to you. Try not to let them get to closer than an arm's length there either. A knife in the side, a syringe in the neck or body could come from anyone. After today you can make all the apologizes necessary to the people you might offend, but you have to keep your distance from everyone today."

"I get the message, Tommy."

"Mr. Big will be here. We've invited him. He's coming and expects to find that the F.B.I. Agents he bought to have succeeded in killing you before he gets here. When he discovers that you are still alive I'm sure that he'll play his trump card. It'll be one that he's been losing sleep over planning. You, I, and the girls are going to stay inside until it's time for the ceremony. Ben, Ray, Chappie, and Danny will take care of the guests when they arrive."

Jennifer's parents, the preacher, and Chantel arrived shortly after Tommy got his promise from Arch. "What happened to the flowers, honey?" Dorothy Curtis asked. They're nothing like what we ordered."

"The delivery van was involved in an accident, mother. It's a surprise that we were able to do with them what we did given the state they were in after the crash," Jennifer replied.

"Thank goodness there is still time. Chantel and I will see what we can do with them."

"We'll take care of it," Chantel assured the girls. "Don't you fret none."

A half-hour before the ceremony was to begin, Chappie showed up with Anne and Archibald Sr., Harry Harold, Lester Gibbons, and Derek Ashworth along with their wives, and Bettie and Bon Bon Bonaventure. Drinks were served, the final preparations were made, and everything was set to go.

"Who are those other people? What are they doing here? How did they get here?" Tommy asked in an agitated voice running to the front door of the house after seeing a group of unrecognizable people walking in from the roadway. "Danny! Could you come here please?"

"There's nothing to fret about, son," said Ray Curtis. "We thought it would be nice if we had some live music and that nice young man Chappie found a fiddle band for us. They followed him out here."

Agent Danny Lee came up the stairs followed by Chappie. "I know. I know, but I took care of it. Chappie told me they were coming and we frisked them all and I personally checked their instruments and their cases and everything is okay. Besides it'll be nice to have a live band playing. They'll add to the ambiance of the occasion," Danny Lee asserted.

"I'll personally vouch for each and every member of that band," Chappie said to assure Tommy that they weren't a threat. "I grew up with most of them and the others I've known for some time."

"All we need now is for a photographer to show up," Tommy said looking around seeing the cringed look on everyone's face.

"I've checked him out too," Danny Lee said. "All his bags, cameras, film canisters everything."

"He's from a very reliable firm in Baton Rouge, dear," Dorothy Curtis said. "Chappie recommended him too."

"He's okay, Mr. Templeton," Chappie said. "He's a good friend of mine and can be trusted to the max and if needed he's very good in a fight. His second job is a bouncer at one of the roughest clubs in Baton Rogue, which doesn't take away from the keen eye he has at events like this."

"You're a good man, Danny Lee and so are you Chappie. Thank you for thinking of them and allowing it. If I live through today I will owe the both of you big time."

# CHAPTER SEVENTY-TWO

**The time had arrived.** Tommy and Archibald Jr. walked down the aisle from the house to set the proceedings into motion. They took up they're position in front of the dock alongside the preacher who was already there clutching the ceremonial book of vows behind him.

The fiddle band started to play the *Wedding March* and Menerva on Ben's arm along with Jennifer on Ray's arm walked down the aisle and upon their arrival taking up a position by their fiancées sides. When the foursome turned to face the preacher he began. "Dearly beloved," and ended with, "You may now kiss the bride." Veils were raised kisses exchanged and those gathered all clapped all save one and that one Tommy noted.

A table suddenly appeared carried and placed before the two couples by Harry and Lester. Upon it were the cake, glasses, napkins, etc. Ray walked around handing out champagne glasses to everyone while Ben followed behind him filling those glasses from a magnum bottle of champagne.

"For the newly weds," Derek Ashworth said uncorking a bottle of champagne that was sitting on the table. Arch, Jennifer, Menerva, and Tommy picked up their glasses, and waited for Derek to fill them. While he waited Tommy looked around.

"Arch don't drink the champagne it's been poisoned" he said taking the glasses from the girls as well as from Arch, dumping out their contents, and setting the glasses back on the table.

"Listen to what you're saying," Derek said picking up a glass and filling it from another open bottle that was sitting on the table.

"Not that one, Derek drink from this one," Tommy said pouring him a glass from the bottle from which he had filled the foursome's glasses with.

Derek suddenly went weak in the knees. Tossing down the one he had poured for himself he said, "I just drank this one why don't you test that one if you're in doubt?" he replied rather feebly. Suddenly he decided to leave and when he turned to do so Danny Lee was standing right there, grabbed, and cuffed him. "Who put you up to this?" Danny Lee said.

"Don't say a word, young man." All eyes turned to see Archibald Ponnard, Sr. approaching them from his seat. "I'm a lawyer and I'll represent you and right now I'm advising you not to say a word."

"Father?" Arch questioned.

"This man is also a lawyer," said Danny Lee.

Ignoring his son, Archibald Sr. said, "but he isn't a noted criminal lawyer like I am."

"Keep him away from me," Derek shouted. "I want to turn state's evidence and I request immunity," he added pulling himself free from Agent Lee and staggered backward onto the dock.

"Don't say a word, son if that's the case not until you get their promises in writing," Archibald Sr. said following Derek onto the dock. "I'm sure that you've worked with the feds before so you know that unless they put it in writing they seldom keep their promises." Derek kept backing up keeping a safe distance between himself and Archibald Sr.

"Stay where you are the two of you," Agent Lee shouted.

"I know everything," Derek shouted. "I may not be a criminal lawyer, but I'm damned good at what I do and I've kept records. I want immunity," he shouted a second time.

"If you cooperate you may get a reduced sentence, but you'll never get immunity," Danny Lee said.

"Hear that, son. They'll hang you as sure as I'm standing here," Archibald Sr. said continuing to advance.

"Derek if you tell us who put you up to this I'll throw the weight of the entire firm behind your defense. We'll see to it that you don't hang. You'll spend some time in prison and I'll keep your job open for you. It'll be there when you get out," Archibald Jr. said.

"Okay, okay if you promise?"

"I promise, Derek," Arch said, "and I always keep my promises."

"Why you god damned son of a whore," Archibald Sr. shouted and rushed at Derek attempting to push him into the swamp. Instead Derek lowered his shoulder throwing it into Archibald Sr. and at the same time sidestepping him. The blow knocked Archibald Sr. off balance and off the end of the dock into the swamp. Danny Lee tore off his jacket and was about to run down the dock and jump in the water in an attempt to save Archibald Sr., but Tommy reading his intentions body blocked him. "You're too late, Agent Lee," he said grabbing both his arms. "The gators have already joined us in the wedding ceremony." He nodded back over his shoulder. "Notice that the swamp has come alive." Agent Lee looked at the churning, frothing waters of the swamp, and realized what Tommy was saying. "You're too good a man to die that way," Tommy added picking up and handing him back his jacket.

"If you want to do something noble go frisk Mrs. Anne Ponnard. I'm sure Arch would like to console his mother at her time of loss and I'd feel a whole lot better knowing that he's safe doing it. Make sure you check for pins and needles too."

# CHAPTER SEVENTY-THREE

**"Danny, Chappie** if you would gather everyone up in the area surrounding the porch when they are ready I'll explain what has happened here today and why we all still have a reason to celebrate?" Tommy said. While everyone was taking a moment to settle down and try to understand what had just happened the after ceremony tables with the wedding cake, plates, drinks, vitals, etc. were moved up and placed next to the front porch away from the area of the dock.

When the shock had subsided and everyone had found a place to sit Tommy began. "What you all witnessed here today was the end to something that began some twenty-plus years ago. Two men who were founding partners of a law firm fell in love with the same woman and is often the case in life one of them finally came out on top winning the woman's hand and marrying her.

"The other man the loser left the firm and started one of his own in another part of the state. A short time into the marriage the woman discovered that she was pregnant and had been for some time and at a later date realized that the child was not the child of the man she had married, but the child of the failed suitor." Arch had been sitting by her side and holding his mother's hand, but now she let it drop and stood up.

"I went to Harry and told him about the pregnancy. He wanted me to divorce Archibald and marry him but I knew that if I did it would destroy Archibald. I also knew that I wouldn't be able to go on living with the knowledge that I had done that. I had made a commitment out of love for him and I needed to stick to that commitment," Anne Ponnard said reaching over and squeezing Arch's shoulder.

"Harry paid a doctor to lie when my time came saying that there was a problem and the child had to be taken by cesarean section even though it was a normal birth to hide the actual date of conception. I kept Harry in the loop as to how Archibald Jr. was doing sending him pictures and a few mementos that he could cherish every now and then.

"As Arch grew older Harry started an account for him in my name to help pay for his education and other things. By this time he had become a very rich man and a person of significance within the state's higher archy. I always suspected that those two facts made Archibald more than a little jealous. When I was asked about the money I explained it away by telling him that I had received an inheritance from a dead relative that I made up.

"The money was there for Arch but my husband started using it in an attempt to advance his own riches and escalate his standing within the state. He liked to think that it was working, but the fact is he never was very good at investing his money wisely. It wasn't long before the inheritance money wasn't enough to cover his spending so he started to borrow and put us severely in debt."

"Then Harry Harold died and the inheritance money stopped coming. In his will Harry a man that had never married himself left everything, his house, all his investments, his law firm, and his vast fortune to his son, Archibald Ponnard, Jr. a fact that he found out from you, Mr. Ashworth didn't he?"

"Yes, I told him. I had gotten into a bit of trouble over a woman and Mr. Ponnard helped me out of it without blemishing my name. It wasn't until sometime later when I was in too deep and couldn't back away from him and his schemes that I realized that I had been set up in order for him to keep tabs on Harry."

"I'm not certain at what point Archibald Sr. found out about the inheritance lie and who was behind the money or the fact that Arch Junior was actually Harry's son, but he did. Now so deep in debt and about to lose everything he came up with a plan. He knew the contents of Arch Jr.'s will and probably helped him draw it up. He knew that if he died before he got married he would receive the bulk of his son's estate, which now amounted to billions of dollars."

"Thank you, Anne," Tommy said taking over the explanation.

"I'm convinced that a man like him thought first that if he killed Jennifer that it would delay for god knows how long Arch's ever getting married. But he also knew the run around, play-boy lifestyle of his illegitimate son might bring him one day to show up on his doorstep married to some floozy. He also couldn't trust that his son if he were told who his real father was would share his inheritance and help him out of the debt that he was in. There was only one way to make sure that all of the billions came to him and that way was that he would have to kill Harry's son. So he hired people to do that, but he wanted it look like an accident so that he would never be suspected in the investigation that was sure to follow.

"When Arch told him that I was going on a riverboat voyage up the Mississippi and that I was coming to see him before I sailed. He consulted Menerva who was misled herself by Arch Sr. and her own abilities. Arch Sr. then arranged it so that Arch would accompany me on that voyage and also paid for the passage of a hired killer to be on that same voyage with instructions to take him out at the first opportunity available. Although his plan failed and his assassin killed other people by accident he also had her kill those that failed in killing Arch to keep them from talking," Tommy saw the look on Derek's face and said to him, "Yes Derek even if you had stuck by him he would have had you killed too."

"When his assassin failed he put pressure on her. It was a she he had hired, a rogue bounty hunter called Frankie Le Cock. In order to earn her high pay she took risks and because of those risks managed to get herself caught. Now he was really in a pickle. He had already bought Derek and several F.B.I. Agents to keep him informed of Arch's whereabouts and kill him, but since they along with everything else he had tried failed he decided to throw caution to the wind by using Derek to serve Arch and Jennifer poisoned champagne."

"But how did you know the champagne was poisoned?" Chappie asked.

"First off the cork didn't pop, which meant it had been opened before. Secondly it was a different brand than all the others that Chantel had brought from *Grumpy's*. Thirdly I saw Derek switch bottles when he filled Menerva's glass after having filled our glasses even though that other bottle was more than half full which cinched it for me. Where you instructed not to poison Menerva, Derek?"

"I was supposed to poison all four of you, but I had heard of Menerva's reputation and the things that she was capable of even after death and I didn't want to have to worry about that."

"I guess that you now know that you wouldn't have had very long to worry about it for you would have died like all the others who were hired to do the man's bidding. I know that Mr. Ponnard Sr.'s demise was a tragic to witness, but it means that all those he killed or had killed finally realized the justice they deserved.

"Arch and Jennifer have known each other for a long time and today is the day we celebrate them and their release from the fear of being murdered. Today we are here to celebrate their beginning of a new life which also begins today for Menerva and myself. We would like it very much if you all stayed and celebrated that new beginning with us."

# EPILOGUE

**The celebration lasted** well past midnight with most of the guests crashing at the *River House*. Agent Lee and the one remaining senior agent after collecting and bagging all the evidence stayed for a couple of hours to help celebrate and hitched a ride back to town with Chappie.

Arch told his mother that he would take care of her, but when she discovered that he and Jennifer were going to be moving to Shreveport she told him that she no longer wanted to live in her New Orlean's home. She asked Arch if he wouldn't mind selling it and buying her a smaller place hopefully somewhere in his neighborhood close by his new home.

True to Arch's call Bettie Bonaventure livened up the evening with her usual flair with her and Bon Bon being among those crashing at the *River House*.

Just before light came to the sky above the swamp Tommy crept from Menerva's side and silently went outside and stood on the edge of the dock. Menerva feeling his absence went to the window to check on him. Standing there she watched Tommy thank Hecate, the Dark One, Goddess of Witchcraft for her part in solving this mystery that had once again been presented to him and saving his friends lives. While thanking her Tommy noticed that the swamp usually an opaque yellowish-green color had cleared and now reflected the multitude of stars looming overhead in the clear night sky. Lowering his eyes back to the water he saw a ring of stars surrounding the heads of the images of Willow and his two daughters, Phoenix and Cricket. Tears came to his eyes as they conversed with him. He thanked them for allowing Menerva to be a part of his life, but assured them that they too would always be a part of his heart. Menerva watching from the open, screened window heard and witnessed everything Tommy said and was himself witnessing.

One by one Willow, Cricket, and Phoenix's image started to fade and the stars surrounding their heads lifted skyward and disappeared in the heavens above leaving the swamp an opaque, yellowish-green color once again.

Silently returning to his bed and Menerva's side Tommy crawled in. Menerva put her arm around him and snuggled in as tightly as was physically possible.

The Templeton's stayed in Louisiana, Shreveport to be exact until the Ponnards all three of them were well situated after which they bid their farewells and returned to New Hampshire.

When Tommy went to the Post Office to collect the mail he had put on hold he noticed the return address on a letter near the top of the pile that was handed to him. When he got back home he showed the letter to Menerva and together they opened it.

## Dear Mr. Templeton,

**In reviewing your previous** application for acceptance into the F.B.I. training facility at Quantico, Va. and in view of the letters that we have recently received form our headquarters in Illinois and Louisiana we are making an exception in your case to our admittance qualifications.

As of this date your acceptance has been confirmed and you are to present yourself to Quantico on the following date.

Printed in the United States
By Bookmasters